OTHER BOOKS BY JAMES CLIFFORD

Double Daggers by James R. Clifford has placed as an Award-winning finalist in the Historical Fiction category for the 2007 National Indie Excellence Awards.

Double Daggers was one of seven books selected by the American Numismatic Association as "a notable and great read for 2006."

"James R. Clifford has been graced with a fertile imagination . . . This is one novel that will refuse to be forgotten long after it has been put to rest on one's book- shelf, as Clifford's characters linger in the readers' minds as well as his scenes that have an icy clarity to them."

–Norm Goldman, Editor Book Pleasures

"*Double Daggers* is very strongly recommended as a complex, superbly crafted, thoroughly entertaining novel from beginning to end."

–James Cox, Editor, Midwest Book Reviews

"History is evoked in James R. Clifford' s novel of intrigue and suspense... Anyone with a love of history will thoroughly enjoy this carefully researched and splendidly told story that spans the centuries."

– Alan Caruba, Editor BookViews

"If you want to read something edge-of-your-seat-engaging, historically fascinating, and really well written . . . This book would make wonderful book club fodder, it is well written and intriguing to end."

–Michelle Boucher-Ladd. FrontStreet Reviews

"...An attractive, enjoyable novel that even provokes thought in those who go for that sort of thing."

- Seabrook Wilkinson, Charleston Mercury

MORE REVIEWS, BIO AND BOOK INFORMATION CAN BE FOUND AT: WWW.JRCLIFFORD.COM

Ten Days To Madness

by

JAMES CLIFFORD

JR Rutherford Books
Cover Design by Toprotype

Bechtler Gold Coin image provided by Stack's Bowers Galleries

Mountain photo courtesy of Rachel Grimes
Rachel Grimes is a freelance photographer from Salmon, Idaho and the owner/operator of Dark Mountain Photography. Salmon's rural location offers her many amazing opportunities for outdoor photography. Rachel also specializes in applying abstract twists to photography. See more at darkmountainphotography.com.

ISBN: 0615589626
ISBN 13: 9780615589626

Books by James Clifford

Blackbeard's Gift

Double Daggers

A Griffin In Her Desk

Ten Days to Madness

Prologue

1853

Near Rutherfordton, North Carolina

Samuel Posten smiled. The five-dollar gold piece felt good in his hand, and he greedily looked it over with a growing sense of pleasure. His plan was almost complete.

He rubbed a finger across the words *Carolina Gold* stamped into the coin's center, and the gold luster gave Posten an immense feeling of satisfaction. His only true love in this world was money, especially gold.

Posten tossed the coin back into the box and turned to face the mint master. Christopher Bechtler was a tall, dour man of few words. Posten didn't care for Bechtler, but that fact wouldn't stop him from doing business with the man. Posten needed him, at least for now.

"Everything in order, sir?" Bechtler asked in a clipped tone.

Posten nodded without taking his eyes off the box of gold coins. "Yes, everything is in order."

Bechtler nodded. "Excellent. I'll gather my things."

With rising jealousy, Posten watched Bechtler leave. He hated being around wealthier men.

Gold had been discovered in North Carolina in the early 1800s, causing a stampede of fortune hunters, criminals, and fools to flood the state, all with the dream of striking it rich. At first, finding the gold had been easy enough, but the miners had no way of converting their raw gold into a negotiable currency without taking enormous risks and expense transporting their hard-earned finds from western North Carolina all the way to the Philadelphia Mint. The hazardous two-week journey was expensive, time-consuming, and filled with constant danger, especially from Indians and bandits who scoured the trail looking for easy prey.

Posten disdained the Bechtler family because he abhorred those who beat him to a business opportunity, and the Bechtlers certainly had done that.

Twenty years earlier, Bechtler's uncle had purchased a tract of land below the mountains in Rutherfordton, North Carolina, where he built a private mint. Then the Bechtlers proposed a deal that the miners couldn't refuse: for a two-percent fee, the Bechtlers would take their raw gold and mint it into coins, saving the miners the expense, time, and risk of traveling all the way to Philadelphia.

The miners jumped at the chance, and the Bechtlers reaped immense wealth from the dangerous efforts of the gold miners.

Posten shook his head in disgust. After all these years, it still burned him up that the Bechtler family had made so much money from their enterprise, but there was nothing he could do about it now. He had more pressing matters at hand.

He had traveled from Charlotte to Rutherfordton to complete the last gold purchase. The trip to Rutherfordton was out of his way, but there was no one else he could do business with in this matter.

The Bechtlers' reputation for honesty and fair dealing had been unsurpassed for decades. But in this instance, it was secrecy and discretion that Posten was paying for, and it came with a steep price. The greedy son of a bitch had charged him a seven-percent fee instead of the customary two percent to melt the gold into new coins, but Posten had no one else he could trust.

He knew he was taking a great risk moving such an enormous quantity of gold at one time, but he had no choice. He hadn't become a wealthy man by sitting around hoping everything would turn out all right. The creditors were breathing down his neck, and the bank's directors were demanding answers regarding money he had siphoned for other investments that had not exactly worked out the way he had anticipated.

And to make matters worse, many of his private investments had completely collapsed. He was in serious financial trouble and stood at the very edge of the precipice.

But Posten was a survivor, and he never forgot his motto, "Better safe than sorry." That was why he was taking the risk of transferring the gold all at one time.

It wasn't just his collapsing business empire that Posten was worried about. He had an odd feeling, an intuition. He firmly believed the United States was actually a land made up of two separate, very different countries, and that this dichotomy could not go on forever. In his opinion, it was only a matter of time before the fragile union of states tore itself apart. And being a banker, Posten knew that paper money was just that—paper. It could become worthless at any time, so he wasn't taking any chances.

He was moving the gold to his brother's farm in Ohio for "safekeeping." The gold was his insurance. If worse came to worst and everything failed, or the country fell into war, he didn't plan on spending the rest of his life as a pauper. He would hightail it back to Ohio, retrieve his gold, then relocate to the upper Midwest, Canada, or, if he had to, Europe, where he would start over.

It wasn't that big of a deal to start over. He had done it before, but a man of his stature couldn't begin a new life without money.

The thought of being run out of Charlotte in disgrace didn't scare Posten. The only thing that scared him was being poor, and that terrified him to such a degree that he literally shook whenever the dreaded thought crossed his mind.

Bechtler returned with the last of his bags. He was hitching a ride with Posten south to Spartanburg to scout out property to build a new home. Bechtler told him he was planning on relocating because, despite the mint's success over the last twenty years, its days were drawing to a close. The government had opened its own mint in Charlotte, and gold had started to dry up in North Carolina.

Posten closed the lid on the chest of gold and pointed to the armed guards. "Load up this last box."

The hired guns grabbed the last box of gold coins and left the room. The trip to Ohio was risky, but that was why he had hired the best gunfighters in the South.

Of course, he had to pay them practically a small fortune for that protection, but the cost was worth it.

Posten turned back toward Bechtler. "I appreciate your, ah, continued discretion in this matter."

Bechtler nodded. "My pleasure. After all, you paid for it."

"Damn right, I did!" Posten sneered.

The two men left the mint, climbed aboard the horse-drawn wagon, and with six armed guards riding next to them, the journey began.

Posten's plan was almost perfect, but he had made one mistake, a detail that would cost him not only his gold, but his life. It had not occurred to him that the greed of one of the hired gunslingers was as large as his own and that the gunslinger had figured, why get paid a little, when, with a little planning, he could get paid a lot.

After gaining Posten's trust and employment, the gunslinger had gone to the Mountain Cherokees and double-crossed him.

The gunslinger's proposal to the Indians was a simple one. He would give them the logistics of the gold shipment, and the Indians would take care of the rest. For their efforts, the Cherokees would get three quarters of the gold, with the rest going to the gunslinger.

In Posten's greed and rush, he hadn't considered the greed of another, and he didn't take into account that to a gunslinger, a small portion of his gold represented a fortune.

Chief Black Fox sat crouched in the thicket, transfixed by the sight of a solitary eagle soaring high in the dark blue sky.

This is a good sign, he thought, as he returned his attention to the band of warriors huddled around him. The sight of the eagle bolstered his confidence. He could sense the spirits of his ancestors around him, and it made him happy.

"The Old Ones have come," he said in a hushed tone to his warriors.

His eldest son, Broken Stream, whispered, "The white men should be near."

The chief stared back up into the sky. The eagle had disappeared, causing a flash of concern.

"Great Chief," his son continued, "won't robbing the white men of their gold cause them to seek vengeance? Won't they travel high into the mountains searching for us? We don't need their yellow metal. We have the mountains to sustain us."

Black Fox forgot about the disappearance of the eagle as he fought back his temper. He didn't want to admonish his son too harshly in front of the other warriors, but the chief was never questioned unless he was the one seeking counsel, especially when it was from his own blood.

His son was not old enough to remember when most of their people were rounded up by the United States government and forced to march to a reservation in a place called Oklahoma.

Years later, Black Fox heard someone call the journey his people faced the Trail of Tears, and even though he didn't face their hardships, he had cried enough tears to last many lifetimes.

Fewer than a thousand Cherokees remained on their land after the removal, with most of the splintered tribes living precariously in small towns along the Tuckasegee River. Black Fox refused to be subject to the whims of the white man and had led his tribe high into the mountains.

Black Fox continued to hold his tongue, letting his anger dissipate. He was getting old. He felt it in his heart and in his bones, and even though his son's nature leaned toward caution, the chief knew Broken Stream would make a good chief one day.

The chief looked at the young warriors who knelt in a circle around him, thinking he could use his son's foolish outburst to prove a point.

The chief spoke. "Our people have always lived freely in these mountains. We have always walked these lands, fished these waters, hunted the great and noble animals. But now, we are almost no more."

Black Fox spread his arms. "We are all that is left. We alone carry the burden of protecting our land, our people, our heritage. The gold we take today is not meant for us. It is for those who come after us. The 'Ones That Know' have spoken in my dreams. They say that one day the great spirits will call upon the purest, most noble Cherokee to reclaim the gold we take today. And when he does, it will set our people free.

"I have selected each and every one of you because I know you are true Cherokee warriors. It is our legacy to protect the gold, to keep it safe in the mountain burial cave next to our ancestors. And each one of you..."

Black Fox turned and stared each of his warriors in the eye, "has given a blood oath to protect the gold for the future of the Cherokee Nation."

Black Fox looked Broken Stream directly in the eyes. "And perhaps your son, or his son, will be called upon by the great spirits to claim the gold and use it to buy back our lands. Lands stolen from us. Only then can we be truly free."

His warriors remained silent. They didn't have to speak because Black Fox could tell by their faces that they understood. They understood that they alone held the burden for the future of their people.

"It is time," the chief said solemnly. The Indians spread out along the trail and waited.

Black Fox watched, crouched in his hiding position as his scout rode past signaling that the armed escort was approaching. The chief looked up into the sky and saw a sight that made his soul scream out in joy. Except for mating season, eagles were solitary birds, so to see a dozen of the majestic birds circling high in the sky only added to Black Fox's conviction that he would save his people.

The chief returned his attention to the path as he heard the unmistakable sound of horses approaching. A few moments later, the wagon and armed guards appeared around the bend. Black Fox imitated the call of an eagle, and with lightning efficiency, the white men were dead before they knew what had happened to them.

Black Fox sprinted over to the carnage and stood next to the gunslinger who had given him the information. The dead man had a strange look of surprise etched across his face, and the chief said a prayer for the man's spirit. He was usually a man of his word, even with white people, but not this time. He had had many dreams telling him that one day the gold would make a difference in his tribe's survival, and he couldn't take any chances by relying on a white man to keep his word. *After all,* he thought, *they had broken their word every time since arriving in the Cherokee's lands.*

Black Fox quickly divided the gold between a dozen warriors who rode off in different directions as a precaution. However, the Indians were headed to the same destination, a hidden cave that only a few of his people knew about.

The sacred cave had always existed high up in the remotest part of the mountains. Only the tribe's chiefs and bravest warriors were buried there, and now the gold would be placed next to the bodies of their greatest ancestors. Black Fox and his warriors would protect the gold forever, if necessary.

Black Fox followed behind his warriors as they rode up the mountain, and for the first time in years, he felt a glimmer of hope. He looked up into the sky. The eagles were gone, but he smiled. A long forgotten sensation of peace came over him.

He truly believed that, now, his people had a future. One day they would get their lands back.

CHAPTER 1

Charleston, South Carolina

Friday, February 1

Charlie Parker stared at his wife with a mixture of exasperation and guilt.

"You want to do what?" she asked again.

He folded his arms across his chest and repeated, "I want to go up to the mountain home for a week. What's the big deal?"

"Without us?" she asked, sweeping a hand across her bangs while giving him that "I'm very disappointed" look—a look that all husbands learn to pick up on early in their marriage.

"C'mon, Susan. It's just for a week. What's the big deal?"

Charlie knew his request was going to make her upset, but he had made up his mind, and he wasn't going to back down. Few times in their marriage had he ever absolutely demanded something, and even though he couldn't understand exactly why he wanted to go to the mountains all by himself, he just knew he did.

And that was that.

Anyway, he deserved it. For months, he had been working sixty hours a week to finish a huge advertising campaign. The deal had been a major coup for Charlie's little firm, and once the contracts were officially signed, it would go a long way toward securing his family's financial security, not to mention giving him a much-needed cash infusion.

So, with the deal now complete, he needed a break, a little alone time. He wanted to go to the mountains for some rest and relaxation, and by God, he wanted to go alone.

Susan huffed and mumbled something he didn't understand. He pretended to read the newspaper while watching her out of the corner of his eye as she began sorting through the day's mail. It was a stall tactic she had begun employing early in their marriage.

A few minutes passed before she broke the silence. "I don't know, Charlie. I hear it's been like the worst winter in decades up there. Why don't you wait till the spring when you can at least go outside and won't freeze to death?"

He shrugged, realizing he would have to wait her out.

They had been married for eighteen years, and they were both pushing their middle forties, that strange in-between time when you're no longer young, but not quite "old," either.

They had two kids, a fourteen-year-old boy and a ten-year-old girl. Charlie assumed that they had the typical marriage for people who were their age and had managed to stay together during this age of "quickie divorces" and "when the going gets tough, everyone splits" type mentality.

He was content, reasonably happy, and despite some rocky periods in their relationship, he was steadfastly loyal to his wife. There was no question that they both shared a deep love for their children, despite all the sacrifices, responsibilities, and frustration that parenthood sometimes carried with it.

He couldn't help himself and gave Susan a beguiling smile that she ignored while opening junk mail and pretending to be interested in the million-dollar guaranteed sweepstake offers.

Oh, what is her little mind conjuring up? he wondered.

Charlie stole a glance as Susan continued to focus on the mail, and he couldn't help but admit that his wife was still a beautiful woman.

He expected his body and face to show signs of growing older, but he felt he had changed drastically, and what disturbed him most was that he could not put a finger on the change. It was strange, because no matter how long he looked at himself in the mirror, he could not figure out what was different.

Charlie stood six feet tall and had started getting a tad chunky in the midsection, but he considered himself to be in "reasonable" shape for someone his age. He knew his eyes and general facial outline looked older than in previous years, probably because he was tired, but that wasn't the cause of his consternation. What bothered him was about a month or two ago, a queer feeling spread through him whenever he looked at himself in a mirror, and it had started to really scare him.

The episodes had become more and more frequent, until about a week ago, he had stopped recognizing himself. It was like a complete stranger was staring back, and the only thing that kept him from screaming was his mind's repeated reassurances that it was the same old body of Charlie Parker.

In fact, sometimes, if he looked long enough, it would frighten him so badly that he had to leave because he started to feel that he was trapped in someone else's body. It had gotten to the point that he stopped looking at photos and even began shaving in the shower so he didn't have to look in the bathroom mirror.

He glanced back over at Susan, who looked exactly like she did in her early thirties. Her eyes were a clear dark blue, and she had thick black hair that to this day drove him crazy. Her skin was delicate, almost unwrinkled, and it maintained a beautiful porcelain complexion that Charlie remembered so vividly the first time they met.

He chalked up her youthful appearance to good genes and an obsession to wear sunscreen, even if it was cloudy or raining outside.

Just staring at her still brought a pang of desire to him. And even though that intense spark of romance had faded somewhat over the years—largely because of jobs, kids, mortgages, and all the other bullshit that goes into living in today's world—Charlie strongly believed the important thing was that they both still loved one another, even if it was a different type of love than when they were first married and had no kids.

Hell, the more he thought about it, their relationship, their love, was probably even stronger compared to those first years of dating and marriage when everything was so new, so blissful.

Time, the silent destroyer of everything—the thought made him flinch involuntarily, like an electric shock had jolted through his entire body.

He blinked rapidly because his brain felt like it had seized up for a second, almost like a computer being rebooted.

His previous thoughts of his wife and kids were replaced with an indescribable trepidation, a gnawing fear, and a sense of impending doom. He wasn't sure what words to use to describe the feelings. All he knew was that he recognized the sense of panic because he had felt it before.

His hands grew clammy, and his heart skipped a few beats. He involuntarily coughed a few times before he forced himself to take a few deep breaths. Some chemical receptors in his brain must be misfiring because they were sending forth memories of a time and place that he preferred to keep locked away in the furthest reaches of his mind.

However, despite his best efforts to train and even trick his mind, from time to time "the bad thoughts" still managed to break free from their prison deep inside his subconscious, sending forth a flood of diseased thoughts to his conscious mind.

He tried to calm himself. His body always reacted in this fashion when memories of his "black days" arose. That period in his life had been more than a decade ago, and as quickly and unexpectedly as the darkness had descended upon him, it also had disappeared.

Well, almost disappeared.

That horrible episode in his life had been equivalent to someone turning a light switch off, and then back on, in his mind.

He remembered one night going to bed, not caring if he woke up the next day, with his mind full of darkness, anxiety, and irrational thoughts. The next morning, he awoke feeling like a completely new man with a bright future, flowing with optimism, hope, and a renewed vigor for his family and life.

The psychiatrists explained that it wasn't unusual for that type of a condition to appear and disappear suddenly. But what the hell did they know? In his opinion, they were all a bunch of incompetent, overpaid doctors.

Charlie believed the whole episode had just been a fluke, a one-time "chemical imbalance." Even the doctor had told him at his last appointment that he felt Charlie would probably never suffer another significant "episode" for the rest of his life.

The passage of time didn't stop unwanted thoughts from creeping into his mind every once in a while, but the psychiatrists had told him a thousand times: "Thoughts are just thoughts. They can't hurt you unless you allow them to."

Sound, logical advice that was impossible to remember during an attack.

He took another deep breath and forced himself to smile, another trick he had taught himself as he began to feel normal again.

This was a quick one, he thought.

Charlie looked over at Susan, who glanced up from her mail and flashed him a smile. He always thought it was amazing that no one could tell what went on in his mind. Inside, he could be locked in the furthest depths of despair, bargaining with God to end the pain. But yet, he could smile and carry on as if he didn't have a care in the world.

No one ever knew, ever.

"What are you smiling about?" he asked.

"Nothing." Susan went back to reading one of her catalogs.

Charlie truly believed he was a lucky man to have won her, and he always tried to remember it. Susan never wavered during his "bad time," and he believed only her strength and dedication to him pulled him out of the abyss.

He shook his head. *Why am I thinking about this now?* he wondered. *Does the trip to the mountains have something to do with it?*

Susan finally ran out of mail and catalogs to look at, so she looked up and asked, "But what about work?"

"The Roth campaign's over, thank God! Trust me. They can manage without me for a week."

Her list of objections was dwindling. Susan walked over to the kitchen desk and picked up a stack of envelopes. "Hold on, let me put these bills in the mailbox."

Charlie nodded with a slight smirk and watched as she walked out of the back door. Work was the last thing he was worried about, because if his employees didn't like it, too damn bad. After all, he was the boss.

He had spent eleven years working for a family-owned construction firm before getting sick of the politics and continually being passed over for promotion in favor of lazy, incompetent relatives of the owners.

So at age thirty-eight, three years removed from his "episode," Charlie took the big plunge and started his own company. The first five years were a struggle, but now his hard work had paid off. The business was successful enough to afford him and his family a comfortable lifestyle. The bills got paid. There was plenty of food on the table. The kids would be able to go to a decent college, and Susan could stay at home if she chose to, which she did.

They didn't spend winter holidays skiing in Switzerland, nor did he ever expect to, but that was all right with Charlie. All in all, he led a happy quiet life.

And with the Roth account pretty much a done deal, he could finally begin to relax a little and enjoy the fruits of his hard work.

In fact, other than his unexplained bout of "mental illness," the only major traumatic event that had occurred in his life was when his parents had been killed in a car accident eight years ago.

They were in their late seventies at the time, but they were in perfect health, and Charlie always felt that despite their ages, their deaths had been premature.

According to the state police, his dad had lost control of their car on the Blue Ridge Parkway. The official police report stated that the car veered off the road, plunging down a steep ravine, resulting in both of his parents being instantly killed.

His stomach began turning into a knot when he recalled walking into the morgue. It was a place he hoped he would never have to visit for the rest of his life. He had wanted to see his parents' faces one last time, but the coroner persuaded him otherwise.

He could still picture that pompous ass who, without a hint of emotion and with a tone and attitude that sounded more like some punk teenager taking an order at some burger joint, presented him with the grisly news that his mom and dad had been burned beyond recognition due to the explosion and fire. His parents' remains were eventually identified through dental records.

God, everything about that morgue was awful! How could anyone work in a place like that? The smell, the glaring fluorescent lights, the stagnant air, and the feeling of death that seemed to permeate everything.

To be surrounded by death at all times— how could anyone who worked there have kept their sanity?

His parents' passing had hit Charlie hard, and it took him a long time to get over it, but he did, at least to the degree that people do when they lose loved ones so suddenly.

He moved on with his life, but something about the facts relating to their deaths bothered him even to this day. The police said it was an open-and-shut case. A simple traffic fatality, but the circumstances surrounding the accident just didn't make sense.

For one, the accident had occurred at approximately three o'clock in the morning. His parents were never up that late. They were early risers who went to bed every single night at exactly nine o'clock on the dot, even on New Year's Eve.

Perhaps even more unusual than the time of the accident was the fact they were traveling on the Blue Ridge Parkway. That didn't make any sense at all. Even if, for some unknown reason, they had decided to go back home in the middle of the night because of a sickness or emergency, they sure as hell wouldn't have taken the Blue Ridge Parkway to get back to Charleston.

Charlie had called the police a couple of times voicing his concerns, and at first, they were cooperative, but as he began to ask more and more questions, they became almost standoffish regarding the matter.

In the end, the police said there was nothing more they could do and that the case was closed. So, Charlie dropped his inquires. What else could he have done? He had to get on with his life. His parents were gone, and there was nothing he or anybody else could do to bring them back. But even to this day, the unanswered questions lingered in his mind.

He looked out the kitchen window and saw Susan talking to a neighbor. He turned back toward the refrigerator and stared at a picture of the mountain house attached to it.

Charlie was an only child, and he had inherited the property. The homestead was a place full of family history, a place of happiness and warmth where he spent most of his summers as a child. A magical place he considered a second home.

He stared over at a picture of his father and unconsciously reached inside his front pocket. He pulled out the gold coin that he always carried with him. Susan thought he kept the coin as a good luck souvenir, but the real reason he always kept it in his pocket was because it served as a daily reminder of his dad. His father had given the coin to Charlie for his eighteenth birthday, and it was the best present he had ever received in his life.

He wasn't much of a coin collector, but he knew his dad loved the coin, and that was why it was such a special gift. His father told him that the coin was minted before the Civil War in Rutherfordton, North Carolina, and that his own father had given it to him when he was a boy, just before he died.

Charlie's only regret regarding his father was that he never got him to open up about his own father. All Charlie knew about his grandfather was that he had "passed" when his father was a young boy and that he had bought the secluded property sometime in the early twenties. Charlie had tried to get his dad to tell him about his grandfather a few times, but his dad made it quite clear that he didn't wish to discuss the matter.

Charlie reluctantly accepted his father's silence and stopped asking questions, figuring there must have been some hidden skeletons in the closet or some sort of family disgrace when it came to his grandfather.

After all, his father had been a supportive, loving man, and later in adulthood, they became good friends, so if his father didn't want to discuss his family, that was all right with Charlie.

He studied the picture of the mountain home. The house was situated on the side of a gentle slope with a spectacular view of the mountain on all sides. Tall, densely packed trees lined the fifty-acre property, with a large well-stocked trout stream running through the northwest corner. It was a great house set in a beautiful place.

Charlie supposed many people would have sold the property if they were in his position. The land was worth a boatload of money, but he would never sell. The mountain was a place of tranquility and peace that was hard for him to find anywhere else in his life.

He felt that his parents' spirits still permeated the home, and even though to this very day, Charlie was prone to unexpected bouts of sadness over their tragic deaths, for the most part, the house brought him happy memories of his parents and the times they had together.

Charlie had lived his entire life in Charleston, South Carolina, which was only a seven-hour drive to the mountains, and during the summer, the cool mountain air was a nice respite from the smoldering humid days of summer along the coast.

The back door opened, and Susan walked in flashing him a self-imposed look of hurt. Charlie couldn't help himself. He smiled, seeing her pouty expression that she gave him when she was displeased or wasn't getting her way.

He walked over to Susan and wrapped his arms around her, giving her a big affectionate hug.

"Honey, I just want a little time to myself, a little time to decompress. You know how hard I've worked the last six months. I just need a little break. It has nothing to do with you or the kids. You know that."

"But Charlie..."

"You go off twice a year with your girlfriends," he cut her off, "to get away for a while. I don't have any problem with that."

"I know you don't. But I'm not going off by myself in the middle of winter. I think that's kind of weird."

He chuckled, and the phone rang before he had the chance to remind her that he was going off to their mountain home, not some Club Med resort or Las Vegas.

Susan grabbed the phone. "Parker residence."

"Hold on." She put a hand over the phone. "Do you want to renew your subscription to the newspaper? You get a free hat."

"That's fine." Charlie walked over to the refrigerator and pulled out a cold Budweiser. He popped open the beer and took a long drink while Susan finished renewing the newspaper subscription.

She hung up the phone. "You're doing your nervous habit again."

He grimaced and looked down at his hands. Somewhere over the last couple of years, he had developed what could only be described as a "nervous twitch." He would rapidly tap his index and middle finger against his thumb on both hands. Susan said he had even begun to do it while he was sleeping.

He forced his fingers to stop their spasmodic dance. "Well, you're making me nervous. I didn't think you would be this upset about me going up to the mountains."

"I ordered you the yellow one," Susan replied nonchalantly.

"Yellow what?"

"Hat."

Obviously, she was still a bit peeved at him because she knew he would never wear a yellow hat. It was time for a different ploy. Charlie knew she would say yes if he absolutely insisted, but that wasn't the point. As any married man knows, never tell your wife what you are going to do in these types of matters. It's always better to get at least a reluctant blessing.

"Honey, listen…"

Charlie walked back over and slid around her backside, where he started rubbing her shoulders.

"There is nothing wrong. I promise you. I just really need to get away. Get some rest. That's all. You know I don't go anywhere the whole year unless it's with you and the kids."

He could feel her body beginning to relax as he moved down to her shoulder blades.

Susan sighed deeply. "I see you've resorted to bribery now. What next, a box of chocolates, some flowers, and a movie?"

Charlie laughed, mostly because she appeared to be relenting.

"But you have to promise me something."

"Anything you want."

"I don't want you drinking a lot. Okay?"

Charlie pressed his fingers deeper into her back. He had never been a big drinker except, of course, during his "bad period" in which he had relied on alcohol to numb his mind and body.

Some of the doctors believed that even though the alcohol hadn't caused his problem, it certainly contributed to its severity. Susan strongly disagreed and felt that the excessive alcohol was responsible for the whole episode.

So he had promised her more than a decade ago that he would drink sparingly, and it was a promise he had kept.

He massaged her neck. "I promise. I'll drink my usual three of four vacation beers in the evening, and that's it."

Susan pressed her back up against him. "And I want a half-an-hour back rub later tonight."

"Done."

"So, what in the hell are you going to do up there anyway? It's the dead of winter. Nothing's even open. It gets dark like at three-thirty in the afternoon. I'd be scared to death all by myself."

"I'm going to sleep late, read my books, and take some long walks. Who knows, maybe I'll do a little fix-up work around the place."

"How can you read those horror books all alone in the mountains in the dead of winter?"

"Easy. I'll sleep with all the lights on."

Susan shook her head, and even Charlie understood his obsession and love of horror and supernatural books to be a strange quirk in his personality. Vampires, UFOs, werewolves, unexplained phenomena, monsters, demons, devils, Satan-possessed children, hobbits, gnomes, evil clowns, sinister dreams. His philosophy was the weirder, the scarier, the more bizarre, the better, and he had a pretty extensive library to show for it.

"You are truly a strange man. You know that?"

"Yes. Yes, I do."

Susan laughed. "Fix-up work...I doubt that. You better not spend the entire week at the Green Man, okay? You promised."

Charlie gave her a sly smile. The Green Man was a bar in the mountains run by an old Englishman named Kingsley. The place had been around as long as he could remember. Even Charlie's old man had visited the place a few times in his younger days.

"You know," Susan said, wagging a finger at him. "I need to check that place out one of these days. I can't believe that I have never been there before. For all I know, it may be one of those strip joints."

Charlie laughed because it was as far from a nudie bar as possible. "Well, I have invited you plenty of times," he reminded her.

Susan drank an occasional glass of wine, but she had never been a big drinker, and, of course, never showed any desire to go to a bar and hang out. So she had never accepted any of his token requests to accompany him to the Green Man.

"Next time we're up there, I'm taking you there, whether you want to go or not. I'm telling you, you'd like it. The place is a Class A joint. It's like a high-end English pub but with real expensive furniture and fixtures and..."

"That's so weird," she interrupted, "a nice place in the middle of the mountains. Why in the hell would that guy ever build such a place? He must be losing his ass."

Charlie laughed. His wife didn't drink much, but she could cuss with the best of them when she felt like it.

"I don't think he cares. He told me he inherited a large sum of money a long time ago, he liked the area, and he liked being a bar owner, so there you go. Hell, he's been there for at least..."

Charlie stopped because he suddenly realized what he was going to say didn't make sense. His dad had gone to the Green Man in his younger days, and he thought Kingsley was in his late sixties, but if that was the case, the math couldn't work.

"Yes?" Susan said.

Charlie shook his head. “Oh, he’s been there for a long time.”

Charlie could tell by her tone it was time to get her final permission once and for all. Enough pussyfooting around.

“So you don’t mind then, huh?”

“I guess not,” she replied reluctantly. “I suppose everyone needs a little break every once in a while. Maybe the peace and relaxation will help you stop doing that, whatever the hell that thing is you do with your fingers. I mean you are doing it now. Will you please quit it!” she scolded him.

Charlie stared at his fingers, and they looked like they were having epileptic seizures. He had to seriously concentrate to get his fingers to be still. And with that accomplished, he kissed her on the forehead.

“Thanks, honey. You’re the best.”

~

CHAPTER 2

Saturday, February 2

"Hey, you two. Come over here and give me a kiss goodbye," Charlie called out to his son and daughter, who were milling around the yard. By the impatient looks on their faces, it was evident they were more than ready to get on with their Saturday plans, and Dad was holding them up.

Jessica walked over with a smile and threw her arms around his neck. "Bye, Dad. Don't get eaten by any bears."

"Thanks, hon. I'll try not to. And thanks for your concern. I appreciate it."

His daughter flashed him a sarcastic smile that made Charlie wonder if she really wouldn't have minded if a bear took a chunk out of him.

Jeffery was still standing in the middle of the yard kicking pine cones. Charlie motioned to him. "Get over here and give your ol' man a hug goodbye."

Jeffery reluctantly shuffled over as if he was about to be subjected to some form of inhumane torture. When he got close enough, Charlie grabbed him in a bear hug.

"Ah, Jeez, Dad," Jeffery yelled, trying to squirm away from his embrace. "Let me go!"

He broke free of Charlie's hold and fled back to the safety of the yard.

Susan walked over to the car laughing at their antics and threw an arm around Charlie's shoulder. "Okay, you'd better get on the road. You want to get there before nightfall, don't you?" She gave him a hug and a kiss.

"Love you," Charlie said.

"Love you, too. Drive carefully."

He got in his car and pulled out of the driveway. His family stood together in the yard and waved goodbye. He was on his way, and as much as he was going to miss his family, Charlie was excited about his adventure.

The drive to the mountains was nice and relaxing. Charlie smiled. To think, in his younger days he used to consider all forms of travel a waste of time. Now, he would gladly pay good money for a chance to hop in his car, all alone, turn on some good music, and drive in peace for a few hours.

He exited the expressway and turned onto the two-lane highway that would take him the rest of the way to the mountains. This was his favorite part of the trip because he enjoyed driving through the small mountain towns. Charlie passed through Rutherfordton and slowed near a highway plaque just on the outskirts of town.

The only reason he knew about the plaque was because his father had told him about it as a child. It marked the area where the Bechtler Mint was located during the early- to mid-1800s.

He didn't know much else about the mint except that he owned one of their gold coins and that it closed down before the Civil War.

The trip passed almost too quickly. He was on the last stretch of the country highway keeping one eye on the road and the other on the mountaintops. Charlie watched the last sliver of the orange-tinted winter sun as it fell behind the mountaintops.

"Damn! What a beautiful sight," he said.

The mountain was covered in a fine white powder, and the last of the day's ebbing sunlight bathed the snow-covered mountaintops in an iridescent blue.

He couldn't remember the last time he felt this good, this relaxed.

He was almost to the mountain home, and for a brief second, he considered stopping off at the Green Man for a couple of beers. He dismissed the idea, figuring it was better to buy some provisions at the store, unload the car, and get settled in. Anyway, he had a whole week to catch up with Kingsley.

The car approached a small wooden sign posted on the shoulder of the road welcoming all into the town of Wellington. The sign had seen better days, and Charlie checked to see if the town's population number was still posted underneath.

He slowed down. Yep, still there. The sign proudly displayed Wellington's current population of 1,437 citizens. Charlie couldn't remember how or why he had begun to always check out the town's population number, but it had become sort of a game he and Susan had started playing years ago. Evidently someone on the town council took the figures pretty seriously because, without fail every season, the numbers had been changed to reflect the current population. Of course, with the small number of residents, the changes were always little: plus two or three, minus one or two.

He did a quick calculation. The last time they had passed the sign, the number was at 1,433. Wow! A regular population explosion must have occurred over the last few months.

Charlie drove into the town limits and slowly made his way down Main Street. Pretty much everything was closed for the day, and only a handful of people milled about finishing up the last of the day's business.

Two- and three-story faded brick buildings lined each side of the street. The buildings housed all the assorted businesses and local government agencies that it took to run the little town—a barbershop, police station, the local attorney, a real estate office, and hardware store. All kept in nice, neat order.

As one would expect, the sidewalks were swept, there wasn't any graffiti on the building walls, and no trash littered the ground. The entire business section occupied only two blocks, and at the end of the street was a small park about the size of a football field with a restaurant, coffee shop, grocery store, and a library behind it.

Charlie drove around the square park and pulled into a parking spot for the grocery store. He walked into the country store and started collecting all the necessities he would need for a few days. The store was closing in a few minutes, and he was the only patron, so he quickly picked up his groceries and headed to the checkout.

"Good evening," he said cheerfully to the checkout girl, whose back was to him.

She turned and began to say something but stopped abruptly.

Charlie couldn't believe his eyes. The girl was breathtakingly beautiful in a very exotic way. Charlie knew he was gawking, but he couldn't help it. She was young, maybe in her early twenties, and appeared to be a Native American. She had flawless dark skin with shiny black hair that fell halfway down her back, but most of all, it was her eyes that he noticed. Her large oval eyes were of a certain color he had never seen before, almost a steel-blue color mixed with emerald green.

Charlie coughed, forcing himself to stop looking at her.

She began ringing up his groceries. "I hear it's been a cold winter so far," he said.

She looked back at him. "Yes, but it is about to get worse," she answered in a delicate voice.

"Really?" he said, wanting to engage her more, but he couldn't find the words. He felt like he was sixteen again trying to ask a girl out for a first date.

She checked the rest of his groceries, and he paid the bill. He didn't want to leave. Something about just being in her presence caused a strange feeling to come over him. A feeling he didn't understand.

But he couldn't stand there staring at her, so he grabbed his bags and walked to the door. He took one last look back. She was staring directly at him.

"See you later," he said.

She had an intense look on her face. "The Nunnehi are watching," she said, almost in a whisper.

"Excuse me?" he asked, not sure exactly what she had said to him.

"Have a good night, sir," she answered, then turned and walked down the aisle.

That was strange, Charlie thought, as he left the store. *What the hell was she talking about?*

He got into his car and headed off to the mountain house, which was a good twenty-minute drive from the center of Wellington. The last stretch of the highway was practically deserted, and he passed only two pickup trucks and an eighteen-wheeler before coming to his turnoff. He turned off the highway, pulling onto a narrow dirt road that led up to the cabin house.

The house was situated three miles from the entrance, and it had always been a bumpy ride. For years, he had talked about paving the road but had never gotten around to it, mostly due to the expense.

He tried to recall the last time he had been up here by himself, probably decades ago. The dark night sky held no moon, and the forest on each side of the dirt road was pitch black. Only the car's headlights provided any light, causing Charlie to feel like he was driving through a tunnel, and for a brief moment, he felt a tinge of apprehension before laughing out loud.

"Jeez! What a sissy-boy," he said aloud.

He was a bit too old to be afraid of the dark. Susan would have thought this was pretty funny. He was already scared, and he hadn't even been up here for five minutes.

He pulled up to the dark cabin, and the car's light caught a sliver of a reflection. Something was sitting on the front porch railing.

"What the hell." Charlie stopped the car. "Well, I'll be."

He put the car into park and sat there staring at his unexpected visitor. He couldn't believe the dang thing hadn't flown off, because sitting on the porch rail was a large owl. The bird stared directly at him.

Maybe it had made the cabin porch its little home and was reluctant to give it up, Charlie surmised.

He sat in the car for another five minutes watching the owl. The bird didn't budge, so finally, he opened the door and got out. He expected it to fly off, but instead, the owl continued sitting on the rail, staring at him, almost as if it was daring Charlie to make him leave.

He slowly inched forward closer until he got only about ten feet away and the giant owl spread its wings and flew off into the darkness of the night.

He looked in the direction the owl had flown. Charlie breathed in the cold crisp mountain air and shivered. It was cold as hell.

He looked up into the stunning night sky. With no moon or any other light around for miles, the stars, all trillion or so of them, seemed to be unleashing all their light directly toward his infinitely miniscule position in the universe.

The sight reminded Charlie of how insignificant he was relative to the great expanse of the universe, and that age old question of "what it all meant" played in his mind. After philosophizing over the stars for a few moments, he gave in to his body's desire to seek warmth, and he unloaded his gear and went inside for the night.

After everything was unpacked, and after he had called Susan to check in, Charlie opened a beer and sat down in an enormous leather chair that had been his Dad's favorite resting spot.

"Damn, that's good," he exclaimed after taking a large swig of the beer. "Finally, a little peace and quiet."

He surveyed the house. It felt good to be back.

He had to hand it to good ol' Pops: there was nothing he would change about the place. The cabin was made from local trees, giving it the appearance of a giant-size Lincoln Log cabin from the outside.

Inside, the main room was large, open, and vaulted, with a massive stone fireplace set against the main wall. The dark hardwood floor was accentuated by a thick area rug in front of the fireplace that added a touch of warmth.

He stared up at a giant stuffed boar's head above the fireplace mantel. Sharp white fangs protruded from each side of the animal's mouth. Susan absolutely hated the stuffed animal heads that lined the walls of the room, but Charlie thought they added just the right ambiance for a mountain house. His father had been an avid hunter in his younger days, and he had tried to get Charlie interested, but he just never cared for it. He had nothing against hunting, but he'd rather read his horror books or take walks.

Besides, Susan hated guns, and she made him get rid of all of his father's rifles after he passed away. Charlie argued with her that they should keep at least one gun in case of an emergency, but she wouldn't have it. Actually, their fight over the firearms had been one of their most serious arguments in years. In the end, he relented because she had been so adamant about the issue, but he still wished he had kept at least a rifle hidden somewhere, just in case.

The kitchen sat adjacent to the main room with a hall leading down to two bedrooms in the back of the house. Directly off the kitchen, an open set of stairs led up to the master bedroom. Between the kitchen and the den, there was a large wooden table.

Charlie's favorite part of the house was the little side room situated off the den that his father had converted into his own mountain library. His dad had also been an avid reader, although their tastes in books were quite different. His father didn't share his penchant for strange horror or the macabre. He preferred to read more mainstream mystery, private eye, or spy-type novels.

The library contained only a sitting chair with wall-to-wall bookshelves filled with varying assortments of books. Charlie had once tried to count them all but stopped after becoming bored at over eight hundred titles.

But probably what Charlie loved best about the place—much to Susan's and his children's dismay—was that there was no television.

He wasn't a prude, but the shit that was on the boob tube today was unbelievable. If he had his way, he would get rid of every television in their home. Well, on second thought, maybe he would keep one for football season.

Charlie walked over to the library and ran a finger across a few dusty titles. He already had the night planned. He was going to build a nice fire, drink a few beers, read a little, and then hit the hay early. He scanned the books and pulled out *Salem's Lot* by Stephen King.

He considered reading it for the third time but instead, settled on one of his dad's old books, an old

John MacDonald book titled *The Busted Flush.* It was an unusual choice for him, giving his penchant for reading almost nothing but horror novels, but he didn't want to scare himself silly the very first night.

He had brought his own cache of books but figured it was better to warm up with a good old-fashioned "private investigator, pretty damsel-in-distress" story.

He went back to the leather chair, opened a new beer, and began to read. The night passed and only after looking down at the side of the chair and seeing eight empty beer cans did he realize how late it had become. Susan would have a conniption fit if she knew he drank that many beers in one night.

He laughed. He had already broken his promise. *Oh well, what she doesn't know won't hurt her.*

He looked up at the clock and yawned. "Damn! It's almost midnight."

He returned the novel to its rightful spot in the library and walked upstairs. *That was a good first night,* he thought, taking off his clothes. He climbed into bed with a content feeling and immediately fell asleep.

∾

I'm going to die! Absolute dread raced through his mind as an overwhelming sense of terror spread through his body. He was blindly running through the dark woods, and he knew he had to get away from what was chasing him if he had any hope of surviving.

He couldn't remember how he came to be in the woods, but he knew an unknown, unfathomable assailant was close behind, and somehow, Charlie understood if it caught him, a slow agonizing death would result. His foot slammed into a tree stump, and he fell to the ground.

An ungodly howl echoed through the forest. It was close, real close.

He could feel his ankle swelling, but fear overpowered any sense of pain. He scrambled to his feet and continued blindly running through the trees. He had no idea where he was, or where he was going, but he knew he had to find somewhere to hide before it was too late.

He ran through a thicket of small bushes, oblivious to the gashes the limbs were inflicting upon his face and arms.

He stumbled out of the brush into a clearing on top of a long cliff that stretched as far as he could see. He feverishly looked around thinking he recognized where he was. He didn't know how he knew, but he was sure there was a cave somewhere underneath the edge of the cliff.

A small degree of hope filled him. If he could reach the cave, he just might survive.

That tiny glimmer of hope faded as another bloodcurdling shriek came from behind him.

He ran faster along the edge of the cliff, desperately searching for the entrance to the cave. His chest and lungs burned, screaming for him to stop. His legs felt like they were on fire, but he pushed on, fueled by pure adrenaline and abject terror.

He saw a strange outcropping of rocks that resembled a wolf on the prowl, and he knew the cave was just behind the rocks. He had found it! The cave opening was only a few yards away. A faint blue light illuminated the opening, which was just under the cliff's face another fifty feet away.

Charlie ran as fast as he could. He was only feet away when a shriek erupted to his left side. He scrambled up the last incline knowing it had to be almost on him. He could feel its hot stinking breath on his neck. An overwhelming dread filled him with the realization that he wasn't going to make it.

An explosion of pain tore through his back. Every nerve, every fiber in his body exploded in an instantaneous ball of searing fire and pain. He collapsed under the weight of the attacker, knowing his chance to escape had failed.

It was upon him—attacking, slashing, biting, tearing—causing him to experience a type of pain that he didn't think possible. Charlie felt his flesh and muscle being savagely torn from his body.

And through the unfathomable pain, Charlie experienced a new type of a terror. A terror that was far worse than the fear of trying to flee or the pain of the savage attack.

He realized that there are indeed worse things than being dead, and Charlie prayed as he had never prayed before. He prayed not for escape but for death, an unconscious, unfeeling death where complete nothingness filled all voids.

~

Chapter 3

Wellington, North Carolina

Day One, Sunday, February 3

Charlie bolted from the bed gasping for air, with a sense of impending doom raging through his mind. His heart felt like it had seized inside his chest, and he desperately looked around the darkened room in utter disorientation.

Where the hell was he?

He clutched his chest. An enormous pressure filled the center of it, and a cold sweat drenched his entire body. A dreadful thought ran through his mind. He was having a heart attack, and he was going to die. Alone.

"Oh Jesus! No!" he prayed. Finally, his panicked mind grasped where he was, and he leapt off the bed clutching his chest.

He stumbled over to the nightstand, grabbed the phone, and started to dial 9-1-1, but then he hesitated. He took a deep breath and gingerly rubbed his chest. The pressure had eased immensely. He could feel his heartbeat beginning to slow and the all-encompassing dread beginning to fade. He sat down on the bed, still holding the phone. Even though Charlie felt a little better, his body shook uncontrollably.

Early morning light streamed in through a crack between the curtains of the bedroom window, and the dream surfaced in his mind. He laughed nervously as it dawned on him that he wasn't having a heart attack. The nightmare must have triggered some type of a panic attack.

He took a deep breath. "Jeez, what a nightmare." He sighed, running a hand through his sweat-soaked hair.

Hell! He had never had a dream like that before. It felt almost too real to have been a dream. He sat on the bed for a full ten minutes breathing deeply, trying to get his body to return to normal.

Finally, he stood. His legs almost buckled. They felt like they were made out of Jell-O. He took a step, and for some strange reason, his ankle hurt like hell. He limped into the bathroom and took a long, hot shower. The steaming hot water helped clear some of the cobwebs out of his mind, but it didn't eliminate the nightmare from his thoughts. He had never experienced a dream so vivid, so real.

After showering and dressing, he went downstairs, fixed coffee, cooked up a couple of eggs and some hash browns. He was ravenous, and after the shower, four cups of hot coffee, and a full belly, the dream and the terror it had brought faded.

Charlie walked outside onto the cabin porch, breathing in the cold mountain air. He slowly exhaled a stream of mist through his mouth and raised his face up toward the morning sun. He closed his eyes, letting the winter sunlight bathe his face in warmth.

He opened his eyes, taking in his surroundings. Charlie felt weird, but he couldn't quite place what was causing the feeling, and it bothered him. After a few moments, he laughed. He realized why he felt so strange—he was surrounded by complete silence.

He looked around. No cars. No kids. No dogs barking. No phones or radios or TVs, only unadulterated, absolute silence. The bright sunlight reflected off the snow, causing him to shield his eyes with his hand. He looked back toward the house. Long icicles resembling sharp daggers hung down from the roof. Tiny beads of melting water slowly dripped from the end of the ice's razor-sharp points. Charlie made a mental note to be careful not to stand underneath one of the dagger-like icicles.

He looked up toward the blue sky and saw a pair of hawks circling high above the mountain peaks, and it struck him: the silence was, well…it was unnerving.

He went back inside and grabbed his car keys. He drove into Wellington, and even though it was not his initial plan, for some unexplained reason, he pulled in front of the grocery store. He parked the car and walked into the store.

A gangly teenage boy was at the checkout counter, and Charlie walked up and down a few aisles pretending to shop. He saw no sign of the girl, so he grabbed a twelve pack of beer from the cooler and walked back to the checkout counter.

"How are you doing?" he said, setting the beer down.

The kid grumbled something incoherent and rang up the cash register.

"Hey, I was in here last night, and a young girl was working. Do you know when she is scheduled to work again?"

"What?" the teenager mumbled.

Charlie knew he probably sounded like some kind of a stalker or pervert. After all, the girl was probably half his age.

"I, uh, well, she's the Indian girl, and I am doing some research into local tribal customs, and I just wanted to ask her a question."

"Indian girl? I don't know what you are talking about. No Indians work here."

"I was in here last night buying groceries. She had long black hair, probably in her early twenties."

"Mister, you must have gone into another store. I've worked here since I was twelve. My dad owns the place. We have never had an Indian boy, an Indian girl, or an Indian chief work here, ever."

Charlie wasn't sure how to respond. "Sorry. I must have been mistaken."

He handed the kid a twenty-dollar bill and took back the change. He picked up the beer. The kid turned his back, and Charlie left. He got into his car thinking that punk kid had to be pulling his chain. Then it dawned on him. *Hell, the kid was probably infatuated with her. Who wouldn't be?* Maybe he saw Charlie as an adversary.

Teenagers. That's okay, he thought. He could check back in later. *She probably works the night shift.*

Charlie ran a few pointless errands and returned back to the cabin in the midafternoon, where he kept busy by chopping firewood. The hard work felt good, and he lost track of time until he realized the creeping shadows from the surrounding trees had started to close in around him.

He looked up. The sun was just above the crest of the mountain.

He set the ax down, and a sense of trepidation filled him as he stared up at the barren mountain. He couldn't explain it, but it was like he was dreading the coming darkness.

That settles it, he thought. It was finally time to go to the Green Man and see Kingsley. He went inside, cleaned up, and grabbed a beer for the road. As he pulled onto the highway, he wondered if he really wanted to go to the bar or if that was just an excuse because he didn't want to be at home alone with the specter of night and the darkness it brought.

Night fell across the mountain as he drove down to the bar. During the entire drive, Charlie kept reminding himself to limit himself on the beer intake. He was already jumpy enough, and alcohol had a strange effect on him. For most people, it served as a relaxant, but for him, if he wasn't careful, it actually had the opposite effect.

He had stopped drinking heavily after his "episode," and the few hangovers he had had over the last decade had been awful. He was perfectly fine when he drank, happy and easygoing, but the next morning brought only misery.

He could handle the typical symptoms of overindulgence, but what he couldn't live with was the extreme anxiety and feelings of severe depression that his hangovers seemed to bring. In fact, usually after suffering from one of his extreme hangovers, it would be months until he touched a drop of alcohol again. That's how bad it felt.

Charlie pulled into the Green Man's parking lot. Only two pickup trucks and a very old Buick were parked in the lot.

Must be a slow night, Charlie surmised.

He walked in and saw a few crusty-looking locals sitting at a table drinking pints of draft beer and playing cards. The men cautiously glanced up from their game to inspect the newcomer invading their territory.

Charlie smiled and nodded in their direction. "Evening, gentlemen."

For his efforts to be friendly, he received a few cursory grunts, and then complete dismissal as the men went back to their card game.

The layout of the pub was exactly how he envisioned an old tavern tucked away in some English countryside would look like. The place was dimly lit with hardwood floors, dark paneled walls, and a tall ceiling.

A long oak bar ran against the back wall of the main room, with an assortment of wooden tables haphazardly strewn around the room. A hallway in the back led to a dining room, rarely used because the kitchen was operated only when Kingsley felt like cooking, which was not often.

But when he did cook, the food was excellent. Usually, there was just one item on the menu to choose from, but it was generally an exquisite English fare such as rabbit, beef Wellington, Shepherd's Pie, and occasionally, fish and chips.

Charlie sat down at the oak bar, and after a minute or two, Kingsley came out of a small office behind the bar. A big smile spread across his face as he spotted Charlie.

"Hell's bells," he cheerfully said in an English accent, despite having lived the better part of the last four decades in the United States. "If it isn't old 'Charlie Boy' himself! How the hell are you doing?"

Charlie returned the smile. "I'm doing great. How's things been treating you?"

"Oh, just peachy." Kingsley reached into the cooler and pulled out two beers. "Here you go, young man."

"Thank you, sir." They clinked their beer bottles together.

"Man, that tastes good," Charlie said, after downing a third of the beer.

"You said it. Hey! What are you doing up here this time of the year?"

"Oh, just wanted to get away for a little while."

"Is the family with you?"

"Oh dear God, no!" he answered, causing Kingsley to laugh. "They're back in Charleston. I have some fix-up work to do around the cabin, plus I needed a little break from work."

"Well, I'll be, Charlie Boy's a bachelor."

"Damn straight." They raised their beer bottles up in a salute.

"Man, you didn't pick the best winter to visit. It's been brutal. I think it has snowed more this winter than the last five combined."

"I've heard it's been bad."

One of the card players yelled over to the bar, "Hey Kingsley, how's 'bout when you two stop kissing, bring us another round, you good-for-nothing lazy bastard."

Kingsley winked at Charlie and replied back to the card players, "Hold on, you bunch of drunks. Can't you see I have an important customer here? If you ever bothered to pay your tab on time or leave a halfway decent tip, I might give you better service."

The card players collectively scowled at his jab and went back to their game.

"Hold on, Charlie. Let me take care of those old fools." Kingsley filled up a pitcher with beer and brought it over to their table.

When he returned, he asked Charlie, "How long you up for?"

"About a week or so. Maybe a little longer if I can convince the missus."

"That's great..." Kingsley's voice trailed off, and Charlie noticed that his usually rosy complexion had suddenly lost all of its color.

Kingsley's eyes were fixed on something over his shoulder. Charlie turned toward the bar's entrance, and standing in the doorway was one of the strangest looking men he had ever seen in his life.

The new arrival stepped into the bar. He was tall, stick-thin, and dressed in an old, out-of-style black suit. The gangly man looked like he could have played a villain in one of those old Clint Eastwood spaghetti western movies. He walked into the middle of the bar staring at Kingsley with a wry smile on his face. Slowly his head turned toward Charlie.

The man's smile resembled a hyena grinning, and it sent a chill through him. The newcomer took off his black bowler hat, uncovering a tangled mass of straw-like white hair. Even from ten feet away, Charlie could see the man's teeth were dark gray, and a pair of black eyes offset his unnaturally pale face.

The man sauntered over to the bar, and even the card players watched his every move. "Kingsley," he announced in a gravelly, almost shrill voice. "It has been awhile."

Charlie studied the man more closely. His skin complexion looked almost albino-like. He couldn't tell if the man was sixty or ninety, but what really struck Charlie as unusual for someone his age was the skin on his face. It was pretty much wrinkle-free.

"Reverend McCellan," Kingsley replied back in an uncustomarily subdued tone.

The reverend turned toward Charlie, obviously waiting for an introduction. Charlie coughed a bit nervously then stuck out his hand. "Charlie Parker."

The reverend's grip was loose, and his hand felt like he was shaking a block of ice. *How could any living person have hands as cold as that?* Charlie wondered.

The reverend stared into Charlie's eyes, causing him to involuntarily look away. Suddenly, the reverend's grip tightened, and Charlie felt talon-like fingernails pressing into his palm. His nails dug deeper. Charlie held back a grimace, wondering what the hell was wrong with this asshole. Charlie forced himself to look back at the man.

"Reverend Stoudemire McCellan. Pleasure to make your acquaintance, Mr. Parker," he said in an old man's Southern drawl.

Charlie pulled his hand away. "Same here."

Out of the corner of his eye, he saw the card players collectively rise and leave.

"You don't happen to be Charles and Katherine Parker's son?"

His gaze returned back to the man with a look of astonishment. "Yes, I am," Charlie answered.

"Such a tragedy." The reverend shook his head.

Charlie felt himself nodding before grasping what he had actually said, as if the man had some type of hypnotic power. "You knew my parents?"

"What brings you into town, Reverend?" Kingsley interjected before the reverend could answer Charlie's question. "I thought your business in Wellington was done."

The reverend turned back toward Kingsley. "A man in my position always has work to complete. You should know that better than anyone."

Charlie was surprised by how much Kingsley's demeanor had changed since the reverend entered the bar. It was almost as if he was afraid of the man.

"Do you plan on staying long…this time?" Kingsley asked.

"Till my business is complete."

The reverend turned back toward Charlie, who took the opportunity to repeat his question. "You said you knew my parents?"

"Yes. I knew them. This is a small town, after all. As a matter of fact, not only did I know your parents, but your grandfather and my father were quite close." He paused before adding, "For quite some time."

Charlie was absolutely dumbfounded. "You knew my grandfather?"

"I know this may be hard to believe by looking at me now, but I knew him when I was a young boy. My father and your grandfather were, eh…good friends, shall we say."

The admission shocked Charlie so much he just stood there with his mouth gaping open like a fool, despite the millions of questions swimming around in his brain.

"Wow," he finally mumbled. "That's incredible, but you don't live here anymore?"

"Until a few years ago, I lived in this area. My family is originally from here. Wellington has been, and still is, a rather tight-knit community."

"Why'd you leave?"

The reverend looked across the bar at Kingsley. "Like the good man said, my business here was complete. But now I have further business."

"What business is that?" Charlie asked.

The reverend smiled, allowing Charlie to see just how ugly and gray his teeth actually were.

"I am an undertaker." The reverend's grin disappeared.

Charlie couldn't help himself and laughed. "I hope you aren't anticipating anyone dying in Wellington anytime soon, are you?" He bit the inside of his lip, instantly regretting his little joke.

"I certainly hope not, but some things are out of my control. It has been a pleasure meeting you, son. I'm sure we'll run into one another again."

The reverend turned back to Kingsley, reached into his jacket, and pulled out a small book. "I came to return this to you."

He handed the book over to Kingsley, who apparently had no inclination whatsoever to take it because the reverend practically had to reach across the bar and shove the book into Kingsley's hands.

The reverend put his bowler back on and bowed slightly. "Good night, gentlemen."

"Wait, Reverend," Charlie called out. "I'd like to ask you some questions about my grandfather, if you don't mind. My father never really talked about him much."

"No, I wouldn't have expected that your father would have had much desire to do that. I am sorry, I have to leave now, but our paths will cross again. That I am sure of."

"But is there some way I could get in touch with you?" Charlie asked, almost in desperation.

The reverend smiled. "Don't worry, son. I'll find you. Rest assured."

Charlie was almost frantic because he realized that he was probably letting the only person alive who knew anything about his grandfather just walk out the door. He'd probably never see the guy again. Charlie watched the reverend leave the bar, and another thought occurred—what in the hell did the reverend mean when he said that he wasn't surprised that his father had never discussed Charlie's grandfather with him?

Charlie sat on the barstool and looked back at Kingsley, who was still white as a ghost. "I can't believe that guy knew my grandfather."

Kingsley shrugged his shoulders with a dismissive look and remained silent.

"Damn, that's one strange dude, huh?" Charlie said, taking a big swig from his beer.

Charlie noticed Kingsley was holding the book the reverend had given him like it was a gift from the devil.

"Kingsley, are you all right?

"What?" He looked up from the book, staring past Charlie. "I'm fine."

"Good. Why don't you give me a beer then."

Kingsley reached into the cooler, set a new beer next to Charlie and walked into his office without saying a word.

Charlie had almost finished his beer before Kingsley came back out. His face had regained a little color, but he still looked unnaturally pale.

"Damn," Charlie kidded. "What's wrong with you? You look like the reverend gave you a case of the willies."

"Nothing's wrong," Kingsley replied in an uncharacteristically nervous fashion. "But I will tell you this: stay away from that man. He's...he's no good."

Charlie laughed. "The reverend? C'mon. What are you talking about? He's just some old geezer."

"You're right about that."

"Is he really an undertaker?"

Kingsley opened a beer for himself. "He used to be. I don't think he has practiced in decades. The old bugger is crazy. He's been searching for gold up in the mountains for half of his life."

"Gold?" Charlie laughed. "He's a treasure hunter mortician?"

"I don't know what he is. Just stay away, and don't ask me any more questions about him. You understand?"

"Okay, but curiosity is killing me. What was that book that he gave you all about?"

"I said to forget it!" Kingsley snapped.

"All right. Sorry," Charlie replied, taken back by the anger in Kingsley's voice. *What's gotten into him?* he wondered.

Kingsley set his beer on the bar and went back into his office. After almost half an hour of waiting for him to come back out, Charlie figured he must have wanted him to leave. *So the hell with him,* Charlie thought, digging a ten-dollar bill out of his pocket. He threw it onto the bar and left.

~

The nightmare came again. An unfathomable evil chased Charlie through the nighttime forest. Once again, he came to the edge of the long cliff desperately searching for the cave. He saw the entrance and sprinted toward it, knowing the beast was right behind him.

He was only feet from the cave when a searing pain exploded from his shoulder, throwing him down to the ground. Raw fear and pain exploded through his body as large chunks of flesh were ripped from his back. The monster's claws shook him violently, turning him over onto his side. This time, Charlie caught a partial glimpse of the monster's ghastly face.

The beast had a human resemblance, and it looked like Reverend McCellan.

~

Chapter 4

Day Two

Monday

The nightmare woke Charlie up at 3:00 in the morning. He sat up in bed gasping for air, but this time he knew he wasn't having a heart attack despite his racing heart and squeezing pain in his chest.

He lay back down and tossed and turned for the next couple of hours. He couldn't get the damn image of the beast and its resemblance to the reverend out of his mind. Finally, with dawn almost upon him, Charlie managed to drift off to sleep, only to have his slumber interrupted by a constant ringing.

Half-asleep, Charlie finally realized the noise was the phone. He reached over to the bedside table and picked it up. "Hello," he mumbled.

A low hissing sound came from the receiver.

"Hello," he repeated, only to be greeted by an eerie static that rose and fell in pitch.

"God damn it!" Charlie slammed the phone down.

The clock read *5:58.* He rolled over onto his back and stared up at the ceiling. Just like the morning before, his chest felt heavy, his hands and feet were clammy, and an uncomfortable trepidation filtered through his body. He couldn't get the night's dream out of his mind.

What in the hell is the deal with the nightmares? he wondered.

His thoughts turned to that weird-ass son of a bitch he had met at the Green Man. The reverend—the undertaker gold hunter. He couldn't believe the guy had known both his father and grandfather.

He tried to shake off the strange dreams by forcing himself to laugh. Didn't doctors say that laughter was the best medicine?

"Just my mind playing tricks on me," he spoke up to the ceiling, positive that the dreams and the fact that he was all alone out in the middle of the woods were the underlying cause of his anxiety. After all, he did have a penchant for reading horror stories. Charlie was certain he was just letting his imagination get the best of him.

He closed his eyes, and much to his surprise, he felt himself drifting off.

He wasn't sure how long he had been asleep when once again; the phone jolted him out of his sleep. Charlie wearily stared at the nightstand, hesitating to pick it up. The bedside clock read *9:30.* He must have been exhausted to have slept this late. The damn thing would not stop ringing, so finally, he reached for the phone, almost forcing himself to answer it.

"Hello!" he snapped.

"Charlie," he heard Susan's voice speak.

"Oh, hey, honey. How's it going?" he replied in a more gentle tone.

"Jeez, you're supposed to be relaxing. What are you so jumpy about?"

Charlie laughed. "Sorry. I was still sleeping. Someone kept calling in the middle of the night and..." He didn't know what to tell her, so he changed the subject. "How're you and the kids doing?"

"Fine, I guess," she huffed.

Charlie instantly recognized the "something's wrong" tone in her voice.

"What's the matter?" he asked, knowing he would regret it.

"Jeffery got into big trouble at school."

Charlie sat up in bed. "What'd he do?"

"It's a long story, but he and that delinquent buddy of his, Donny Butler, they started a mud ball fight during recess, and let's just say Principal Jones was not too happy about it."

Charlie tried not to laugh because he knew Susan took these matters seriously. Jeffery was a good boy for the most part, and hell, kids will be kids.

"C'mon, Susan. Principal Jones...That old biddy probably hasn't laughed once in the last fifty years."

"That's beside the point. You didn't let me finish," she admonished him. "Jeffery hit a girl in the eye with one of the mud balls, and there must have been a rock or something in it because it cut her pretty badly."

"Shit," Charlie muttered. "Is she all right?"

"No, she isn't. She had to get stitches. And who knows, if it had hit her a half-inch lower, she might have lost her eyesight."

"God damn it!" Charlie cursed, realizing for once Susan wasn't being overly dramatic about something. "And Jeffery and his buddy started all of this?"

"Yeah, they suspended him for a week, and he is on probation for the rest of the year. The principal told me they were close to expelling Jeffery, and they would have if it hadn't been for his outstanding grades and good behavior."

Charlie sighed. "Sorry you had to deal with this by yourself. Ah, do you want me to come home?" He hated asking her that and held his breath as the line went silent.

"No," Susan finally answered. "There is nothing you can do now. It's all right."

Charlie took a deep breath. "I'll have a long talk with him when I get home."

"Well, his ass is grounded for the rest of the month, so he will have plenty of time to think about it. So are you enjoying your little vacation?" she asked in a sarcastic tone.

"Yeah, it's been relaxing so far," he lied.

"Sure didn't sound like it by the way you answered the phone."

"Like I said, some idiot kept calling and hanging up last night. Must've been a wrong number or something."

"Everything else okay?"

"Just fine."

"All right, have fun today. I have to go."

"I'll call you later tonight. Love you."

"Love you, too," Susan replied. "Bye."

Charlie rolled out of bed, took a quick shower, and headed downstairs for coffee. As the pot was brewing, he turned on the radio because he needed some noise to fill the silence.

He walked outside onto the porch and breathed in the fresh air. He stared off into the countryside, taking in the tranquility, the stillness of the woods surrounding him.

Dark gray clouds hung low in the sky. They looked like snow clouds, and Charlie could almost feel the moisture in the air. It was going to snow later in the day. He breathed deeply. The nightmares were still vivid in his mind. It had all seemed so real. He had had nightmares before, but they had never felt like this, so frightening, so real.

He laughed. "It's too damn quiet here," he yelled out to the woods. The sound of his voice breaking the quiet stillness startled him.

Charlie walked around the side of the house to the back. The fresh layer of snow crunched loudly underneath his boots. He stood in the back yard surveying the property. He looked back toward the house and felt his breath catch. Underneath his bedroom window was a set of animal prints, and they weren't from a small animal.

He slowly walked over and crouched down to get a better look. The prints stopped right up against the back of the house. Charlie turned on one knee and looked back. The tracks led out into the woods and appeared to go up the mountainside.

Was it a bear? Black bears were pretty common in the area.

He stood wondering why in the hell an animal would walk all the way up to the house directly below the window to his bedroom. Was it looking for food? Did the animal sense he was up there sleeping?

The thought unsettled him, and even though he figured he must be out of his mind, he couldn't resist the urge. Charlie ran back inside and grabbed his heavy coat, winter hat, and gloves. He was determined to see where those tracks led to.

As he walked toward the edge of the woods, a thought occurred to him. What if he came face to face with the culprit? What would he do then?

He ignored his own mind's warning and followed the prints through his property down to a stream, where they disappeared. The water was only about knee-deep, but he wasn't going to risk frostbite to follow some damn animal. Charlie walked along the side of the stream for a few hundred yards, where he found a log to cross over. Then he backtracked to where the prints had ended on the other side.

Charlie smiled. *Not too bad for a city boy,* he thought. The tracks started again on the other side.

The higher he hiked up into the mountains, the more he began to second-guess his decision about going so far into the woods. What if he did run into a bear? Or what if he fell and broke something? He might not even be able to make it back home.

Stop! his mind shouted. *Talk about a big baby.* He was acting like he was scared of his own shadow.

Despite his growing apprehension, he felt a tremendous urge to continue on, and he was determined to do so, no matter what fears his mind conjured up.

The trees grew thicker, and the terrain turned harsh and rugged as he pushed higher up the slope of the mountain. He emerged from a thick crop of trees and froze dead in his tracks.

A hundred yards directly in front of him were two men kneeling down over something. They were frantically chopping something, and both of the men wore clothes that appeared to be made out of animal skins.

What in the hell were they doing?

An intense fear filled Charlie, followed by a sense of immediate life-threatening danger. He didn't know why, but he couldn't let them know he was there. Their backs faced him, so he hadn't been seen yet. He could still get away.

Charlie slowly began to back up toward the trees and had just reached the perimeter of the forest when he saw a large black raven perched on a tree branch over the heads of the Indians.

The raven turned toward Charlie's direction. Then it squawked loudly. Both men turned and looked up at the bird, then down the slope at Charlie.

He had been spotted.

Charlie began to wave but stopped. Fear tore through him as he got a better look at the men.

His mind couldn't comprehend what his eyes were seeing. They appeared to be native Indians, but something was horribly wrong with their faces.

Even with the distance between them, Charlie could tell their faces were hideously disfigured.

Charlie's body froze in terror as one of the Indians flashed an evil smile, causing a wave of hot bile to rush up from the pit of his stomach into his throat.

What in God's name was wrong with them?

Both Indians slowly rose to their feet, giving Charlie a gruesome view of what they had been kneeling over. In between the Indians were the disemboweled remains of some animal, or at least he hoped for his sake it was an animal.

The warm bile moved from his throat into his mouth, and he felt like he was going to vomit. His eyes returned to the disfigured faces of the Indians and he looked down to their hands holding long bloody knives.

The raven gave another high-pitched squawk, and one of the Indians raised his head toward the sky, letting out a bloodcurling scream.

Charlie's heart seized in his chest. The two Indians began running toward him with their knives raised. For an instant, he stared, almost transfixed by the bloody knives, before self-preservation took over, causing him to bolt through the trees with the comprehension that he was in a race for his life.

The fear was so strong, he couldn't even process a clear thought except that if those Indians caught him, he was going to end up sliced open with his guts hanging out like whatever it was they had been mutilating.

He was a long way from home and doubted he could outrun them, but what alternative did he have? He sprinted down the jagged slope, zigzagging between trees for fifteen minutes straight, not once looking back.

He was too afraid to.

He reached the stream bordering his property and jumped straight in without a moment's hesitation. He waded across as fast as he could, not giving a thought to the freezing cold water. He crossed back onto his property and allowed himself to think that he might actually live to see another day.

Only after catching a glimpse of his roof did Charlie risk a look back. He saw no sign of the Indians. He ran the last stretch to the cabin, where he burst in through the front door, collapsing onto the floor.

Charlie desperately tried to catch his breath, but his lungs burned, and it felt like he was trying to suck a noodle through a straw. His chest heaved, with his breath coming in ragged gasps.

He slammed the door shut and barely managed to lift his hand up to turn the lock on the handle. Charlie slumped back down and sat on the floor with his back against the door, trying to get oxygen into his lungs.

After a few minutes, he managed to catch his breath somewhat. And once he realized he wasn't going to die from suffocation or a heart attack, his fear turned back to the Indians.

Did they follow him all the way here? For all he knew, they could be scouting out the place now, looking for a way to attack him inside of his home.

Charlie crawled over to the window and peeked above the ledge. No sign of them. He half stood and ran crouched all the way over to the back of the kitchen. He fell down underneath the window. Slowly, he peered out into the back yard. Still nothing, but he wasn't going to take any chances. He reached up, grabbed the phone, and dialed the sheriff's office.

"Sheriff's Department," a lady's voice answered. "How may I assist you?"

"This is Charlie Parker," he said breathlessly. "Can you please connect me to Sheriff Thomas?"

"Sorry, sir. The sheriff is at a Rotary Club meeting. Can I take a message?"

Rotary Club! He was on the verge of being killed, and the sheriff was at a Rotary Club meeting.

"Listen," he practically screamed into the phone, "this is important! I've been...Is there any way to get a hold of him?"

"Is this an emergency, sir?"

Charlie hesitated for a second. The sight of the gruesome faces of the Indians was still fresh in his mind. "God damn right, it is," he answered. "Please get him on the phone and tell him that Charlie Parker out at the Parker residence off Highway 107 has been..." He paused.

"Yes...Sir, are you there?"

"Just tell him to get out here as fast as possible. Somebody's trying to kill me." Charlie slammed the phone down and looked around.

He needed something to protect himself. God damn Susan! This was exactly why he should have kept one of his dad's guns. He should have never listened to that stupid bitch. He was going to get killed, and it was all her fault.

He grabbed the fire poker, and once again checked outside. Nothing.

The phone rang, almost causing him to faint before remembering that it was probably the sheriff calling back. He ran over to the table and picked up the phone. "Hello."

"Mr. Parker, this is Sheriff Thomas," a calm, reassuring voice said. "What's the problem?"

"Sheriff, thanks for calling me back. I know this sounds crazy, but some damn Indians tried to kill me!"

"What!" the sheriff replied with a tone of disbelief. "Can you repeat that?"

"I was attacked by two Indians."

"Inside your house?"

"No, ah, I was up in the mountains, and they attacked me."

"Attacked you?"

"I mean they were going to. They had knives, and they began to chase me. I outran them back to my house."

"Hold on, Mr. Parker. I want you to take a deep breath, okay?"

"Okay." Charlie tried to calm himself.

"Did these men follow you?" the sheriff asked in a very calm, professional manner.

"I haven't seen them, but this all just happened. They could be right outside my house for all I know."

"Have you been..." The sheriff didn't finish the sentence, but Charlie knew that he was going to ask him if he'd been drinking.

But instead, the sheriff said, "I'm leaving now. I'll be at your place in less than eight minutes. Are you hurt or injured?"

"No."

"Is anyone with you?"

"No."

"Mr. Parker, do you have a phone in your upstairs bedroom?"

"Yes."

"Good. Are your front and back doors locked?"

"Yes."

"Fine. I want you to hang up the downstairs phone. Go up to the bedroom. Lock the bedroom door, and I will call you right back."

"Okay." Charlie hung up the phone, ran upstairs, and was locking the bedroom door when the phone started ringing.

He grabbed it. "Sheriff."

A low hiss crackled over the line. "Sheriff?" he repeated. The hiss continued. Then Charlie thought he heard words through the noise.

"Sheriff!" he screamed.

The hiss stopped, and a garbled voice began whispering, "Nun He. Nun He. Nun He." Over and over, the words without meaning were repeated.

"Who is this?" he yelled into the phone.

"Nun He. Nun He. Nun He." The chanting grew louder, faster.

Then it struck him, those were the same words the Indian girl at the grocery store had said to him—Nun He.

What in the hell did those words mean?

Charlie slammed the phone down. Two seconds didn't pass before it rang again.

"Shit!" he cursed, not wanting to pick the phone back up.

Then he remembered he had to answer it. It might be the sheriff.

He grabbed the phone and said hesitantly, "Hello."

"Charlie?" the sheriff asked.

"Yes." He breathed a sigh of relief.

"Why didn't you pick up the line? It just kept ringing."

"What! I don't know, I..." Charlie didn't know what to say because if the sheriff had called, he would have heard a busy signal because they didn't have call waiting.

"Never mind 'bout that. Are you up in the bedroom?" the sheriff asked.

"Yes."

"Good. Do you have a firearm or any other type of weapon on you?"

"No. My damn wife made me get rid of them. I can't believe that..."

"That's okay." The sheriff cut him off. "We are less than five minutes away. I have my deputy with me, and I'm going to turn the siren on when we turn down your road. You'll be able to hear it."

"All right." Charlie peered out of the bedroom window trying to see if there was any sign of the Indians.

"Now," he heard the sheriff say in a relaxed tone. "Let's leave this line open. Tell me if you hear anybody trying to break into your house or if you see anything, but don't hang up the phone until I tell you to. All right?"

"Okay."

Charlie remained on the line. Three minutes later, he heard the police siren in the distance, and for the first time since his run-in with the Indians, he felt reasonably safe. He waited for thirty seconds. "Sheriff, I'm heading downstairs," he said into the phone. "I'll meet you at the door."

"See you out front." The phone line went dead.

He was at the bedroom door when the phone rang. Surely that wasn't the sheriff calling back. He took a step back into the room but stopped. A voice inside of him told him not to answer it.

He left the bedroom with the phone still ringing. Charlie cautiously walked down the stairs and peered around—nothing. He opened the front door just as the police cruiser pulled up.

Charlie stepped out onto the porch with a tremendous feeling of relief. The cavalry had arrived.

"Thanks for getting here so quickly," he called out to the sheriff and the other policeman as they jumped out of the car. They surveyed the yard before returning their attention to Charlie.

"Charlie, this is Deputy Johnny Ridge." Charlie shook his hand.

The deputy was an Indian. He was young, probably in his late twenties, and he was dressed in a crisp khaki policeman's outfit, with a black tie and a silver star pinned over his heart. He took off his black cowboy hat, unveiling short, cropped black hair. His face was chiseled, and his demeanor was all business.

"Charlie, why don't you go back inside for a few minutes while we take a quick look around? When we're done, you can tell us exactly what happened."

"You want me to go with you?"

"No. Let us make sure the property is secure. Then we'll talk."

Charlie grudgingly went back inside. After a few minutes, there was a knock, and the door opened. The sheriff, followed by the deputy, walked inside.

Deputy Ridge spoke first. "There was a wolf here last night."

"What?" Charlie replied, before remembering the animal tracks outside of his house that had caused him to go up into the mountains in the first place. "I thought they were from a bear," Charlie said.

The sheriff pointed at the deputy. "He doesn't look like it, but Johnny here is the best tracker in the county. He's a full-blooded Cherokee. They call him Big Bird." The sheriff laughed at his wisecrack.

"My Cherokee name is Soaring Eagle," the deputy corrected him.

The sheriff smiled. "Right."

"So those prints in the back yard are from a wolf?" Charlie asked the deputy.

"Yes, sir."

"I didn't think wolves lived up in these mountains anymore."

"There aren't supposed to be any," the sheriff said. "I haven't heard of anyone seeing a wolf in these parts in over twenty years."

"There are a few left," the deputy rebutted. He pointed up toward the top of the mountain. "They live up high, in the most remote parts of the mountains. It is very rare for one to come down this far, though. Very unusual."

"Okay, enough with the wolf," the sheriff said impatiently. "Why don't you tell us what happened."

Charlie gathered his thoughts. "Well, that's why I went up the mountain in the first place. I saw the tracks. I thought it was strange, so I followed them."

The sheriff took off his jacket and set it on the kitchen table. "You went up the mountain by yourself?"

"I know it probably was not the smartest idea in the world, but I was curious."

"All right." The sheriff gestured toward the couch. "Why don't we all take a seat, and you can finish telling us exactly what happened."

"Y'all want a cup of coffee or something?" Charlie asked.

The sheriff looked over at the deputy, who shook his head. "No, we're fine, thanks," the sheriff answered.

The two lawmen sat down on the couch, and Charlie took a seat in his dad's leather chair.

Charlie recounted his story. Well, almost all of it. He just couldn't bring himself to tell them about the deformed condition of the Indians' faces. He knew he probably already sounded like a lunatic, so he left that part out, for now.

He finished, and they briefly glanced at each other. Charlie could tell by the expression on the sheriff's face that he had doubts about what had happened.

The sheriff fiddled with his tie. "Do you think these, ah, Indians' intent was to harm you?"

"Hell, yes. They chased me halfway down the mountain with knives. I thought they were going to kill me."

"Sir," Deputy Ridge interjected. "I don't doubt you saw two men up there, but in all likelihood, they were probably just trying to scare you. You know, have a little fun with you."

"Fun! It sure as hell didn't feel like fun to me. They had goddamn knives as big as your arm," Charlie replied angrily.

The deputy raised his arm in a conciliatory gesture. "I understand, Mr. Parker. I don't blame you for being pissed at these guys. You say you thought they were skinning an animal?"

"I didn't say 'skinning.' It looked to me like they were mutilating it."

"Well, remember, Charlie," the sheriff said, "you said you were quite a distance away from them. You know what I think?"

"No. What?"

"First, I believe you ran into some men. And I believe they were skinning the hide of an animal, maybe a protected animal. I think you might have run into a couple of poachers, and they were taken by surprise. But, I also think they probably just tried to throw a scare into you."

"I guess that could have been the case," Charlie mumbled doubtfully, because the Indians he saw sure as hell didn't look like poachers. But what was he going to tell them, that he saw two mutant Indians whose faces looked like they had been mauled by a grizzly bear?

"It wouldn't have been the first time something like this has happened," the deputy added. "You were at the wrong place at the wrong time."

"I don't know, maybe," he muttered.

"Tell you what," the sheriff said. "Me and old Yellow Bird here…" He pointed a thumb at the deputy who, by his look, didn't appreciate the jabs about his Cherokee name. "We'll track up the mountain and see what we can find. Trust me, if anyone was up there, the deputy will know it."

Charlie nodded. "Do you want me to go with you?"

"No. You'd better stay here." The sheriff smiled and pointed down toward Charlie's feet. "Why don't you get out of your wet shoes before you catch frostbite."

Charlie looked down at his shoes, realizing his feet were still wet after running through the stream. Suddenly, he could feel the cold numbness stabbing from inside of his feet, almost like tiny pins jabbing away at his flesh.

"Okay, I guess. You sure you don't want me to go with you?" he asked, shifting nervously in the chair.

"I think we can manage." The sheriff stood. He smiled reassuringly at Charlie. "Look, if I thought you were in danger of any harm, I wouldn't leave you here by yourself. We'll be back in no time. Just lock your door, and I'll keep my cell phone on. If anything happens, just call me." The sheriff handed him his card. "There's my direct cell phone."

Charlie put the card in his pocket. "Okay. I'll sit tight."

The sheriff put on his jacket, and they left. Charlie went to the kitchen and watched them trudge through the back yard until they disappeared in the trees.

Great, Charlie thought. *They think I'm some kind of big baby, or worse, they think I'm crazy.* And the more he thought about it, the sillier his story seemed. Thank God, he hadn't told them about the Indians' mutilated faces.

What in the hell would they have thought then? Serious doubts began creeping into his mind. Maybe the sheriff was right. Maybe they were just skinning an animal, and in the process, blood had sprayed onto their faces causing them to appear deformed. After all, he had been a long way from them, but he was almost certain that…

Shit. Maybe he *was* losing his mind.

There was nothing more he could do, so he went upstairs, changed his socks and shoes, and returned to the chair in the kitchen and nervously watched for the sheriff and his deputy to return.

After half an hour, Charlie grew restless and began pacing the kitchen. It was taking almost all of his willpower not to fix a drink.

An hour passed, and he began to get worried. Where in the hell were they? What if the Indians attacked them? He seriously contemplated calling the sheriff's cell phone to check in, when they emerged from the woods.

The deputy followed behind the sheriff carrying a large black plastic bag with both hands. Charlie went outside and jogged over to them.

The sheriff pointed toward the bag. "Well, Charlie, looks like you were right. We located the spot where you were at, and we found this about a hundred yards farther up the slope."

The deputy lifted the bag up. "Here's what's left of that wolf that was on your property last night."

"The Indians did that?"

"Yep," the sheriff answered.

"I'm not so sure they were Indians," the deputy cut in.

"Why?" Charlie asked.

"For one, wolves are sacred animals to the Cherokees. A Cherokee would never kill one unless..."

"So, like we thought," the sheriff interrupted, "you stumbled upon a couple of guys doing something illegal. Hell, you probably scared them more than they scared you."

"But…" Charlie didn't know what to say. "Are you going to try and find these guys?"

"We'll take the remains in for evidence, but whoever it was up there, they're long gone by now."

"But…" Charlie began to protest again.

"Charlie, look," Deputy Ridge said in a calming manner. "I don't think the men you saw were Indians. But for argument's sake, let's say they were. That means they're part of the Eastern Band of Cherokees."

The sheriff pointed to the deputy and winked at Charlie. "That's Crazy Bird's tribe."

The deputy ignored the comment and continued, "The Eastern Band has a community living past the western ridge of the mountains over in the Qualla Boundary. They've been there forever, and they don't bother anyone. They live off the land and don't really follow our rules when it comes to the land and its resources. The wolf might have been sick and threatened them, or, less likely, they might have needed the fur for clothing. And if they weren't Indians, they were poachers trying to sell the pelt for profit. Anyway, I don't think those men are any threat to you."

"Always the white man's fault." The sheriff snorted in a not-too-friendly manner. "If it was your folk, they were only living off the land, and if it was some white guys, they were just aimlessly killing for monetary gain."

"What I meant, Sheriff, was that…"

The sheriff raised a hand. "Let's just drop it."

Charlie tuned out their argument. He was confused, not only by what he saw, but by the actions of the sheriff and his deputy. He didn't care if the men he had seen were green in color. Didn't these two chuckleheads understand his life had been in danger? That's all that mattered to him.

"I didn't mean to insult anyone," the deputy continued their squabble.

"Gentlemen," Charlie interrupted. "I don't care if they were Indians. I don't care if they were black, white, yellow, or whatever. It doesn't matter to me. I saw what I saw. These men tried to kill me. That's all I care about."

"Whoever they were"—the sheriff shot the deputy a disapproving look—"we both agree. They put a fright into you to scare you off. But either way, Indians or not, I don't think you have to worry about them anymore. They won't bother you. You were just at the wrong place at the wrong time. It's that simple."

"So, that's it?"

"Well, there really isn't anything more we can do. If you don't feel safe staying here, I recommend going back home, and certainly, if anything more happens, don't hesitate to give us a call."

There was really nothing Charlie could say at this point without sounding like a lunatic or a scaredy-cat.

"You're probably right. I appreciate you coming out here as fast as you did."

"No problem." The sheriff grinned.

The men walked around to the front of the house. "Hey, you mind if I use your restroom real quick?" The sheriff patted his stomach. "I had too much coffee this morning."

"No. No problem. It's past the kitchen, down the hallway, on the right."

"I know. I've been there before," the sheriff said. He turned and headed toward the house. Charlie had forgotten that the sheriff and his father had been somewhat friendly in their younger days.

Charlie watched Deputy Ridge walk to the back of the police cruiser, where he unlocked the trunk and threw the bag with the wolf remains into it. Charlie followed him over. He wasn't exactly positive, but he felt like there was something the deputy wasn't telling him.

"So you're a pretty good tracker, huh?"

The deputy slammed the trunk top down and shrugged. "I guess."

"Hey, how far down did those guys chase me?"

"I don't know."

"What do you mean you, don't know?"

"Hard to say. Not far."

Deputy Ridge turned so they were facing each other, and for a brief second, something passed in the deputy's eyes that caused Charlie to believe that there was something he wasn't telling him, or the sheriff.

"There's some other reason why you didn't think they were Indians. What is it?"

"It's nothing."

"There's something you aren't telling me," Charlie said calmly.

Deputy Ridge looked back up at the house. "Something didn't make sense. The…" He stopped abruptly. Charlie saw the sheriff coming out of the house.

"Here." The deputy handed him a card and squeezed it into the palm of his hand. "Don't hesitate to call if you need anything."

Charlie was going to press him about it but stopped. Obviously, whatever he wanted to tell Charlie, he didn't want the sheriff to hear for some reason.

Charlie stuck the card into his shirt pocket. "Thank you. I will."

"Okay, Charlie," the sheriff called out. "Mystery solved. Don't hesitate to call us if you need anything. Just lock your doors, and you should be just fine."

"Sheriff, can I ask you an unrelated question?"

"Sure, what is it?"

"Do you happen to know a man named Reverend McCellan?"

The sheriff's jovial expression instantly disappeared. "Why?"

"Just curious. That's all."

The sheriff looked uncomfortable. "I haven't heard his name mentioned in years. He used to be an undertaker in these parts, but that was a long time ago. Why the interest?"

"No reason. His name just came up."

The cool smile returned to the sheriff's face. "Okay, Charlie, my boy, we have to go. Have a good day."

Charlie wanted to ask him more about the reverend, but he held his tongue. McCellan had struck an obvious nerve with the sheriff, and something was telling him to drop the subject, at least for now.

The sheriff and deputy got into the cruiser, and Charlie watched them drive away, thinking that his little trip to the mountains was becoming more bizarre by the hour. He began to feel like one of the characters he read about in one of his horror books.

What could Deputy Ridge possibly have been trying to tell him? And perhaps even more importantly, why wouldn't he have wanted the sheriff to hear?

Charlie looked up into the sky, and true to his earlier intuition, snowflakes began to fall.

~

Chapter 5

Charlie spent the rest of the day pacing around the house, constantly making sure the doors and windows were locked. He even cautiously ventured outside a dozen times or so to check around the property. He knew what he had seen and didn't care what the sheriff or deputy said because there was something wrong with those damn Indians.

He felt like a caged animal and needed to get out of the house. He considered going down to the Green Man for a couple of beers, but Charlie quickly dismissed the idea. The roads were likely to be a bit dicey with the new snow, plus Kingsley had acted so weird the other night, he really didn't feel like seeing him.

"It looks like it is just me and you, kid," he mumbled to himself.

Charlie walked out onto the porch. The snow had let up for the moment, and a layer of thick gray clouds hung low over the top of the mountain. Normally, he would have contemplated the beautiful sight. Instead, he was consumed with the Indians.

Where were they? What were they doing? Had they already forgotten about him, or were they lying in wait, ready to attack?

After a few minutes of scouting out the area for the hundredth time that day, he felt somewhat satisfied. "I guess the mutant Indians aren't lurking around here." He burst out laughing at the idiocy of his statement. "I've lost my mind!" he shouted out to the trees.

Charlie shook his head. Maybe the sheriff was right. Just a couple of poachers, that's all. He supposed the deputy had acted all twitchy because the Indians were probably his cousins, and he was just covering up for them so they wouldn't get into trouble.

He busied himself by stacking enough logs on the porch to take care of the fire for the night. Charlie settled in watching with growing anxiety as darkness crept down from the mountain. Large snowflakes drifted slowly down from the dark sky, and the tree limbs made low swooshing noises as the wind picked up.

Charlie sat for a while staring out of the window, listening to the silence. His heart pounded in his chest. What he really wanted to do was to go back to Charleston, but he knew it was too late now, and it was going to be a long night. He threw a couple of more logs onto the fire and walked over to the library, deciding he needed a good book to get his mind off those Indians.

He traced a finger across a row of book titles. He had read most of them, so he knelt down and began looking at some of the books on the bottom shelf. He came across *The Shining* by Stephen King and pulled it out. He had read the book at least a half-dozen times, and it was a horror classic in his opinion, but he resisted the urge to read it again. He was already jumpy enough, and *The Shining* would not do his nerves any favors.

He smiled as he pulled out his father's old copy of Bram Stoker's *Dracula*. He fondly remembered one lazy summer during his childhood—he probably wasn't older than nine or ten—and he had since read this same exact book three times.

The legendary vampire story began Charlie's love affair with the macabre.

He began to put the book back on the shelf when something caught his eye. "What the heck," he mumbled.

He pulled out a few more books, and behind them was a small wooden box. He grabbed it and blew a thin layer of dust off the top. There were no markings, with only a gold latch on the top. The box looked really old. He turned it over, and on the bottom, the word *McCellan* was carefully carved into the wood.

He could tell by the box's weight that something was inside it. He took it over to the kitchen table, and after studying it for a few more seconds, he carefully opened it.

Inside was a small hard-leather book.

He picked it up carefully. The binding was stiff, with no titles or words on either the front or back.

Charlie opened the book. The first page had turned a yellowish-brown color from the passage of time, and again there was no writing. He turned the page, and in neat, large handwritten print were the words *Ezekiel McCellan.*

He turned to the next page, and the date *September 13, 1927,* was handwritten in the upper left corner. Underneath the date, the book began:

> My name is Ezekiel McCellan, and my story begins, or should I say ends, in the year 1927 after the death of my family from the Blue Death. The pain and agony of their passing is almost too much to endure. I can't believe my beautiful wife and two daughters have been taken from me so cruelly. God is an evil, wicked being who deserves a punishment far worse than having to live on this hell known as Earth.

"Ezekiel McCellan," Charlie said aloud. He was certain the strange man who had entered the bar the other night, the reverend, had said his last name was McCellan.

Surely these two men weren't related?

He flipped through a few pages. The book appeared to be a diary of some sort, and Charlie wondered how in the world it ended up in his father's library.

Charlie turned back to the first page and continued reading:

> I have chosen to live the rest of my wretched days high in the mountains, alone, away from those who wish to destroy me and everything I have worked so hard for. I denounce all those who have betrayed me, and I shall seek vengeance upon them. I have sold all my possessions and purchased a tract of land where I have

employed local craftsmen to help me construct a suitable cabin. I have no choice in their employment, but still, I despise these men being on my property and will have to watch over them carefully. They might try to steal the secret from me, but I won't let them, no matter the cost. I have nothing to lose.

What in the hell had he stumbled upon? Charlie turned the page, and the date skipped ahead two weeks to the end of September.

I have had to abandon my search for the time being in order to see that my house is completed before winter sets in. But more importantly, I have to keep a continuous watch on the carpenters. I grow more suspicious of their intentions with each passing day.

The next entry was dated October 8, 1927.

The house has been completed just in time. Cold weather is approaching, but I have adequate living quarters and enough provisions to get me through the winter. I will spend my remaining days fighting to receive what is rightfully mine. I intend to retrieve the gold or die trying. I thought I had taken care of the Injuns once and for all, and I can't figure out where the new ones have come from and how they knew about the cave. I suppose that doesn't matter. What is done is done. They are there, and I will have to deal with them just like I dealt with the others.

I feel no remorse over my actions since the Cherokees stole the gold to begin with. It had to be done.

Charlie closed the book and stared up at the ceiling. Gold! He reached into his pocket and pulled out his Becthler gold piece. The coin felt cold, heavy in his hand, but he liked the feel of the gold, and for the first time since his father had given it to him, he wondered how much money it was worth.

He looked at his watch. It was almost 8:00. Reluctantly, he put the coin back in his pocket, set the book down, and dialed his home number.

Susan answered, and he said, "Hey, honey, how you doing?"

"Good. I hear you're getting a bunch of snow up there."

"Yeah, it really started coming down this afternoon."

"How many inches have you got?"

Charlie stood up, walked over to the window, and peered out into the darkness. "About seven or eight."

"Wow. You're not planning on going anywhere tonight, are you?" Susan phrased it like a question, when really it was meant to be a statement.

"Nope." Charlie didn't feel like explaining that the weather wasn't the real reason why he didn't feel like going down to the Green Man. He was about to ask her about Jeffery, when a movement from outside the window caught his attention.

"What the…" He walked back over to the window and pressed his eyes up against the glass. His heart felt like it was flipping over in his chest. With the blowing snow and darkness, it was hard to see, but he thought saw an outline of a figure standing up against a tree next to the driveway.

A surge of fear ran through him. Had the Indians come back?

"Charlie? Hello, are you there?" he heard Susan ask over the phone.

He squinted, trying to make out who or what was out there. He couldn't ever remember a darker night. It was as if a black blanket had been placed over his home. He wasn't certain, but he swore something moved around to the back of the tree.

"Charlie!" Susan repeated.

"Hold on." He set the phone down and walked outside. The howling wind blew snow sideways, stinging his eyes and making it hard for him to see more than a few feet.

He cupped his hands to his mouth and yelled, "Anybody there?"

Only the howling wind answered. With his body lowered against the biting wind, Charlie forced himself to walk until he was about six feet from the tree, where he stopped. He wrapped his arms around his midsection for warmth. Without the proper clothes, a person couldn't survive more than a few hours out here.

"Hello, anybody there?" he called out again.

He waited but saw no signs of movement. He cautiously circled the tree. Nothing. He looked down, and there were no footprints or signs that anybody had been there, even though Charlie swore he had seen something standing up against the tree.

His mind must be playing tricks on him. Who the hell would be out here anyway, in the darkness, with the blinding snow and hurricane-force winds?

He shook almost uncontrollably. The freezing temperatures and fierce wind actually caused physical pain, and he remembered Susan was holding on the phone. He ran back into the cabin, quickly locking the door behind him.

He picked up the phone. "Sorry, honey. Gosh dang! It's freezing out there!" he said through chattering teeth.

"Where the hell did you go?"

"I thought I saw a...deer or something outside. I just was checking it out."

"You don't think it was a bear, do you?"

Charlie laughed. "No." He always got a kick out of her apprehension of bears. A few summers ago, a couple of harmless black bears had gotten into one of their garbage dumpsters, and ever since then, she had developed a real fear of the animals.

"You sure?"

"Yes, honey, it wasn't a bear," he answered, wishing in fact that it had been one.

"Well, just be careful. You hear me?"

"Yes, I will. How are the kids?"

"Fine. Jessica is at the movies with some friends, and Jeffery is upstairs sulking because of his grounding."

"Do you want me to talk to him?"

"No, I think he just needs a little time...one of those teenage things. I think he is partly embarrassed and partly defiant about the whole thing. But hopefully, he's learned his lesson."

"Well, I'll be home in six days. Hey, by the way, do you ever remember seeing an old wooden box in the library?"

Susan laughed. "Charlie, there are a million books in there. A box...why?"

"Well, it's weird. I found it on the bottom shelf behind a row of books, almost like someone hid it there. Inside was an old book, some guy's diary or memoirs from the early 1900s."

"It's probably your dad's."

"It's not his writing, but I guess he must've got it from somewhere." Charlie didn't want to be quick with her, but he wanted to get back to the book. "Okay, I'll call you tomorrow. Love you."

"Love you, too. Watch out for the bears."

Charlie forced a laugh. "I will. Bye."

He stared at the black book on the table. Where the hell did it come from?

He sat down and continued reading.

October 22, 1927

The first snow of the season came. It started early last night and has not let up. Almost a foot and a half has fallen, and there appears to be no end in sight. I am thankful that I have chopped enough firewood to get me through the season, as it is sure to be a long and cold one.

I am all alone now, but that doesn't frighten me, nor do the cold or hardships I am sure to face the rest of the winter. Only the betrayal by

> those who are my own flesh and blood tortures my nights when my mind has time to think and remember.
>
> I don't need my brother. I will find the gold without his help, and then I will take my revenge.
>
> But I miss my wife and daughters, their laughter, their moods, their feminine ways. I didn't expect my mind's reaction to the quiet and isolation that the mountains have brought. The silence seems to be playing tricks on me, especially at night.

Charlie shivered and felt the hair on the back of his neck stand straight up. He read on.

> The noises are unexplainable, and for weeks now, late into the night, I think I see some type of a man, a beast in the shadows of the trees, hiding. Every morning, I check my property but find no prints. Perhaps it is one of the Cherokees I have been tracking. Is it possible that they have turned the tables on me? Am I the one now being followed? Have they discovered where I live?
>
> I have to be more careful not to give myself away, but the Indians are cunning, resourceful creatures. Curse them. The Cherokee are the spawn of Satan. I have no doubt that it is God's will to destroy them, which I intend to do if they stand in my way.

Charlie set the book down and laughed nervously. Cherokees! Things that go bump in the night, haunted forests. It looks like he and Ezekiel had something in common after all, a vivid imagination that seemed to grow in isolation.

He stood, stretching his arms and legs. Charlie walked over to the kitchen sink, reached underneath, and pulled out a dusty bottle of old scotch. He had given up hard liquor years ago, but he needed something stronger than a beer to help settle his nerves.

He poured a healthy dose of the scotch into a glass and added a little water and ice. He took a big sip and almost choked on the alcohol. He poured another measure, forcing it down, but after the third drink, his palate adjusted to the raw, searing taste, and he welcomed the burning sensation the liquid brought to his throat and stomach.

He took the drink over to the chair and sat back down.

He continued reading:

> *November 22*
>
> I haven't written any words for some time because I have been preoccupied with my plans. I had to be careful because these Indians are hard to fool, especially in the woods, but I have learned their patterns after months of careful study. They may have escaped their punishment for now, but they will feel God's wrath soon enough.

Was this guy crazy or what?

Charlie read on, and Ezekiel spent the next couple of chapters describing in excruciatingly boring detail his daily life. He rose with the sun, fixed breakfast, did his chores around the property, and then would set off into the woods, where he spent the rest of the day trapping and spying on a group of Indians before returning at sundown.

Charlie shook his head. This guy had a bizarre obsession with the Indians.

Finally, Charlie came to the chapter that explained the man's obsession with the Indians. Ezekiel wrote that he thought he knew where a large amount of gold was hidden, and the Cherokees stood in the way of his retrieving it. Ezekiel also kept repeating that he was deathly afraid of being out in the woods after sunset. He was scared of some strange beast that he believed was tracking him and would eat him if it caught him.

Charlie closed the book, yawning. There was one thing Charlie was certain of—this Ezekiel character was off his rocker.

Charlie rubbed his bleary eyes. The book was fascinating, and he wanted to read more, but he could barely keep his eyes open. After all, it had been one hell of a day. He couldn't stay up any longer, so Charlie put the book back in the box and set it in the table drawer.

He went to bed and fell asleep instantly. Luckily, no Indians or nightmares interrupted his sleep for the remainder of the night.

But even in the midst of sleep, the subconscious never stops working, and deep in his slumber, Charlie's mind kept repeating the words, "Nun He, Nun He, Nun He," over and over and over again.

∾

Chapter 6

Day Three

Tuesday

Charlie's eyes opened. His internal clock told him it was early in the morning. Then his aching head and racing heart told him he drank way too much last night. He rolled over, and the first rays of dull gray light filtered through the crack in the window curtains. A gnawing anxiety ate away at him. He took some deep breaths, but it didn't help. He couldn't make his body relax.

"Shit," he cursed. This is what he deserved for drinking hard liquor. What in the hell was he thinking? He knew his body couldn't handle that shit.

His heart felt like a runaway locomotive, and no matter how much he tried to go back to sleep, it was no use. His body felt like a ragged ball of pent-up anxiety ready to explode at any second. As much as he prayed to be able to fall asleep and end his misery, he knew there was no way that was going to happen.

His heart flipped a few times, and he sprang from the bed. Every nerve, every cell in his body felt like it was on hyper-alert, and there was nothing he could do to stop it, except to maybe have a few drinks to quell the panic.

"What are you doing?" he screamed. It wasn't even seven o'clock in the morning, and he was thinking about having a drink.

He went into the bathroom and turned on the light. He caught his reflection in the mirror and flinched. Then he did something he hadn't done in a while: he stared at his reflection. His skin looked ashen, and his eyes were bloodshot.

"Who's in there?" he whispered.

Did anyone else know he was changing? Could they see it? Surely his wife had noticed. Why hadn't she said something?

The bathroom light was almost unbearable. He flipped the light switch off and took a long shower in the dark. Only after the hot water had run out did he get out of the shower. His churning stomach reminded him that he hadn't eaten dinner last night. No wonder he was so hungover.

He went downstairs and didn't bother making eggs or toast. Instead, he cooked up an entire packet of sausage because his body needed some grease and fat to counter the alcohol still roiling through his system.

Charlie ate enough sausage to lower his life expectancy by a few months and was pouring his third cup of coffee when he heard the unmistakable sound of a car coming down the road.

Who in the hell could that be? Maybe the sheriff was coming to check up on him.

Despite his hangover and raging anxiety, he felt a little foolish about the previous day's "episode." The rational part of his mind began to rectify and accept the sheriff's account of what had happened to him up in the mountains.

He set the coffee down and went out on the porch. The storm from the night before had ended, leaving close to ten inches of snow. But the passing front left crystal blue skies and the bright sunlight stung his swollen eyes. He had to shield his eyes with his hand to see the car pulling into sight.

His anxiety suddenly sprang up a notch. It definitely wasn't the sheriff because the car approaching was an old fifties-style black hearse.

Then he caught a glimpse of the driver. "Jesus H. Christ!" he cursed. Behind the steering wheel was the man from the bar, the reverend.

What is he doing here? Charlie wondered. And how'd the reverend know where he lived?

Charlie walked down the porch stairs as the black hearse pulled up and stopped. The reverend stepped out of the car. He was wearing the same black suit that he had on at the Green Man the other night. He removed his bowler hat.

"Good morning, Mr. Parker. I hope I have not come at an inconvenient time."

"Ah...well, I was just..." The reverend was the last person he wanted to talk to, but he was so surprised by his appearance that he didn't know what to say.

"I promise, I won't take much of your time," the reverend interjected. "Do you mind if I come in?"

"I guess not." Charlie answered.

The reverend followed him into the cabin.

"Would you care for a cup of coffee or something?" Charlie asked.

"No, thank you."

"Have a seat." He motioned toward the couch.

Charlie glanced over at the kitchen counter, spotting the almost empty bottle of scotch. The palms of his hands were soaked in perspiration. Man, he desperately needed a drink of that, especially now.

His face felt hot, bloated, and his skin crawled. He couldn't remember the last time he felt this bad.

The reverend sat on the couch, and Charlie took a seat directly across from him on the leather chair. Even though a good six feet separated the two men, Charlie had an uneasy feeling that he was too close to the strange man.

He had an odor that was hard to place. Musty? *No,* Charlie thought, *it's more like decay or rot.*

"So, what can I do for you?"

"You look just like them. You know that?"

"Excuse me?"

The reverend grinned. "I was just commenting that you look exactly like you father and grandfather."

Charlie shifted uncomfortably in the chair. The reverend was staring directly at him, and it was damn unsettling.

Charlie coughed. "I wanted to ask you about that. How could you have known my grandfather? He died in the twenties. That would make you well over..."

The reverend cut him off. "I'm older than I appear. But that isn't the reason why I have come here today. I wish to discuss another matter with you."

"Okay. What is it?"

"Your father had something of mine that I have been looking for...well, for quite a long time. I was wondering if you could help me retrieve it."

"Huh, are you serious? What could my father possibly have of yours?"

The reverend's eyes continued to bore into him, adding to Charlie's discomfort. "Well, actually your father had..." the reverend paused. "It is a complicated story, but I am looking for a book that your grandfather took from me when I was a child."

"My grandfather! I thought you said it was my father's?"

"That is correct. Your grandfather took it, and it was given to your father, who kept it all these years."

"Wait a second. You say he took it? You mean borrowed, right?" Charlie asked, as warning bells began sounding in his head.

"Borrowed is fine, but nonetheless, it is by all rights my property. I don't begrudge you for your ancestor's misdeeds, but as his blood relative, I think it would only be fair if you returned it."

Charlie felt his neck starting to burn. "Reverend, I don't know what you are talking about, and I certainly don't appreciate you coming here and accusing my grandfather of being a thief."

"I didn't say he was a thief, Charlie. I just stated the truth. He took a book from my father, a book that by all rights is mine, and I want it back. That's all. It is of no value to you."

"What kind of a book?" Charlie asked, knowing full well he was referring to the strange leather book he found in the library. Even with his terrible hangover and still foggy mind, it wasn't hard to put two and two together. After all, the reverend and Ezekiel had the same last name.

"The book is old. It is bound in black leather, and it is a story written by my father, Ezekiel McCellan. Although, if you were to read it, you might incorrectly assume he was writing his memoirs. But it is all fiction, of course."

Charlie couldn't believe his ears. Could the reverend actually be telling the truth? He struggled to keep his emotions in check and once again looked over at the bottle of scotch.

He turned back toward the reverend. "But if my grandfather stole it from your father that long ago, how would you know what the book is about?"

The reverend flashed an evil-looking smile revealing his gray teeth. "I didn't come here to play games. You know what I am talking about. I can see that."

"No, I…" Charlie began.

The reverend waved a hand, cutting him off midsentence. "The book is of no value to anyone except me. As I explained, I place no blame or fault upon you. I just would like it returned. I would consider it a personal favor, and all would be forgiven."

"All what would be forgiven?"

"I am only asking that you return it to me. No punishment will come if that is done."

"Punishment?"

"It is a crime to steal, is it not?"

Charlie thought for a second. Something didn't make sense. In the book, Ezekiel had written that his whole family had died from the Blue Death which Charlie learned that was what they called a bad flu epidemic back then, so how could the reverend have been his son unless, maybe, Ezekiel had remarried later on and had had a second family. But he couldn't ask the reverend about that because it would prove he had the book.

"Will you please return the book to me?" the reverend asked again.

Charlie ignored his question. "What makes you think my grandfather stole it from your father? And why in the world would he have taken a book from you in the first place?"

The reverend's face twisted into a ghoulish expression. "Those events happened a long time ago and are not important, but I will tell you, your father hid the book from me for years, also claiming he didn't have it. For a long time, I believed him, although I had my suspicions. Then I discovered that he had been lying to me. I am growing tired of playing games with the Parker family. It is in your best interest to give me the book. Or else."

"Or else what?" Charlie stood. "Reverend, I don't know what you are talking about! I have nothing to give you, and I don't like being threatened in my own home. I would appreciate it if you left."

The reverend started to say something, but must have thought better of it. He stood, and Charlie still couldn't believe how tall he was. He stepped closer to Charlie so that they were only a few feet apart.

God! What was that smell?

"I could offer you a reward, Charlie. A handsome one at that. Is it money you want?"

"I don't want your money! I told you I don't know what you are talking about, and I want you to leave, now!"

The reverend smiled. His evil grin reminded Charlie of a hyena laughing. He put his hat back on and walked past Charlie toward the door.

He opened the door, turned and pointed a crooked finger at him. "I warn you, Charlie Parker. Your time is short. I won't wait like I did with your father. I want the book returned to me. You have until the end of the week."

And then what? Charlie wondered.

He held back his temper and said as calmly as possible, "I assure you, I will search the house, and if I come across any book…" He hesitated for a moment before saying, "I will give it to you. Now please go."

The reverend walked out the door, and Charlie watched him get into the hearse and drive off.

He couldn't help but wonder, was it possible that his grandfather had really stolen the book from Ezekiel and that his father had also hidden the book? *And if they had—why?* His father was one of the most honest men he had ever known. *What could he possibly have wanted with it?*

Charlie walked over to the kitchen counter and grabbed the bottle of scotch. He took a long sip, forcing down the alcohol. He clenched his teeth, trying to keep down the poison his stomach was attempting to reject.

Charlie went to the table where he had put the book. He stared down at the closed drawer. He hesitated, debating about whether he really wanted to open the drawer and take the book out.

Warning bells as loud as a tornado siren rang in his head. He put his hands up to his ears unconsciously before realizing the excruciating noise was coming from within. A strange realization formed in his mind. He understood that his decision to open or not open the damn thing was akin to one of those major life decisions that will forever and inexplicably change the course of one's life.

This was his Pandora's Box.

He reached down despite the voice screaming in his head to throw the book in the fireplace and go back to Charleston before it was too late.

His fingers touched the drawer's handle, and he took a deep breath, slowly opening it. He wished it had just disappeared overnight, but the black book was still there, beckoning him. Charlie picked it up with the understanding that he was sealing his fate.

He opened Ezekiel's book and began reading.

He read for the next four hours straight, only stopping to use the bathroom. Late in the afternoon, he finished as the sun began its daily trek of sliding behind the mountain to slumber for yet one more night. Charlie watched as the sun drifted below the mountain peaks, scattering a spectrum of orange-blue light across the sky. He was transfixed by the beauty, realizing, with an almost unfathomable knowledge, that the sun's daily descent began billions of years ago and was unending, like time itself.

Time lasted forever, but he wouldn't because his place upon the timeline of the universe was so short that it was practically immeasurable.

The thought scared and excited him, all at the same time.

He carefully put the book back in the drawer and went into the kitchen. The scotch was long gone, so he dug a beer out of the refrigerator.

His hands shook. He almost couldn't comprehend what he had read in Ezekiel's book. Could it be true? Or was it just the ramblings of a man who had gone mad? And for God's sake, how did Charlie's family fit into all of this?

He knew he would have to find out.

CHAPTER 7

Day Four

Wednesday

Charlie awoke with an unusual feeling. He felt good, refreshed. It was just after sunrise, and he was awash with a sense of urgency, excitement, and even a hint of danger.

He felt like he was eighteen again, when experiencing the uncertainty and spontaneity of life was a daily event, unlike the almost never-changing mundane pattern that middle age brought with it.

He hastily pulled a sweater over his head, realizing with a sick feeling that he had done almost the exact same thing every day of his life for the last twenty plus years, and for what? A lifestyle he couldn't afford and didn't want anyway.

Who was he doing it for? His wife? His kids? He figured at least there had to be some selflessness and honor in that, right? Those sacrifices had to make up for some of his flaws and misdeeds. He had lived his life for others, but now, this was his time.

Charlie finished tying the shoestrings of his boots and bolted down the stairs two at a time. He grabbed his jacket on the way outside, where he spent the next two hours tromping through his snow-covered property, looking. He wasn't exactly sure what he was searching for, but he wanted to get an idea of his surroundings. It had been years since he had surveyed the entire property.

He didn't come across anything unusual, only snow, trees, and silence. At first, the silence had been disconcerting, but Charlie was getting used to it. He discovered that it actually had a language of its own, and it had started speaking to him.

He looked at his watch. It was already past nine o'clock, so the library would be open in less than half an hour. He made his way back to the cabin and hopped into his car. Hopefully, the research would provide some answers.

Charlie drove into town and pulled up to a weathered one-story brick building. A large sign in front read *Wellington Public Library*, and it dawned on him that, despite his love of books, he had never stepped foot into the local library. He walked in, and except for an old man asleep at a table with a stack of books and magazines scattered around him, he appeared to be the only patron.

He strode up to the main desk, and after patiently waiting for five minutes without seeing anyone, rang the assistance bell.

A few moments later, an elderly lady appeared from the back room. Charlie almost had to stifle a laugh because she looked exactly like anyone from central casting would depict a small-town librarian.

She wore her neatly coifed gray hair tied up in a bun and possessed a slender, almost frail, physique. A pair of reading glasses sat halfway down a slim nose, and she wore a gray cardigan sweater, along with an attached gold bug pin.

"Good morning." Charlie smiled.

"Good morning." She returned his smile. "How may I assist you?"

"I am doing a little research, and I was wondering if the town's newspapers were kept on a computer database?"

The librarian pushed her glasses back to the top of her nose. "Sir, I don't know what big city you're from, but we have two dilapidated computers, and I have one part-time employee who gets out of junior high school at three and works till four, three days a week."

"Hmm…right. Well, do you keep any copies of the town's newspaper?"

"I said we lacked resources, but we still do our job." Her admonishment made Charlie feel like he was in the third grade again. The charming looking elderly librarian was quickly turning into the Wicked Witch of the East.

"What years are you looking for?" she asked.

"Well, it would be for the years…How old is the newspaper?" Charlie asked, suddenly realizing that the paper might not even have been around that far back.

She wrinkled her nose. "*The Mountain Gazette* has been in continuous weekly circulation since 1902."

Damn, Charlie thought. *Not even close.*

But then the librarian added, "Of course, we have copies that go all the way back to the paper's first publication in the early 1800's. From 1821 to 1902, the *Gazette* was published sometimes weekly, sometimes monthly, and a few years went by without a single issue. Many times, the *Gazette* was just printed as the news dictated or when someone was interested in doing it."

"That's perfect. Can I see the years, say starting in 1851?"

"Of course, but as I said, the newspaper was published sporadically during those years. Those issues have been sealed for protection, but copies have been made and placed on microfiche reels that you can search through."

"That'd be great. Thanks."

"Please give me five minutes to locate them." She turned and disappeared into the back room.

Charlie doubted Ezekiel's claim of gold being stolen by the Cherokees, but he figured he'd start researching before the Civil War and work his way to the 1920s. He looked over at the old man, who had begun to snore loudly. He watched the old man sleep until, true to her word, the librarian returned exactly five minutes later. She led him to a small table in the back of the library.

On top of the desk sat a microfiche machine, and after giving a quick tutorial on how the machine worked, she left. Charlie thought it was kind of odd that the librarian never inquired as to why he wanted to see old newspapers from the 1800s, but he figured it must have been some type of a librarian's code not to ask the business of its patrons.

He cracked his knuckles. "Let the search begin."

First, he wanted to check out Ezekiel's story that a murderous band of Cherokees stole a fortune in gold outside Rutherfordton. Ezekiel had written that the Indians had ambushed a transport carrying a large shipment and hid it in some cave up in the mountains. Certainly, if his claim was true, it would have made the newspaper.

Supposedly, that happened before the start of the Civil War, so to be sure he went back far enough, he started in 1851.

The first hour was slow going, with the majority of news stories devoted to regional events pertaining to the local community. Predominantly, the articles centered on crop reports, weather stories, and birth and death announcements.

Just when he started to get really bored, figuring he was wasting his time, a headline caught Charlie's eye. It was dated January 1822, and the headline read: *GOLD FOUND IN THE MOUNTAINS.*

The article was written in dramatic prose excitedly recounting the story of how a trapper had come across a large cache of gold nuggets while wading in a back country stream. His find had set off a minor gold rush in the area.

Charlie sat back in his chair. *Gold in the North Carolina Mountains.* Then that meant at least Ezekiel's crazy ramblings about the gold in the mountains had some truth to it. But then again, Ezekiel had also written that the stolen gold coins had been stashed in some mystical cave located high in the mountains, and that cave was protected by a fierce band of warrior Indians. Obviously, there was some fiction mixed in with the facts.

Charlie peered between the bookshelves and saw the librarian sitting at her desk. He got up and walked over to her.

"Yes, can I help you?" She flashed him her sweet grandmotherly smile again.

"Yes, Ms.…I'm sorry, I don't…"

"Mrs. Taylor," she interjected.

"Ah, Mrs. Taylor. I was wondering if I could ask you a question about some local history?"

"I'd be glad to be of help if I can."

"I came across a news article about gold being found in the mountains in the 1820's. Was there ever a substantial amount found in the area?"

Her face drew up as if he had asked a stupid question. "Mr.…"

"Parker."

"Mr. Parker, as a matter of fact, yes. It has been an almost forgotten fact, but the first gold rush in the United States actually occurred in North Carolina."

"It did?"

"Yes. My facts may not be completely accurate, but until the gold rush in California in 1848, North Carolina was the leading gold-producing state in the nation…primarily just north of the Charlotte region, but substantial finds did stretch up into the mountains. And, of course, even to this day, there are fortune seekers who claim that the mountain still holds vast quantities of gold. As a matter of fact, every year, we get at least one of those types coming in here and pouring over old maps and such—really a waste of time if you ask me."

"Wow," Charlie replied. "My family has had land here for generations. I never knew."

She peered over the top of her eyeglasses. "You're not looking for gold, are you, Mr. Parker?"

He laughed. "Hardly. I am just..." He paused, trying to think of what he should tell her because he wasn't really sure himself. "I'm doing a little family research, and I am also interested in the Bechtler Mint that was located in Rutherfordton before the Civil War. My father gave me one of their coins."

That seemed to improve her mood, and she smiled thinly. "I can help in regard to the mint." She opened a desk drawer and pulled out a card. "Here. This man knows more about our local history, including the Bechtler Mint, than anyone I know." She handed the card over.

"Thanks," Charlie said, tucking the card into his pocket.

"Discovering your family roots and who your ancestors are is important," the librarian added. "Of course, on the other hand, sometimes you might find out things that you wish you hadn't. Hopefully, you won't discover any hidden skeletons in your family's closet."

Charlie couldn't figure this woman out. He forced a smile. "I guess I'll have to take that chance."

"Good luck in your search, and let me know if I can be of any help."

"Thanks," he said cheerfully then he mumbled. "You crazy old bag."

He returned to the microfiche and sped through 1852 and the first part of 1853 until a headline from the summer of 1853 caught his eye. He'd hit the jackpot.

BECHTLER KILLED IN AMBUSH.

One of Rutherfordton's finest citizens was murdered last week in a horrific attack that has left all of Wellington and the surrounding areas on extreme edge. Mint operator Christopher Bechtler, Charlotte businessman Samuel Posten, and their armed guards were ambushed and killed in an early morning attack twenty miles south of Rutherfordton. Mr. Bechtler was on his way to Spartanburg for business when their transport was evidently ambushed in an attack that had obviously been planned. Sheriff Thomas stated that the men all died from injuries consistent with an Indian attack, leading to speculation that a rogue Cherokee tribe is responsible for the murders.

Sheriff Thomas is at a loss to explain the motive for the murders, although he speculated that the killings could have been an act of revenge caused by the Indian Removal Act that forced most Cherokees in the area to be relocated to reservations in Oklahoma in 1838. The sheriff went on to say that he adamantly assures the public that those responsible will be brought to justice in a swift manner.

The Bechtler family emigrated from Germany in the early 1780s, and each generation had been a pillar of the community since Christopher

Bechtler Sr. moved his family from New York to Rutherfordton in the late 1830s. The Bechtler reputation is known throughout the South for its mint located in Rutherfordton and the gold coins they produced.

The Bechtler Mint produced the first one-dollar gold coin in the United States, and it was the Bechtlers' ability to convert raw gold into a negotiable currency that helped shape the economy of the entire South. Three generations of Bechtlers produced coins at their mint, and they were universally known for their craftsmanship and fair, honest dealings.

Rutherfordton Mayor Vail Miller stated, "Without the Bechtlers, the Carolinas never would have experienced the prosperity they have enjoyed over the last four decades. Mr. Bechtler will be missed. It is a tragic day for all of us."

Charlie pulled out his Bechtler gold coin and looked it over. The edge was ridged. On the obverse along the top was the inscription *C BECHTLER*, with the words *FIVE DOLLARS* in the center, and underneath that was *RUTHERFORDTON*.

He flipped the coin over. *CAROLINA GOLD* was stamped on the top, with a large star in the center, and the date *1853* was underneath the star.

He put the coin back in his pocket and thought for a second. What the article didn't report was whether the transport was carrying a large amount of gold like Ezekiel claimed. Could he just have made that part up? Certainly the newspaper would have reported that fact.

Charlie grinned. He was a bit surprised that the first part of Ezekiel's crazy tale held up. There was, or at least had been, gold in the area, and Christopher Bechtler had been killed by Cherokees. He continued scanning the dates for any related news stories about gold or Indians.

He found a few sporadic mentions of small gold discoveries here and there but no mention of any sizeable finds or any huge interest. What was really odd was that there was not one more mention of the Bechtler heist and if the Indians were caught.

After the Civil War started in 1861, the paper was printed sporadically, and toward the end of the war, it was hardly printed at all.

Once the war ended, the newspaper went back to reporting about the weather, crops, births, and local interest stories. Charlie yawned and started flipping ahead by years until he reached World War I.

His research was definitely slow going. After searching all those years, he had found only two stories of interest.

Charlie stood up and stretched. His body was stiff from sitting all day. The old man was still in his chair, but he was awake, reading a woman's fashion magazine. Charlie looked over at the wall clock and couldn't believe the time. It was already two o'clock.

"Man, I must have been in some type of time warp," he said, trying to figure out how four hours had passed by. He was hungry, but he didn't want to take the time to go eat, so he sat down and continued searching through the microfiche.

After a fruitless hour and a half, Charlie's eyes and back were killing him, and he was losing interest. He abruptly changed gears and began searching the papers in the twenties for any stories or information on Ezekiel McCellan, the reverend, or his family, since for some inexplicable reason; they all seemed to be connected in some bizarre way.

After scrolling through a few more years, he found an article dated April 28, 1927. Charlie grinned and hit the desk with his fist, making a loud thump. "I found you, Ezekiel, you ol' bastard." He looked sheepishly over at the librarian's desk. Luckily, she wasn't there to admonish him.

The headline read: *CHEROKEES MASSACRE MCCELLAN FAMILY!*

> Tragedy has descended upon the Western Carolina Mountains, and it has brought with it panic and fear. Late yesterday, Ezekiel McCellan returned home after a day of trapping, and what he discovered has sent a wave of fear and anger through the whole area. Inside his house, he discovered the gruesome remains of his wife, Tabitha, and two daughters, Isabella and Sandra.
>
> Sheriff Thomas and his deputies immediately went to the scene. After a thorough investigation, the sheriff has issued an arrest warrant for a group of Indians he believes are responsible for the crimes. Thomas told the *Gazette*, "The evidence is beyond doubt, and I intend to bring these savage beasts to a swift justice."

The Indians responsible for the brutal murders are part of a small tribe that splintered off a group known as the Eastern Band of Cherokees. The Eastern Cherokees remained in western Carolina after refusing a government order to relocate to reservations in Oklahoma. The Indians are confined mostly to the Qualla Boundary north of the Smoky Mountain National Park, but small splinter tribes are spread throughout remote areas of the mountains.

Local authorities believe some of these tribes have lived obscurely high in the mountains for decades, and for unknown reasons, it is one of these obscure tribes that attacked and killed the McCellan women.

The total number of Indians involved is unknown at this time, but Sheriff Thomas has reason to believe that this is only the beginning of a desperate act by desperate savages.

A distraught Ezekiel McCellan told the sheriff that the Indians had been stalking his property for some time, but he didn't think much of it because they had never acted in a threatening manner in the past.

The last known murder by Indians in this part of the country occurred back in 1853 when a group of Cherokees ambushed and murdered a transport on the way to Spartanburg, South Carolina. One of the men killed was Christopher Bechtler, the last mint master of the famous Bechtler Mint located in Rutherfordton. Ironically, that investigation was led by Sheriff

> Thomas's own father, but the Indians suspected of the killing were never brought to justice.
>
> Sheriff Thomas has stated, "These killers who are responsible will not go unpunished. I will spend the rest of my days making sure the Cherokees who murdered those poor defenseless women hang from the gallows."
>
> The sheriff went on to call for any and all able-bodied volunteers to help search the mountains and bring the Indians responsible for such a heinous crime to justice.

Charlie crossed his arms across his chest. The article was perplexing because in his diary, Ezekiel wrote that his family had died from a flu epidemic and that he had retreated high into the mountains to start a new life. Charlie didn't know what to make of the contradiction, and if the reverend was Ezekiel's son, why was there no mention of it in the article?

He rubbed his sore eyes, which burned from reading hours of fine print. His stomach rumbled—partly from nerves, partly from hunger. He had to get something to eat, but first he needed to find out what happened to the Indians.

Three issues later, he found out.

> *SAVAGE CHEROKEE MURDERERS CAPTURED! WELLINGTON RESIDENTS BREATHE THE SIGH OF RELIEF.*
>
> Four days after the murders of the McCellan women, the band of Indians responsible was trapped and captured Thursday by a group

> of local men led by Sheriff Thomas, Ezekiel McCellan, and his brother Jeremiah.
>
> After a brief skirmish high in the mountains, two Indians were shot dead, three were apprehended, and four were trapped in a large cave. The sheriff gave the trapped Indians numerous chances to surrender. After all options were exhausted, the cave was blown up with dynamite, and the Indians were sealed to their fate.
>
> Judge Prescott proclaimed the captured Indians guilty and waved court proceedings, saying, "Justice needs to be carried out swiftly and with a severe punishment so that this type of crime is never perpetuated in our community again." The Cherokees are to be hung at sunrise Saturday.

Charlie reread the last chilling sentence: "The Cherokees are to be hung at sunrise Saturday."

He pushed the scroll button on the machine, taking him to the next newspaper issue. A grainy picture covered the entire front page, with only a one-word headline: *JUSTICE!*

Charlie leaned closer to the machine to get a better look at the haunting photo.

Three Indians hung from the gallows, with a group of men standing in the background. One of the Indians appeared to have been almost decapitated by the rope, and the necks of the other two Indians were twisted at horrific angles.

Charlie stared at the eerily unsettling picture for a long time. The first man on the left was clearly the sheriff because Charlie could make out the large silver badge on his chest. Next to him were two deputies holding shotguns, and on the right side of the gallows were two men in regular clothes who must have been Ezekiel and his brother Jeremiah. Standing in front of Ezekiel was a young boy.

Was that the reverend? Charlie thought.

He sat back in his chair staring at the image of Jeremiah McCellan. He looked familiar, but Charlie couldn't put a finger on who the man reminded him of.

And why in the hell had Ezekiel written that his family had died from fever rather than being murdered by Indians? Why would Ezekiel lie? But that brought up another point. The reverend had told him the book was really just a fictional account, but it didn't seem that way to Charlie, especially after discovering all of this.

Then it occurred to Charlie that perhaps the only way Ezekiel could deal with the murder of his family was to invent an illness to mute the emotional pain of what really had occurred.

The more he considered it, the more he realized that that was probably the reason behind it. He thought of Susan and his kids, and he couldn't imagine what he would do if something happened to them.

But what about the Cherokees? What could have caused them to murder a family in cold blood, especially after living peacefully in the mountains for decades? Why all of a sudden would they kill a man's wife and daughters for absolutely no reason, or as best as Charlie could make out, with no motive? Surely they would have known what the ramifications were going to be. What could possibly have provoked them into such a suicidal act?

Charlie stood. His joints and muscles ached. That was enough for today, he decided. He walked between the bookshelves to the front of the library. He smirked. The old man was still there, only he was asleep again with his head down on the table.

Charlie looked around. He wanted to say thanks to the librarian for her help, but she was nowhere in sight. He started to ring the bell, when he heard a strange sound coming from behind him. He turned to see the old man staring directly at him with an odd look on his face.

"Nun He," the old man said with a blank expression on his face.

Charlie took a step closer to the old man. "Excuse me?"

"Nun He," the man repeated.

The man had to be in his eighties. His face was criss-crossed with wrinkles, and his eyes were so glassy he looked like he was completely out of it or on drugs.

"Sir, what do those words mean?" Charlie demanded.

"You will find out soon enough," the old man said in a hushed tone, then put his head back down on the table.

Charlie went over to him and shook his bony shoulder.

The man's head snapped up. "What, what do you want? Is the library closing?"

"Why'd you say those words to me?"

The old man looked confused. "What words?"

"You said something like, 'Nun He' a couple of times. You don't remember?"

"I did? Uh, I was probably just talking in my sleep, that's all."

Charlie stared down at the man, who looked confused and tired. Charlie wanted to question him more but thought better of it, so he turned and left, figuring there was no point in harassing the old guy. He opened the library door and was about to step out, when he heard the old man call out, "Nun He."

Charlie stopped but didn't turn.

"Nun He," the old man repeated in a weird tone.

Charlie clenched his fists and left without looking back.

~

Chapter 8

Charlie peered cautiously over the steering wheel up toward the gray mountain peaks. Giant white storm clouds billowed high into the sky.

He whistled. "Man, this is going to be a bad one."

He flipped the radio to the local weather channel, and a computer-generated voice continuously relayed a blizzard warning for the area. The forecast called for a foot of snow with near hurricane-force winds throughout the night.

That's okay, he thought. It would give him a chance to search the cabin. He had never seen Ezekiel's book until two nights ago, so who knows what else might be hidden away somewhere. Hopefully, he could find something more to shed light on the mystery confronting him.

His cell phone rang, causing Charlie to jump in the car seat. He pulled the phone out of his coat pocket. "Hello."

"Hey, Charlie, my boy, it's Kingsley. How's it going?"

Charlie grimaced. Kingsley was the last person he wanted to talk to. "Hey. Not too bad. What you up to?"

"Looks like a big storm is a coming."

"Yep. Sounds like it."

"Man, this winter keeps getting worse and worse."

"Yeah."

"Well…listen. I called to apologize."

"Apologize? For what?" Charlie pretended not to know what he was talking about.

"You know, when the reverend came in. I was awful short with you. I was calling just to say sorry."

"No problem. I had completely forgotten about it," Charlie lied, but he felt relieved. Maybe Kingsley was just having a bad night after all.

"So you're not mad?"

"Nah, it was no big deal."

"Okay, great. Hey look, the bad weather is not supposed to come down until after midnight. Why don't you pop on down, and I'll buy you a couple of pints."

Charlie stared up at the mountain and the building clouds. "Kingsley, I…" Even with the apology, Charlie wasn't so sure it was a good idea to go down there, with the weather and all.

"C'mon, it's a slow night," Kingsley interjected. "I could use the company."

Charlie looked at the clock on the dashboard. The weather report did say that the heavy stuff wasn't expected for hours, and Kingsley had been a good friend over the years. No reason to burn a bridge over one bad moment.

"All right," Charlie hesitantly replied, not sure if he was making the right decision. "I'll be down in a few minutes."

"Great, see you then."

Charlie closed his cell phone, and a surge of what he used to call the heebie-jeebies tore through his body. He slammed his fist on the steering wheel. "No, God damn it!"

He forced himself to take deep breaths. The feeling scared the hell out of him. He hadn't felt like that since his breakdown more than a decade ago—the raw fear, the darkness that suddenly consumed his entire being lasted only for a few seconds, but it was enough to make Charlie wonder if he should just go home, now. Forget everything and just drive straight back to Charleston tonight.

No! He couldn't do that because then he would be giving in to it. It was just a feeling, and feelings can't hurt you, at least that was what all the doctors had told him. What he needed was just a few beers and a good night's sleep, that's all.

He pulled into the empty parking lot and walked into the Green Man. The looming storm must have scared everyone off because there wasn't a single person in the bar. Kingsley came out of his office with a big smile.

"Charlie, my boy," he exclaimed with exceptional good cheer. "Glad you could make it. Let me get you a beer on the house."

Charlie forced a smile. "Sounds great." He sat down on the barstool while Kingsley opened up two beers and passed one over.

Kingsley saluted. “Cheers.”

Charlie took a big gulp, and after four beers, their little row from the previous night appeared to be long forgotten. They discussed the usual—football, politics, the terrible weather—but the more beers Charlie drank, the more he felt the need to try and find out more information about the reverend. It was like an itch that scratching couldn’t relieve.

Charlie decided to test the waters. “Hey, by the way, I know you didn’t want to talk about it, but that man who was in here that night, the reverend…”

Kingsley raised a hand. “Look. Like I said, I’m sorry about that. The guy just rubs me the wrong way, and I took it out on you.”

“That’s okay, but do you mind if I ask you a question?”

“Shoot.”

“Who is that guy?” Charlie laughed, trying to keep the tone of their conversation lighthearted.

Kingsley’s eyes seemed to dart nervously around the room, and once again, his face went pale. He sighed loudly. “He really is just some crazy old coot. There are some wild stories about him. I don’t know how true they are. He’s one of those lunatic gold hunters. He believes there’s a fortune in gold hidden up in the mountains.”

“Really?” Charlie said, thinking about the articles he had read at the library. “What’s he digging around in, some old mine?”

Kingsley laughed. “No. The guy’s crazy all right. He believes that his father discovered a fortune in buried gold hidden in some cave. The fool has been searching for it for over forty years, best that I know of. Wasted his whole damn life, if you ask me.”

"You mean, like hidden treasure?" Charlie asked, trying to play dumb because a piece of the puzzle had just been connected, and he now knew the real reasons why the reverend was so desperate to get the book back. Obviously, the reverend believed his father had left clues in the book to where the cave was located.

"I guess," Kingsley answered.

"But who would bury a fortune in gold up in the mountains?"

Kingsley shrugged. "I don't know, Charlie. I'm just telling you what the crazy bastard thinks. There is an old legend that a shipment of gold coins was stolen by a group of Cherokees back before the Civil War."

"Cherokee gold," Charlie mumbled, with a growing tightness building in his stomach as he thought about the Indians that chased him down the mountain. Then he remembered the gruesome photo of the Indians hanging from the gallows, and a shiver went through him.

Something weird was definitely going on here.

"How exactly do you know the reverend?"

"Forget that, Charlie. Listen, I know this is going to sound crazy, but…since you brought it up, I was wondering if I could ask you a favor."

"Sure. What is it?"

Kingsley seemed to hesitate for a second. "We both agree that the reverend is half off his rocker, but he is old, and, well, he's been pestering me."

Charlie's defenses suddenly shot up a notch. "Oh yeah? About what?"

"By any chance, have you come across a book at your place? It's really old, supposedly written by the reverend's father."

"Huh?" Charlie stammered.

"An old leather book. Handwritten by a man named Ezekiel," Kingsley repeated.

Charlie drank what was left of his beer, stalling for a little time. "No, I haven't. But my father has a pretty big library. There are a million books in there. Why do you care?"

"I don't. The reverend asked me if I could convince you to return the book to him. You don't even have to give it to him. Give it to me, and I'll pass it along to him."

"Are you saying I'm lying?"

"C'mon, Charlie. You're the one who started asking me questions about the reverend."

"So?" he said defensively.

"Look, you're misunderstanding me. I'm not saying you know where the book is, but I know your father had it. He told me so. I was just asking if you would mind looking for it. That's all."

"My father told you he had the book!"

"One time after he had a few bourbons, we got to shooting the shit, and he told me some crazy story that his father gave it to him and told him to..."

"To what?"

"To hide it from the reverend."

Charlie laughed. "What! Have you lost your mind? Why would he have done that?"

Kingsley held out his hands, smiling in an unconvincing manner. "Maybe he wanted to keep the reverend from finding the gold."

"Are you serious?"

"No, of course not, but I don't want to be involved in y'all's fight. I mean, the damn book doesn't mean anything to me, or you. Why don't you just give it back to the old cooter? Look at it this way—you probably will be the only person in the last forty years who did something to make the guy happy."

Charlie felt his neck growing hot. "Is this what this is about? Is this why you asked me down here? What is there between you and the reverend?"

"Hold on, Charlie, I'm on your side. But there are things you don't understand."

"Things that I don't understand," Charlie stammered. "What are you talking about?" Charlie was getting the distinct feeling that there was a lot more than Kingsley was letting on to.

"Things that are best left, well…left alone."

"Like what? Try me."

Kingsley shook his head. "People, towns have pasts, sometimes bad pasts that never seem to die."

"I still don't know what you're talking about."

"It was before my time, but there are stories that the mountains are…The world was a different place eighty years ago. Things happened."

"What things, Kingsley?

"I can't believe you've never heard the stories."

"Obviously, I haven't."

Kingsley took a large swig of his beer. "A bunch of Indians got themselves hung a long, long time ago for killing some white folks. As a matter of fact, the folks killed were the reverend's mother and sisters. Some idiots believe the Indians were innocent. It's all an old tale, but some people think that the Cherokees have placed some type of a curse on Wellington, especially on the McCellan family."

Charlie took a deep breath, remembering the photo he had come across in the library. "Are you talking about the Indians that murdered the McCellan women back in the twenties?"

"Yes."

"Why would people think the Cherokees were innocent?"

"Don't know."

"Well, who killed the women if the Cherokees didn't?"

"Jesus, Charlie. You just won't let it drop, huh?"

"If the Indians were innocent, who killed the McCellan women?" Charlie asked again.

Kingsley sighed heavily. "Some say Ezekiel and his brother killed his family and set it up to look like the Cherokees did it."

"What! Why would they do that?"

"I don't know!" Kingsley shot back.

"Do you believe they killed their own family?"

"Hell no, that's insane. It's just an old story. That's all. Don't take everything so literally."

"You're the one who brought it up."

"Here." Kingsley set a new beer down next to him.

"You know, the reverend came to see me," Charlie said.

"He told me. Like I said, he just wants the book back, and he thinks you have it. I'm on your side. I am looking out for you. It's just a stupid book."

Charlie leaned back in his chair. "I know he was an undertaker, but you didn't answer my earlier question. Who exactly is the reverend? Why do they call him 'Reverend'?"

"He's not really a 'reverend' in the traditional sense. That's what people in the old days called an undertaker around these parts."

Charlie smirked. "You should see that old black hearse he drives. Man, this is some crazy shit."

Kingsley nodded but remained silent.

"Why?" Charlie asked.

"Why, what?"

"Why is he no longer an undertaker?"

"Damn it, Charlie! Just drop it. He's crazy...been searching those mountains for some gold hidden in a cave for decades. Who knows? I don't know why you are making such a big deal out of this." Kingsley abruptly stopped.

"Does he think the book holds clues to where the supposed 'gold treasure' is hidden?"

"You'd have to ask him."

"Where does he live?"

"I have no idea, and I don't want to know. Just give the man his dang book back. It is of no value to you."

"I don't have it," he lied.

"Charlie. I am only going to say this one more time. You don't know what you are getting yourself into. I'm begging you. Give him the damn book!"

Charlie stood and threw a twenty down on the bar. "Thanks for the beer."

He left the bar and got into his car, thinking that the dots were starting to connect but in a very strange way.

Then something occurred to him. Kingsley had called him on his cell phone earlier, but he had never given him his cell phone number. How could Kingsley have known his number?

He looked over at the passenger seat and grabbed the brown bag. He pulled the bottle of whiskey out and unscrewed the top. He knew he shouldn't be doing this, but he took a long drink, and the liquid burned all the way down his throat into his belly, followed by a relaxing warmth that started in his midsection, and then spread throughout his body down to the ends of his fingers and toes.

He drove home sipping the whiskey like it was water the whole way.

∾

CHAPTER 9

The storm arrived earlier than expected. A stream of large snowflakes fell as Charlie pulled off the highway onto the dirt road leading up to his cabin. No matter how hard he tried, he couldn't get the conversation with Kingsley out of his head.

What the hell was going on in this town?

The wind had really picked up, and with the blowing snow and darkness, visibility was almost nonexistent. Charlie drove at a snail's pace, keeping a constant eye on the edge of the forest. He kept imagining the Indians waiting for him under the cover of darkness. For the second time that day, he seriously thought about going back home, but it was too late. He was snowed in for at least the night.

As he pulled up to the house, for a brief second, the headlights caught something next to the back of the building. Charlie slammed on the brakes, causing his head to jerk forward. He rubbed the back of his neck and stared ahead. Whatever he thought he had seen was gone.

"Not again!" he muttered, because he could have sworn he saw a wolf standing by the side of his house.

He sat in the car for a full five minutes with the bright lights on, staring off into the trees on each side of the cabin. He took three rapid drinks of the whiskey, and only then could he finally muster enough liquid courage to get out of the car. He ran up to the front door and reached into his pockets for the keys.

Holy shit! They weren't there. He frantically checked his coat pockets. Where had he put his keys?

A guttural howl erupted from the forest. He looked back over his shoulder as panic set in. Where were his keys? Then it dawned on him—he probably left them in the car's ignition. He ran back to the car, certain he was about to be attacked by some unimaginable beast at any moment. He reached inside the car, grabbed the keys, and ran back to the house at a full sprint.

He reached the door as another howl filled the night. It seemed to explode from all directions and was so loud that it felt as if the sound waves had permeated his skin, traveling down to the very marrow of his bones.

"C'mon," he yelled, fumbling the keys. His hands shook so badly, it took him three tries to finally get the key into the lock. He burst through the door, slamming it behind him.

He stood in complete blackness, and a new wave of terror consumed him. He couldn't stand the dark because the blackness only brought the unknown, the unthinkable, and Charlie's mind could not tolerate that possibility.

What if the Indians were waiting for him inside? He groped for the light switch, expecting to feel the sharp blade of a knife at any moment. After what seemed like an eternity, he found the switch and flipped the lights on.

He took a deep breath. Wonderful, glorious light filled the room, and he was all alone.

Charlie looked back outside. No sign of whatever had been next to the house, if in fact there even had been anything. But he had heard its howls from the forest. He went to the back door in the kitchen and turned on the outside light and peered outside. Nothing.

He double-checked the door lock, went to the refrigerator and pulled out a beer.

Screw it, he thought. *The reverend can have the damn book back.* He decided he was going to drop it off at Kingsley's the next morning. Too many weird things had been going on, and he was now convinced the book was the main cause of it.

He went over to the nightstand and pulled Ezekiel's book out of his hiding spot behind the drawer. He flipped through it, casually reading certain sections.

The diary or story was as good as any horror novel he had ever read. Maybe it served as some type of emotional outlet for him, because that's when the idea hit Charlie.

He laughed.

What the hell, he thought, *it wouldn't hurt.* Charlie went back into the kitchen and retrieved a legal pad. If it worked for Ezekiel, maybe it would work for him. He figured he should be recording all the strange events that had been happening anyway, just in case. Who knows, maybe he could pen his own horror novel.

Charlie Parker, novelist. He liked the ring to that.

He spent the next four hours furiously writing about all the events that had occurred since his arrival in the mountains.

When Charlie had recounted everything up to the present, he stopped writing and counted twenty-one pages. Not bad for one night's work. He went into the kitchen and mixed a fresh whiskey and water. He had run out of beer two hours ago. He shook his head in disgust when he looked at the almost empty bottle of whiskey.

A shrill cry exploded outside of his house, causing Charlie to drop the glass of whiskey. The glass shattered on the hardwood floor. He inched his way toward the back door, with broken glass crunching underneath his shoes.

"Jesus H. Christ! What in the hell was that?" he mumbled, absolutely terrified.

He peered out of the window. The cry sounded as if it came from right in the back yard. He never would have believed that a noise could scare him so badly. It sounded like something only the devil could make.

He turned as panic started to overcome him. His heart skipped a beat, followed by a hard thud inside his chest. Something was scratching at the front door. He looked around for a weapon.

God! Why did he get rid of the guns? He slowly made his way over to the fireplace. The scratching grew louder, followed by silence. Charlie took a step closer to the door. Suddenly, the door began rattling violently then it just stopped.

Silence followed. Charlie picked up the fire poker, and forced himself to walk over to the front door.

He pressed his ear against the door but heard nothing. He grabbed the door handle, taking a deep breath. His palms were drenched in perspiration. He didn't want to open the door. There was no logical reason to open it, but some force he couldn't resist was driving him to do it.

Slowly, his grip on the handle tightened. *Why am I doing this?* his mind screamed. He didn't want to know what was on the other side of the door.

But his body was not obeying his mind's commands, and with one quick motion, he flung open the door and stepped back, with the fire poker raised, ready to strike.

Only silence and gently falling snow greeted him. He lowered the poker to his side, stepping into the doorway.

"What do you want?" he screamed out toward the woods.

Charlie lowered his head and saw what looked like a little wooden statue sitting on the porch. He reached down and picked it up. It was about two inches tall and looked like a miniature totem pole.

Where did this come from?

He studied the object. A wolf's body had been carved into the wood around the entire statue, and its mouth was open, baring sharp fangs. A figure of a man's head sat above the top of the wolf's head. He looked closer with growing shock because the face carved into the wood was a perfect depiction of him.

A howl erupted from deep inside the forest, followed by a gust of freezing wind that blew a spray of cold snow into his face.

Charlie began to shake uncontrollably. He looked at the amulet and then threw it as far as he could into the woods. He stepped inside and slammed the door shut.

Charlie began searching. He was positive his father had left something else behind, another clue, more information. He tore through drawers, looked under dressers, and even checked in the attic crawl space, but he didn't find a thing.

He walked back into the library, admonishing himself for not looking in here in the first place. After all, this is where he had found Ezekiel's book. He started at the far end of the bookshelves and started pulling out every single book, looking at its title, checking to see if anything was inside the book or hidden behind it.

Charlie spent hours sitting on the floor pulling out book after book with no luck until he came across a small book titled *Hidden Treasure in the Appalachians,* written by Brack Culler. He had never heard the title, but it definitely could have some information he might need. He opened it to the table of contents, which contained thirteen chapters on various myths, legends, and historical accounts of lost, stolen, or hidden treasure in the Western Carolina Mountains. Chapter Thirteen was titled "The Lost Bechtler Gold."

His palms grew sweaty as he began reading. The chapter provided details about a Cherokee legend that a band of Indians in the mid-1800s stole a large cache of gold coins outside of Rutherfordton, North Carolina, and that these Indians stashed the loot in an ancient burial cave in the vicinity of Grandfather Mountain. The legend went that a small band of ferocious Indian warriors were to stand guard over the cave and the gold until the time the spirits of deceased elders granted the tribe the right to reclaim the gold.

The author claimed that a corrupt businessman named Samuel Posten from Charlotte looted his own bank and conspired with Christopher Bechtler to melt down the hijacked gold into Bechtler coins so they would be harder to trace.

The year this supposedly took place was 1853, and according to records, no Bechtler gold coins were minted that year. But the author claimed that during his research, he came across a Cherokee Indian chief who showed him an 1853 Bechtler coin, a coin that was not supposed to exist.

Charlie set the book down. He knew the legend of the Indian gold was no myth because he had seen the proof firsthand. He reached inside his pocket and pulled out his Bechtler gold piece that his father had given him. He stared at the date stamped onto it—1853.

Charlie spent the rest of the night sitting in a chair by the window, drinking whiskey and staring out into the darkness. He was too scared to leave his spot by the door, so he just sat there fighting the urge to sleep. But as the night grew late and the alcohol set in, he could feel his eyelids no longer listening to his mind's command to stay open. He started to drift...

~

Charlie was trapped deep inside the earth with only a small lantern providing any light, and that was not enough to quench his absolute terror of the darkness that surrounded him. The air was cold, dank, and a fear he had never felt before raced through his body. He was trapped in an underground maze of tunnels.

No matter which tunnel he took, they all led in a big circle back to the same spot—a large cavernous room where hell had runneth over.

Charlie feverishly ran through another tunnel, praying for a way out but all the time knowing there was none. He rounded a bend and stopped dead in his tracks. He was back at the burial chamber.

He crouched low against the cold rock wall and slid down to his knees. The chamber's walls were filled with brightly colored paintings of animals and Indian warriors. A large circle of stone was located in the center of the room. Inside the stone circle, stacked in large piles, was a fortune's worth of gold coins.

But Charlie couldn't care less about the gold. What good was it when death was imminent? After all, he couldn't take the treasure to hell with him. Outside the circle, stacked together in rows a dozen deep were the mummified burial remains of Indians.

How did he get here? He didn't remember going into the cave. If only he could remember.

A howl reverberated through the tunnels. *God help me,* Charlie thought. *It's returned! It knows I'm here.* He turned the lantern off, forcing himself to accept the absolute darkness that seemed to creep into every pore of his body. He crouched lower against the cold rock wall.

The beast howled again.

He knew his fate. The beast was getting closer, and when it found him, he was going to be ripped to shreds.

But death was not his real fear now. There were things far worse than an eternity of silence. Far worse, and he had knowingly traveled the path to discover that terror. Why had he gone into the cave? Why was the answer so important? Somehow, he knew his only chance was if he remembered…

The beast was close. He could feel it.

He heard air being snorted through its nostrils. An ungodly smell permeated the air, and then there was silence. He could hardly breathe. The beast had to be only feet from him, but why had it grown so silent?

Think! Why did he come here?

Charlie felt movement to his right. Something brushed up against him. A thunderous pain exploded through his hand. It felt like a steel bear trap, and he screamed.

~

Charlie jerked up in bed, clutching the fire poker in his hand. He dropped it to the floor, flexing his aching hand. He gasped for air and looked around the room in a desperate frenzy. His body was covered in a cold sheen of sweat. How did he get up to the bedroom? He was almost positive he had fallen asleep by the kitchen door.

He looked around the room. Nothing appeared out of place, but that didn't mean anything. Maybe he had gotten up in the middle of the night and just didn't remember it. That had to have been it, that and another nightmare.

He reached over to the nightstand to grab the bottle of aspirin but stopped. Standing on the table was the wood statue he found outside of his door. The one he thought he remembered throwing into the woods.

His head throbbed in a way that he had never felt before. He grabbed the aspirin bottle, taking out three pills, forcing himself to chew them between his teeth. A bitter taste filled his mouth, making him cringe. Somewhere, he had read that if you chewed aspirin, they acted faster.

Charlie stumbled into the bathroom, where he took a shower and brushed his teeth three times to get the awful taste out of his mouth. He changed and went downstairs.

He looked at the beer cans lying on the floor and shook his head when he spotted the empty bottle of whiskey. He had drunk the entire bottle in one night. No wonder his head felt like it was going to explode, and his whole body felt like a ball of anxiety.

He picked up the empty bottle, and somewhere in the back of his mind, a voice screamed—it screamed for him to get out before it was too late.

He chewed two more aspirins before grabbing his wallet and car keys. He was going back to the library. Maybe he could find the final answers.

~

Chapter 10

Day Five

Thursday

Charlie sat at the microfiche for hours, trying to locate any bit of information about Ezekiel that would somehow tie everything together, but the search was proving elusive. Charlie knew the key lay with Ezekiel and that his grandfather was somehow connected, but finding the answers was proving to be a difficult proposition.

He was about ready to give up for the day when he came across a photo dated August 20, 1932. The picture showed a man of medium build with a thick mustache standing outside a store. A little boy held his hand.

He read the caption accompanying the photo:

> Samuel Parker and his seven-year-old son, Charles, proudly pose at the grand opening of Mr. Parker's hardware store located at the corner of Main and Elk. Mr. Parker moved to Grandfather Mountain after bravely serving as a

> second lieutenant during World War I, where he was awarded the Medal of Honor, the nation's highest military award for acts of bravery and heroism on the battlefield.

Charlie's hands began shaking. Why hadn't his father told him this? His grandfather was a war hero, and all this time, his father's silence had made him think that he had been a man of ill repute or some type of a criminal.

Why? Why would his father have practically disowned his own father, a war hero, a successful businessman?

It didn't make any sense.

He furiously began scrolling the microfiche, trying to find any more stories related to his grandfather, when he caught a whiff of a horrible odor that smelled distinctly like a long-dead animal.

A tap on his shoulder caused him to almost jump out of his chair. He turned, and to his dismay, standing behind him, flashing his gray toothy smile, was the reverend.

"Hello, Charlie," the reverend said in a slow drawl.

"What are you doing here?" he stammered.

The reverend made a grand gesture of looking around the room before replying, "This is a public library, isn't it?" He moved closer to Charlie and peered down at the microfiche machine. "Trying to figure it all out, huh?"

Charlie flipped off the machine. "Figure what out?" he said defensively.

"You'll know when you come across it."

"I don't believe this is any of your business." Charlie stood and began gathering his things to leave.

"What do you want to know about your family?"

"What?"

"I'll tell you anything you want to know."

Charlie stared into the reverend's black eyes. "You'll tell me about my grandfather and everything else?"

"Your father should have told you, but I guess he left it up to me. Even I don't know everything." The reverend scowled. "But I will tell you what I do know. It is time you learned."

Charlie relaxed for a second, but the tone of the reverend made him cautious. He didn't trust the son of a bitch one bit. "I'd appreciate that. There's a coffee shop just down the block. We can go there."

The reverend nodded. "All right."

They left the library. The bright sunshine had given way to a bank of black clouds hanging low in the winter sky. Charlie stole a glance at the reverend. Things always seemed darker when he was in the man's presence. Charlie followed the reverend down the sidewalk to the coffee shop. They took a table near the front window. There was no one else in the shop, and neither man said a word until the waitress came over to take their order.

"What can I get y'all?" she asked loudly, smacking a wad of gum.

"A cup of coffee, please," Charlie said.

She looked over at the reverend with a strange expression on her face. Charlie knew what she was thinking. *What was wrong with this guy?*

The reverend never even looked up at the waitress and said in almost a whisper, "A glass of water."

She nodded and hurriedly left. Charlie didn't blame her. He didn't want to be in the reverend's presence, either.

The two men stared across at each other in an awkward silence. Charlie spoke first. "How exactly do you know my parents?"

The reverend moved an ashtray to the other side of the table. "Your grandfather and my father…" The reverend paused. He looked out the window for a few moments before returning his stare to Charlie. "They were brothers."

The statement practically sucked the air out of Charlie's lungs. "What the hell are you talking about? That's bullshit. I knew this was a waste of time."

Charlie stood to leave.

"Hold on. Please sit back down," the reverend said almost politely. "I promise you, I will provide you with the answers you are looking for."

Charlie hesitated but found himself taking a seat again. "Brothers!" Charlie snapped. "What kind of crap are you trying…" He paused as the waitress came back, set their drinks on the table, and left.

Charlie moved his coffee out of the way and leaned across the table. "Okay then, how do you explain the fact that our last names are different? How could that be if your father and my grandfather were brothers? We'd have the same last name. Wouldn't we?"

The reverend laughed. "C'mon, Charlie, I really thought you would have discovered this on your own by this point. The evidence was right in front of you at the library. I know you saw it."

"What do you mean?"

"The photo from the newspaper. You found all the evidence you should need."

"I don't know what you are talking about. I mean, I did find a photo of my grandfather in front of his hardware store, which only proves that you are completely out of your mind."

The reverend flashed a wicked-looking grin that certainly meant to mock him. "That photo proves me right, not you, you fool."

"What are you talking about?"

"What's your last name?"

"C'mon, you know my last name is Parker."

"That is your given name, not your family name."

"What the hell are you talking about?"

"Your real last name is not Parker. It's McCellan."

"You're crazy!" Charlie slammed his fist on the table. "I saw the photo of my father and grandfather. The article in the library said that Walter Parker, my grandfather, was a war hero. My father, Charles, was standing right next to him. So what nonsense are you trying to pull?"

The reverend laughed in a sinister tone. "Charlie, that photo is the proof I am talking about. Think about it. If Samuel Parker was a war hero, a successful businessman, and a loving family man—who by all accounts he was—why do you think your father never mentioned him to you?"

Charlie frowned. His heart pounded, and he was confused. *What is the reverend getting at?* "I don't know," he mumbled.

The reverend picked up the glass of water and swirled the liquid around before setting the glass back down on the table without taking a sip. "I'll tell you why. Walter Parker was your dad's stepfather, Charlie. Your real grandfather's name was Jeremiah McCellan, and he was a scoundrel and a drunk. He failed at every lousy scheme he ever devised. He cheated his family, his friends. He was a complete failure."

"I..." Charlie didn't know what to say. "I don't believe you."

"Then go down to city hall and have them pull the marriage and birth certificates. What you will find is that your grandmother, Eloise, married Jeremiah McCellan in 1922. Your father was born in 1923. Jeremiah died in 1928, and your grandmother married Walter Parker in 1930. It is all there in black and white right on official state government documents."

Charlie didn't know what to say. He didn't think the reverend was bluffing because all he had to do was to check the records.

"How did my grandfather die?"

"You really want to know?" the reverend asked.

Charlie wasn't sure he really wanted to know, but at this point, he found himself nodding anyway.

"He got drunk one night, as was his custom," the reverend continued, "and passed out up in the mountains. When they found him the next day, he was frozen solid. Your grandmother was so disgusted; she didn't even pay for a proper burial. Your grandfather was buried where he fell, in an unmarked grave, alone out in the wilderness. Your grandmother remarried, and she was so ashamed of her first husband, she took Parker's last name and proceeded to erase any memory of Jeremiah McCellan."

"But how do you know all this?"

"Because, Charlie, how many times do I have to tell you this? Your grandfather and my father were brothers. I am your great uncle."

The thought that he was actually related to this man sent a wave of revulsion through him. He couldn't think clearly. He needed to stall for time to try and figure it out.

"So why do you believe Walter Parker, my step-grandfather, took the book from your father?"

"Charlie, I know you are an educated man, but you don't seem to be getting it. Now, I know this information is upsetting, and certainly it is confusing, but Samuel Parker did not steal it. Your true grandfather, Jeremiah McCellan, stole it."

"But my father was just a child when McCellan died. How would he have gotten it?"

"That's a good question. I don't know the answer to that myself. I gave your father the benefit of the doubt over the years because I believed him when he said he didn't have it. That was until I found out otherwise."

"But why would he steal something like that from his own brother? And what's so important about this book?"

"I've tried to put it as delicately as possible, but you don't seem to be grasping the truth. Your grandfather was a despicable human being. Who knows why he stole it? Spite. Jealousy. Sheer meanness. Does it matter? He lied. He stole. He cheated. He drank. That was who your grandfather was."

"What happened to your father?" Charlie asked.

"You're not going to like the answer."

"What's the difference at this point?"

"Your grandfather killed him. Murdered his own brother in cold blood."

Charlie's head throbbed. No, that wasn't exactly an accurate description because it felt like his blood vessels were expanding and all billion or so of them might burst at any second. The information was too much. He thought back to the article about Ezekiel's wife and his daughter's murder.

"When did this supposedly happen?" Charlie asked quietly.

"January 13, 1928. I guess you didn't get that far in your search. I was left an orphan."

Charlie rubbed his temples and closed his eyes. He could see the photo of the Indians hanging from the gallows. He opened his eyes, praying the reverend would have vanished and that he was dreaming. But this was no dream. The man who looked like death still sat across from him, and Charlie felt as if he couldn't catch his breath. Could his grandfather really have killed his own brother?

"Why did Jeremiah kill Ezekiel?"

"I suppose you could call it brotherly love."

"How did he kill him?"

"Blew him up. Set off dynamite while my father was inside a mine. They never found his body, said he'd been blown to smithereens."

"Jesus! I can't believe this."

"I was raised in an orphanage. I don't even want to tell you what that was like. That's why I want the book back, Charlie."

Charlie desperately needed a drink, not just a drink but a giant bottle. Better yet, a swimming pool filled with whiskey so he could jump in and let the alcohol seep into every pore of his body.

"I've answered your question, so let me ask you one. Have you ever felt alone?"

Charlie picked up a sugar packet and played with it. "Alone? I don't understand what you mean."

"That's what I thought because you wouldn't know it unless you felt it. No one does unless you have experienced the worst feeling imaginable. Think what it would be like to wake up every day with no one, and I mean no one. No one to talk to. No one to nag at you to finish chores around the house or to plan the day or future with. No one who cares if you come home at night. No one who cares if you are dead or alive. To truly be alone in this world is akin to not even living, not even mattering. Almost as if your existence on earth doesn't matter one bit. I have no one, Charlie, and I have had no one for a long, long time. I don't ask for your sympathy. I suppose my condition is partly my fault. But I need the book. I am an old man, and I have nothing to remember the only person I had in my life except for the book, and that is why I want it back. Will you please give it to me?"

Despite his intense disdain for the man, Charlie couldn't help but feel some sympathy toward him. His words did seem heartfelt, but he still had to know more before he agreed to anything.

"Why'd you become an undertaker?"

"I had to work. I figured if I couldn't find what I was looking for among the living, maybe I could find it among the dead."

"And did you?"

"I found death and nothing more, because there is nothing more after this existence."

"Do you really believe that?"

"I don't believe it. I know it. And I see it in your eyes, Charlie. You fight it, but you know the awful truth."

"And what is that?"

"Why, it's all about nothing. Life, death, what lies in between and after—there is nothing."

"I don't believe that," Charlie said, wondering what he actually did believe.

Charlie changed the subject. "Have you been searching Grandfather Mountain for gold all these years?"

"Yes."

"Why?"

"It's exciting. It gives me something to occupy my time rather than preparing dead corpses for an eternity in dirt."

"Searching for gold was a hobby then, an escape?"

"Yes."

"I've heard stories about a hidden treasure stolen by a group of Cherokees. Is that the gold you're looking for?"

"Charlie, there are hundreds of old legends, stories about untapped silver mines, large veins of emeralds, and yes, gold. I know people think I am a crazy old fool, but hunting for it gave me something to do, a purpose, a reason for living. Because if you give up the desire to live, only the cold steel table of the mortician's table awaits you. And I'm not quite ready for that."

Charlie looked down at his untouched coffee. He was deeply shaken by the information, and his initial anger had turned to a type of resignation that left him physically exhausted. "Can I call you tomorrow?"

The reverend studied him intently. "I am a reasonable man. I'll get in touch with you."

The reverend stood and looked down at Charlie. "I'm sorry I wasn't more honest with you in the beginning, but maybe now you can understand why. And I apologize if I have caused you any pain, but everything I have told you is the truth. Try to remember, your grandfather may not have been a good man, but your father was and so was his stepfather, and that is all that matters."

The reverend left Charlie sitting at the table, staring into his cup of cold coffee. Charlie threw a twenty-dollar bill onto the table and didn't bother to wait for the change. His mind couldn't take it anymore, and he decided he needed a drink, perhaps a few dozen.

There was no way he could go to the Green Man. He definitely didn't feel like seeing Kingsley, especially now. A creeping anxiety that part of his life had been one gigantic lie began to settle over him. Charlie now understood why his father had never told him the truth about his grandfather.

He walked down to the restaurant at the end of the street, where he knocked back drink after drink. After a while, he started having trouble focusing, although he could comprehend enough to notice that the bartender was getting edgy about his excessive consumption. Finally, Charlie figured he'd better go while he still could navigate his way home. He paid the tab and left.

He was completely drunk, but his mind had passed the point of no return. He didn't care—he was going to drive home and get even drunker. He pulled out onto the highway. He was trying to drive straight, but the more he concentrated, the worse his driving became.

Thank God this is a little-traveled road, his inebriated mind surmised.

He was almost at the turnoff when he heard a siren. He looked in the rearview mirror and saw blue lights flashing right behind him.

"Shit," he cursed. It was a policeman. He was going straight to jail. Do not pass go. He wasn't in any condition to even try to fake it. For a brief second, he thought about flooring it and trying to outrun the cop, but whatever rational part of his mind remained managed to quell that absurd thought. Charlie pulled over to the side of the road. He turned the ignition off and waited to be handcuffed and hauled off to jail.

What was Susan going to say about this?

He looked in the rearview mirror and groaned. The policeman walking up to his car was Sheriff Thomas.

Great, he thought. Why couldn't it have been some damn highway patrolman? Now, he would have the added humiliation of being arrested by the sheriff.

He rolled his window down. "Evening, Charlie," the sheriff said, peering in through the window.

"Evening, Sheriff," he slurred.

The sheriff looked over at the passenger seat while shining his flashlight directly onto the bottle of whiskey Charlie had bought earlier.

"Charlie." The sheriff shook his head. "Give me your keys."

Charlie pulled the keys out of the ignition and handed them to the sheriff through the window. "Please step out of the car," he ordered.

Charlie managed to get out of the car without falling over, which he considered a major accomplishment. Time to go to jail.

The sheriff looked him over with a disappointed expression on his face. "Do I even need to ask you to take a sobriety test?"

"No, sir. I'm drunk. I'm sorry. I have no excuse. I won't contest the fact in a court of law."

"All right. Step over here."

Charlie moved aside, and the sheriff got in the car, started the engine up, and moved it farther off the side of the road. He got out and locked the car.

"Come on."

Charlie obeyed without comment. He got into the back of the sheriff's car at least grateful that the sheriff hadn't added to his disgrace by handcuffing him. The sheriff pulled out onto the highway without saying a word. Charlie saw him glance in the rearview mirror, and he looked down, too ashamed to look the sheriff in the eyes.

The sheriff shook his head. "Um. Um. Um. Charlie, my boy. You are a lucky man. I shouldn't be doing this, but I'm not taking you to jail, where you damn sure belong. I'm going to take you home."

Charlie didn't know what to say, nor could he properly formulate any words of gratitude except to mumble, "Thanks, Sheriff. Sorry 'bout all this."

"Yeah, well, I'm only going to say this once, and I want to make sure you remember it, even after you sleep off the gallon of alcohol you consumed. Are you listening to me?"

"Yes, sir."

"Good, because if I ever pull you over again, and I even so much as think you had a beer with lunch a day earlier, I am going to take you straight to jail, and I'm going to leave you there for a while. Understand?"

"Yes, sir," he repeated.

"Good boy. Now that that is over, we can have a nice chat while I have you."

Charlie took a deep breath, not believing his good fortune. Susan wouldn't even find out about this. He was one lucky son of a bitch.

"Kingsley told me about your run-ins with the reverend."

"Huh?" Charlie sobered slightly.

"I said I heard about your run-ins with the reverend. I suppose by now the old coot has told you that the two of you are related?"

"You knew that?"

The sheriff looked back at him while driving. "Charlie, we both come from old Wellington families. This is a small town. Sometimes I think it is too small."

"So my grandfather was a McCellan?"

"Yes."

"And my grandfather killed his brother. The reverend's father."

"I don't know why people around here don't ever let sleeping dogs lie. The reverend believes that. Of course, your grandfather was never arrested. He died before that could happen. If you ask my opinion, I'd say he more than likely did it, but I can't say I'm one hundred percent sure. You have to understand it was a very unsettling time for the town. A lot of bad things, injustices, occurred. Of course, all of that was a long time ago."

"But if he did it, why wasn't he immediately arrested and thrown in jail?"

"The law worked differently in those days. There were conflicting circumstances, shall we say. Plus..." The sheriff paused.

"What?" Charlie asked.

"The town has a way of taking care of things in its own way. A lot of people didn't care much for Ezekiel and thought he got what he deserved."

"Got what he deserved? Why would anyone have thought that?"

"There were a lot of people who felt that your grandfather had actually done the town a favor by killing Ezekiel."

"Why?"

"They just did."

"C'mon, Sheriff, I'm drunk, but I'm not an idiot. There had to be a reason."

The sheriff looked in his mirror, and this time Charlie didn't look away. "Because some people believed that Ezekiel murdered his own family and then set it up to look like a group of Indians had done it."

"Oh, my God!" Charlie mumbled, thinking about the photo of the Indians hanging from the gallows. The ghastly image had been etched into his mind. "Why in the hell would he do something like that?"

"Because he was crazy, that's why!" the sheriff snapped, before adding in a calmer fashion, "Ezekiel was a lunatic, and so is his son, the reverend. Both of them wasted their lives tromping through the mountains looking for some damn gold that doesn't exist."

"Do you believe Ezekiel murdered his own family?"

"It doesn't matter what I believe. His family is dead, Ezekiel is dead, the reverend's..." He stopped and turned around to face Charlie. "And you're going to be dead if you ever get behind the wheel of a car in that condition again."

The sheriff turned off the highway onto Charlie's dirt road. They remained silent until the sheriff pulled up to the front of the cabin.

"What about my car?" Charlie asked.

The sheriff glared at him. "You can walk your hungover ass down there tomorrow and get it." He flipped the keys into Charlie's lap.

"And one last thing, Charlie." The sheriff turned so they were looking directly at each other. "I don't care for the reverend, and I want him out of this town. In order to do that, I need you to give him that damn book back."

"But..." Charlie started to protest but was cut off by the sheriff.

"I don't give a shit about the 'hows' or the 'whys.' Just give him that book back, or give it to me if you want, and I'll hand it over to him. I'm serious about this because if you don't, I'm going to arrest you for possession of stolen property. Are we clear?"

Charlie nodded. He had already begun to feel sick from the alcohol and couldn't imagine the pain tomorrow would bring, but he supposed it could have been worse. A lot worse if he had woken up in jail.

He got out of the police car and stumbled toward the house. The sheriff's window rolled down. "Night, Charlie," he called out a bit too cheerily.

Charlie waved a hand and went inside.

~

Chapter 11

Day Six

Friday

Charlie sat at the breakfast table in absolute misery, but that was what he deserved for drinking a fifth of alcohol. His elbow rested on the table, propping up his head. He was trying to think, but his aching head prevented him from doing much of that. He chewed two more aspirins, chasing them down with cold coffee. He flipped the deputy's card for the hundredth time.

That's it, he decided. *I'm going to call Johnny Ridge.*

He picked up the phone and dialed the police station. After two transfers and a five-minute wait, the deputy answered, "Hi, Mr. Parker. How may I help?"

"Deputy Ridge, how are you doing?"

"What can I do for you?" the deputy said in a less than enthusiastic tone, causing Charlie to wonder if he had misread him.

"Mr. Parker?" the deputy repeated.

"Yes, ah, I was wondering if we could get together. There are some questions I'd like to ask you."

Now it was the deputy's turn to be silent.

"Look, just a couple of questions. It's important."

"About the poachers?" the deputy asked.

"Yes and a couple of other things. I promise I won't take up a lot of your time."

"I really am busy."

"Please, Deputy, it's important."

After a few seconds of silence, the deputy finally responded, "I'm on duty till six o'clock this evening. I can meet you after that."

"Great. How 'bout the little bar next to the library? I'll buy you a couple of beers," Charlie replied, even though the absolute last thing he needed was a couple of beers.

"Fine. I'll see you after six."

Charlie hung up the phone and looked over at the clock. It was 11:00. He needed to go find his car. He still couldn't believe that he had been pulled over by the sheriff, but it could have been a lot worse. He was damn lucky he hadn't gotten his ass thrown in jail.

He tried to remember where he had been pulled over, but his memory was a little hazy. He figured the car had to be at least a couple of miles down the road, maybe farther. He opened the refrigerator and stared at the beer. Man, he needed one badly, just to settle his nerves.

What was happening to him? His mind was already rationalizing that it would be okay to have one, maybe two beers. He slammed the refrigerator door shut.

The phone rang, causing Charlie to jump. "It better not be the deputy canceling on me," he swore aloud. "Hello," he answered.

"Charlie, hey, it's Simon. How's things going?"

Simon was his right-hand man at the company and was in charge when he was out. "Good," Charlie answered. "What's up?"

"Well, I don't know. I just got off the phone with Roth, and he was pissed."

Charlie's heart lurched. "What about?"

"He said there are some issues with the bid and the contract."

"What the hell is he talking about? He signed those contracts; it's a done deal. Did he say what the issues were?"

"No, he wouldn't tell me. He wanted to talk to you directly, but you know how those contracts are, Charlie. Until they're ratified and the checks have been cashed, what can we do? I mean we can sue him, but it wouldn't be worth it. It would take years, and the legal fees... I know Roth is a tough SOB, and maybe he was giving me some grief, but I think you should call him as soon as possible."

Charlie knew it was a big deal if Phil Roth was calling directly. He was a busy, powerful man who didn't waste his time calling with trivial matters.

"I'll give him a call and see what's going on. How's everything else?" Charlie asked, as if anything else really mattered.

"Fine. Just a little nervous about Roth, though. What do you think has made him so uptight all of a sudden?"

Charlie didn't even want to begin to think about that possibility. "Who knows?" he said, trying to sound nonchalant about it. "I'll call you back after I talk to him. I'm sure it's nothing I can't straighten out."

Charlie hung up the phone and grabbed his car keys. He had no intention of calling Roth at this moment because if his worst fears were true, there was nothing he could say to fix the situation anyway.

Plus, he didn't feel too good. In fact, he felt like he was dying. Partially, because of his raging hangover, but something else was going on inside of him. It was like he was having an internal war with himself, and both sides were losing.

He left the house and began the long walk to his car, wherever it was. Luckily, it was a reasonably nice day. The sun was shining, and it wasn't too cold.

But the temperate weather didn't help improve his mood. His mind raced with anxiety. He would have to talk to Roth sooner or later, and Charlie knew he had gone too far this time. He had built his business from scratch with no help from anyone. He had worked like a slave for years to build his business, oftentimes undercutting his competitors just to get the business, even if it meant barely making money on the project. He had also engaged in some less than ethical business practices, but that's what it took to compete in business these days. Everyone did it, and Roth was to be his coup de grace, but in order to win the account, he had to take some major shortcuts.

He shook his head. Man, who did he think he was kidding? He had to cheat, and that's what he did.

The problem was if Roth had discovered his fraudulent activities, he was ruined. Charleston was the type of city where everyone knew everyone. If you screwed somebody over, not to mention someone like Roth that meant everyone from the mayor down to the garbage collectors knew it.

He approached the end of the dirt road, turned left, and began hiking down the side of the highway with his hands tucked inside his pockets and his eyes on the ground. He grudgingly walked for about an hour and a half when he saw the bend in the highway.

He didn't see his car. He was already winded and began wishing he had brought some beer to at least ease the pain.

He trudged on, expecting to keel over from a heart attack at any moment until mercifully he reached the bend and spotted his car pulled over on the side of the highway about an eighth of a mile ahead. He walked up to the car, kicked the bumper, and got in. The bottle of scotch was still in the passenger seat. He screwed off the top, forgetting about his earlier pledge of sobriety, and slugged down three large drinks.

He sat in the car for ten minutes sipping the scotch, staring at his cell phone lying on the floorboard, trying to muster the courage to call Roth. Finally, he decided to get it over with. Charlie picked up the phone and dialed his number. He was put directly through to Roth.

"Hey, Mr. Roth, it's Charlie. How are you doing?" he said in his best "let's be friends" voice.

"You have a big problem," Roth replied angrily.

Simon was right. Charlie could tell just by his tone that he was pissed.

"I do?" Charlie replied, with his heart slamming full throttle against his chest.

"Don't give me that shit, you little asshole! You know exactly what I'm talking about. Don't play games with me."

"Mr. Roth, I don't have any idea what you're talking about."

"I knew your father for thirty years. He was a good man. I don't know what trouble you are in with your business or personally, but you cheated on that bid. I signed that contract under false and illegal pretenses."

"Mr. Roth," Charlie began to plead.

Roth cut him off. "Shut up and listen, you little prick. Only because of your dad am I going to give you a one-time offer. Void the contract, and we part ways. If not, I will see you in court, and we both know that not only will you lose, but you will also be facing serious criminal charges. And another thing, if we go that route, I personally will see that not only will you never get another contract in Charleston ever again, but that you also get a few years locked up in jail to think about it."

Charlie was screwed and he knew it. He was in no position to bargain. "Fine, the contract is void."

"And Charlie, consider this another warning. If we meet socially—I don't care if it is at a party, at church, or on the side of the road—I want you to stay as far away from me as possible. I will not speak to you. I will not acknowledge your presence. Your father would be completely disgraced if he was alive, and I want you to think long and hard about that. I hope I have made myself clear."

The line went dead before he could answer.

Charlie threw the cell phone on the floor of the car and grabbed the bottle. He poured the whiskey down his mouth, choking on the burning liquid. Then he did something he hadn't done since his parents died. He cried.

Charlie drove home in a fog of despair. Roth's last words about his father—those hit him the hardest because Roth was right. He went inside and collapsed on the couch, where he fell into a slumber.

~

Chapter 12

Charlie woke in late afternoon. After a cold shower, he drove down to the restaurant to meet the deputy.

He walked into the dimly lit place and spotted Deputy Johnny Ridge sitting at the bar. The deputy nodded as Charlie walked over.

"Deputy," he said as the two men shook hands. Charlie sat next to him and motioned to the bartender to bring him a beer. Luckily, it was a different man than the one who had served him the night before.

Charlie turned to face the deputy, and it didn't take a detective to understand that the deputy didn't look all that happy to be there.

Charlie tried to lighten the mood a little. "I appreciate you taking the time to meet me. So you are a full-blooded Cherokee?"

"Yep."

"Your family live around here?"

"My mother lives over at Qualla Town. My father's no longer around. He worked for the Department of Transportation, basically digging ditches, when he wasn't drunk. Which wasn't all that often. He's been dead a long time."

"Sorry to hear that," Charlie said, surprised at the deputy's admission. Obviously, he was not succeeding in lightening the mood between them.

"How long have you been a deputy?"

"Nine years."

The bartender set their beers down. Charlie reached for his beer with a trembling hand, hoping the deputy didn't notice.

"How do you like the work?"

"It's a paycheck."

Charlie knew this line of discussion was fruitless. They weren't here to drink beers and exchange pleasantries like they were lifelong friends at some reunion. He decided to get straight to the point. "When the sheriff went to use the bathroom at my house, you said, 'Something didn't make sense.' So, what didn't make sense?"

The deputy turned in his chair so they were facing each other. "I think you misunderstood what I said."

Charlie smiled. "Don't bullshit me."

"Okay, there were no tracks."

"What do you mean, there were no tracks?"

"Footprints. You said you saw two Indians skinning something, and then they chased you. Right?"

"Right. So what do you mean there were no footprints?"

"We found what was left of the skinned wolf, but there were no footprints other than our own and yours."

"What!" Charlie said defensively. "You think I made up the story about the Indians...the men chasing me?"

"I didn't say that."

Charlie thought for a second before asking, "Wait a second, why didn't the sheriff mention anything about any other footprints?"

"The sheriff? C'mon, the man's in his mid-seventies," the deputy scoffed. "He was a good law enforcement man in his time. Now, well, he's just old. He didn't even notice."

"What do you mean, he didn't notice? How could he not have noticed?"

"I'm sure the sheriff figured I would have pointed something like that out to him."

"We walked up to the skinned animal, starting looking around. Anyway, he didn't lie to you. He really believed you probably had run into a couple of poachers, and they just meant to scare you. Hell, even if one of them had left their driver's license right there for us to find, the sheriff would have only given them a warning, if that."

"So why didn't you tell the sheriff about the missing footprints?"

"I don't know."

Charlie sat back in his chair. "What'd you mean, you don't know? Do you think I made up the part about the Indians?"

"I'm not sure."

"Well, I'm not too sure why you didn't mention this to the sheriff. So what do you think happened then?"

The deputy took a swig of his beer. "I found something."

"What?"

The deputy reached into his pocket and pulled out a small wooden statue. "Here." He handed it to Charlie.

Charlie hesitantly took the object. It was exactly like the one that he had found outside of his front door the other night, except there was only a wolf carved into it and no likeness of him.

He wanted to tell the deputy about the one he had found, but he decided to hold off, for now. "You found this up in the mountains?"

"Yes. Next to the remains of the wolf."

"What the hell is it?"

"It is a Cherokee amulet. The figure it represents is called a Nunnehi."

"Nun-a-he," Charlie repeated, looking more closely at the wood figure. Those were the same words he had heard over the phone line that one morning, the same words the old man in the library and the Indian girl at the grocery store had said. "What is a Nunnehi?"

"Old Cherokee folklore. A Nunnehi refers to a tribe of spirit warriors. They are immortals who live in another time, another dimension than ours. The Cherokee translation is 'people who live anywhere.'"

"Wait a second. Are you saying you think I saw a Nunnehi? Some demon from another world?"

"Not a demon, an immortal," the deputy corrected him. "A Nunnehi inhabits this world on a different plane than we do and is not usually seen by humans unless it wants to be seen."

"Are these Nunnehi good or bad ghosts?"

"Not ghosts. The Nunnehi are generally peaceful and especially kind to lost travelers. But they can..." The deputy stopped.

"Can what?"

"They are fierce fighters, and there are ancient stories about their best warriors being summoned to assist in fighting battles, especially if it is considered a matter of the survival of the Cherokee people."

Charlie laughed nervously. "I don't know what all this means. You're telling me the Indians that I saw were not really there? And that I saw 'spirits' from another world?"

The deputy looked around the bar; obviously making sure no one was listening. "I'm telling you what I found. And I am telling you a Cherokee myth."

"So who do you think skinned the wolf?"

"Wolves are sacred animals in Cherokee folklore. They are believed to be noble creatures…great hunters. No Cherokee, even today, would kill one unless the chief grants permission, and then the sacrifice can only be done by the tribe's wolf hunter."

"This is crazy," Charlie said.

The deputy shrugged and went back to drinking his beer.

Charlie slumped back in his chair wondering if he was losing his mind. He had come here expecting a few answers, not this.

Charlie sat back up. "What do you believe happened?"

"The Cherokee people are very superstitious and cognizant of the physical and spiritual world around them. Everything in the Cherokee world has a supernatural element to it. I was raised in the Cherokee nation. Some of their myths and beliefs, I take with a grain of salt, but this…Something doesn't make sense. I think you should maybe go back to Charleston for a while. Let things cool down."

"I'm not going back. I can help you."

"Help me? What do you think I'm going to do?"

"Find out who or what was up there and why. If what you say is true, I would think you would want to find out why the Nunnehi have been summoned."

"Sometimes, some things are best left alone."

"What do you know about Reverend McCellan?" Charlie asked, changing subjects.

"I don't know anything about him."

"Has the sheriff ever mentioned anything about him?"

"The only time I remember the sheriff saying anything about a Reverend McCellan was..." The deputy stopped.

"Was when?"

"Eight years ago, after your parents' car accident. We were driving back into town, and the sheriff said something kind of funny, which I didn't even register at the time, but now, with all this going on, well...I don't know."

"What did he say?"

"I don't think the sheriff even knew he was talking aloud, but he said, 'I bet that damn reverend had something to do with this.'"

"I asked the sheriff what he meant, and he just blew it off."

Charlie felt his stomach turn into a knot. "Do you think the reverend had something to do with their accident?"

The deputy shook his head. "I've got no idea, but in hindsight, it looks like the sheriff thought he might have."

Charlie mulled over the deputy's admission for a moment with anger swelling inside of him. He'd kill the son of a bitch if he had something to do with his parents' deaths.

He took a deep breath, forcing himself to calm down. "Okay, listen, you have been up front with me. I know you know more than you are letting on, and that's fine. When you trust me more, you can tell me whatever it is that you are holding back. Since you've been honest with me, I'm going to tell you everything that has happened and what I have discovered since I've been up here."

For the next twenty minutes, Charlie recounted his story. He told the deputy about his meeting with the reverend, the discovery of the book and its contents, the newspaper articles about the gold, the story of the Indians being dynamited inside of the cave, and the murders of Ezekiel's family. He told him about the amulet that he found outside his front door and even went so far as to tell the deputy about the disfigurement of the Indians who had chased him.

After he was finished, he felt like a great burden had been lifted, and as crazy as he knew his story sounded, the deputy didn't act like he was some lunatic who needed instant hospitalization.

"Charlie, I'd like to take you somewhere tomorrow."

"Where?"

"Over to the Qualla Boundary."

"What's the Qualla Boundary?"

"I guess you could call it a reservation. It is about an hour and a half west of here. It's the main home of the Eastern Cherokee tribe. I want you to meet the chief. He lives past the town."

"You think he might have some answers as to what's going on?"

"We'll see. Something is happening in the mountains. I can feel it. What it is, or means, I don't know."

The deputy stood and threw a twenty on the bar. "The beers are on me. I'll pick you up at seven tomorrow morning."

Charlie watched the deputy leave with growing anticipation and excitement. The deputy's reaction proved to Charlie he wasn't going insane, and maybe the chief could explain more tomorrow.

He thought about ordering another beer but stopped. Charlie forced himself to get up and leave. He desperately needed a good eight hours of relatively alcohol-free sleep.

∾

Chapter 13

Day Seven

Saturday

Charlie sat on the porch waiting for the deputy to arrive. He had just talked to Susan, and it had not gone well. She spent the entire conversation bitching and moaning because he was going to stay for a few extra days.

He blew some steam from the top of his coffee. Too damn bad, he thought, because he didn't care if she liked it or not. He was staying.

He took a sip of the hot coffee. The day broke bitterly cold, with heavy gray clouds and a freezing wind. He thought about the meeting with the deputy the night before. Their talk had left him with more questions than answers. He looked out at the dark sky, and for the first time since he arrived in the mountains, he almost felt good.

Maybe it was because, other than the beers with the deputy, he didn't have anything more to drink. And thank God, there were no animals or bad dreams lurking about, so finally he got a solid eight hours of semi-alcohol-free sleep.

His conversation with Roth filtered into his thoughts. That situation was going to be a disaster when he got back home because he knew rumors and hearsay would drift out. He supposed it could have been a lot worse. At least he wasn't going to be sued or thrown in jail, but Charlie wasn't naïve. Charleston was a tight-knit city, and Roth carried a lot of influence. Charlie knew his business was going to suffer drastically because of it.

Shit! Who was he kidding? His business was history, finished, over.

Charlie couldn't help himself and laughed, which surprised him, because he realized he didn't really care about Roth, or his own company, anymore. They could all go to hell.

He set the coffee mug down and rubbed his hands together. There were going to be some big changes when he got back home.

He heard a car approach and watched as the deputy pulled up in a beat-up black pickup truck. Charlie walked over to the truck and opened the door.

"Morning," the deputy said.

"Deputy." Charlie jumped into the truck. "So how far to the reservation?"

"Hour and fifteen minutes."

"Want a cup?" Charlie raised the thermos of coffee.

"No thanks."

The deputy turned the truck around and pulled out onto the highway. They were off.

They drove in silence for a while. Charlie—for the first time since he had been up in the mountains—felt as if he had a mind not clouded by alcohol or internal turmoil.

He finished his coffee. “It’s been quite a week so far. I know this sounds crazy, but until this week, I never knew that North Carolina used to be the gold capital of the country or that the Cherokees held such a large place in the history of this area. Hell, I thought Cherokees were from out West or the plains.”

The deputy shrugged. “I don’t think Cherokee history is widely taught in schools these days.”

“I know, but…I mean, we are going to an Indian reservation less than two hours away from here. I never even knew it existed.”

“Most people don’t know it’s there.”

“Did you grow up on the reservation?” Charlie asked.

“We don’t really call it a reservation.”

“Oh, sorry.”

“It’s no big deal. The area is known as the Qualla Boundary. I grew up outside the town of Cherokee on the Tuckasegee River. My grandfather had some property, and we had a small ranch house.”

“How long did you live there?”

“Till I was eighteen. Then I went to the community college. After I graduated, Wellington had a law enforcement position available, and I’m still here.”

“Why’d you choose to be a policeman?”

A small smile appeared on the face of the deputy. “My grandfather basically raised me. My father was drunk most of the time, while my mother worked her ass off to support us. Ever since I was a little boy, my grandfather always told me to grow up and become a police officer. So I did."

"I'm sure he was proud of you. Is he still alive?"

"Yep."

"Does he still live on the property?"

"He wouldn't have it any other way."

"Tell me a little bit about Cherokee history, its culture."

He watched the deputy light up a cigarette. Man, he wanted one of those badly. The deputy looked over at him with a strange expression. "You really want to know?"

"Yeah, I'm interested."

"You've heard of the Trail of Tears?"

"Yes."

"Well, afterward, there were less than a thousand Cherokees left in the area, most of which gravitated to towns along the Oconaluftee and Tuckasegee Rivers. These Cherokees were later called the Eastern Band of Cherokees. A few small tribes retreated into the mountains and lived in complete isolation."

"Do you think any of these tribes still exist up there?" Charlie asked.

The deputy shrugged. "Who knows? The Smoky Mountains encompass an enormous amount of land. Much of it is pretty uninhabited. I guess it wouldn't surprise me if a few still lived up there, living off the land and trying to avoid civilization."

"How many people live in the Boundary?"

"About thirteen thousand tribal members spread out over fifty-five thousand acres."

Charlie whistled. "Y'all own all that land?"

"It's not as much as it sounds. And it is only a tiny portion of what we inhabited before the white men came."

"I've read the Cherokees have some pretty interesting beliefs," Charlie said, trying to steer the subject away from the stolen lands.

The deputy grinned. "The old Cherokees believe that at the beginning of time, the earth was an island floating in a huge ocean, suspended by a cord hanging down from the sky. When the world grows old and dies, the people will also pass, the cord will break, and once again, the earth will sink back down into the ocean. And all will be water as it was in the beginning. Most Cherokees are afraid of this. Some believe the cords are frayed, ready to break."

"Pretty fatalistic, huh?"

"I guess."

"Do you believe that?"

"I believe in…" The deputy paused. "…the now."

"What the hell does that mean?"

"I believe our entire existence is only one moment in the present followed by another moment, a million successions of moments, one after the other after the other. I don't believe in the past or the future. If the cord breaks…so be it. It is beyond my control or understanding."

Charlie leaned back in his seat and stared out at the highway. They drove in silence for a while before Charlie asked, "What about the history of your people? I thought that was important to you?"

"I didn't say it wasn't."

"What was all that 'in the present' existential shit then?"

The deputy grinned. "Our history is important. It's funny, Cherokee isn't even our name. Our true name, the name we call ourselves, is Tsalagi. Our tribes settled in the Allegheny Mountains when the earth was young, when the cord was still tight and strong, as the Old Folks would say. Our ways and culture didn't change for thousands of years. Then in the course of one hundred and fifty years, it changed completely. I think most of the present-day Cherokees are reasonably satisfied, but I think there is an underlying sadness."

"Why?"

"I think deep down, most Cherokees just want our lands back." The deputy looked over his shoulder and turned on his blinker. "Hold on. There is something I want to show you."

He pulled over to the side of the road, parking the truck next to the guardrail. "You recognize this?"

Charlie looked over the edge of the steel rail with rising anxiety. He had been here one time before and vowed never to return.

The deputy turned toward Charlie. "This is the site of your parents' accident."

"I know. Why are we here?"

"I'll show you. C'mon."

The deputy unfastened his seat belt and got out of the car. Charlie followed, wondering why the deputy had brought him here.

Charlie walked around to the side of the truck, following the deputy to the edge of the guardrail. His earlier contentment had quickly faded, replaced with sadness and a little anger.

He didn't like being here. He looked out over the horizon, and the gloomy skies seemed to grow even darker, matching his inner turmoil. Charlie peered over the rail down the steep ravine. A pang of sadness swept through him. This was where his parents' lives had ended.

The deputy hopped over the rail and started to traverse down the steep embankment. A gust of freezing wind from the peaks stung his face.

"Be careful," the deputy shouted back.

Charlie guessed he had no option but to follow, so he stepped over the rail with more than a bit of trepidation. He had always been afraid of heights, and he cautiously followed the terrain down for about a hundred feet until it flattened out to a small ridge overlooking an even steeper drop down to the bottom.

The deputy stood at the very edge of the cliff.

Charlie wondered what his parents' final thoughts had been in those brief seconds as their car plunged down to the bottom of the ravine.

"Why are we here?" he asked again.

The deputy pointed up, back toward the guardrail. "The official state trooper report states that your parents' car left the highway traveling at a high rate of speed." He turned and pointed to where the guardrail ended by an embankment on the left-hand side.

"Twelve feet separates the embankment and the guardrail. The official cause of the accident stated that your dad lost control and left the highway in excess of eighty miles per hour. Their car struck the side of the embankment, caromed off of it, traveled directly in between the guardrail before going over the cliff, where the car exploded upon impact."

"I know all this," Charlie snapped. "So what? Why are we here?"

The deputy bent down and picked up a rock. He threw it off the cliff and turned toward Charlie. "The sheriff called me at four-thirty that morning, an hour after your parents' accident. We met at the police station and drove out here together. Charlie, you can say whatever you want about the sheriff, but he genuinely cared for your mom and dad. I specifically remembered because he was very shaken up about the accident. You know he didn't need to come out here. The accident was the jurisdiction of Avery County and the state highway patrol, but he...he really felt bad."

Charlie took a deep breath and nodded his head.

The deputy continued, "I know this is a strange question, but did anything strike you as odd or maybe wrong about their accident?"

"How 'bout they were driving in the opposite direction from Charleston, it was three o'clock in the morning, and my dad was going over eighty."

"Did you say anything to the highway patrol?"

"Of course. I made numerous inquiries, but I didn't get anywhere. Eventually, they started blowing me off, so I stopped asking. What else could I do?"

"The sheriff had his own doubts about the accident."

"Do you think there is something more to the accident? Some type of foul play? You mentioned the other night about the sheriff saying something about the reverend. Do you think he had something to do with this?"

"I don't know." The deputy motioned to him. "Come on."

Charlie followed the deputy fifty feet along the ridge in the direction of the embankment and the beginning of the guardrail. The deputy pointed up toward the rail.

"A car could fit through there if it hit the embankment at exactly the right speed. Your parents' car never hit the guardrail. We know that because there was no damage or paint marks on it."

"So?"

"The sheriff and I looked, and we couldn't find any signs of the car striking the embankment, either. There should have been tire marks, destroyed sod, something."

Charlie looked up at the embankment, thinking the deputy was right. If a car had struck it at eighty miles an hour, there should have been something. "I'm confused. That doesn't make any sense."

"I know."

"The reverend has to be connected to this," Charlie said.

"Hold on, there's more." The deputy turned back around and pointed down at the bottom of the ledge. "See that small tree way over to the left."

Charlie forced himself to look over the ledge. It was a long way down, and his legs felt like they had turned to butter.

"Yes," he answered, backing away from the edge.

"That's where your parents' car impacted the ground, exactly five feet to the right and three feet in front of the tree. I personally marked it off. "

"Okay, and..."

"Well, for your parents' car to leave the highway, carom off the embankment, and miss hitting the guardrail entirely..." The deputy pointed down to another spot directly in front of them about a hundred feet down. "The car should have landed about there. Not over by that tree."

Charlie looked at the space and distance. "I don't understand. How could that be?"

"I don't know. But that's the difference of one hundred and twenty feet from where the car should have been and where it actually was. Even with a little fudge room, even by miscalculating by twenty feet, which would be an astronomical mistake, it..." He stopped.

"It what?"

"It's goddamn impossible. Your parents' car would have had to have defied the laws of physics to land where it did. That is, if you accept the state trooper's report."

"Did the sheriff know all this?"

"It was the sheriff who checked it all out because he thought the state police screwed up. He didn't believe foul play was involved, but he thought your father had lost control of the car and hit the guardrail at a high rate of speed and at an unusual angle, which caused their car to flip over the railing, which then would've explained how it ended up where it did."

"If it was so obvious, why didn't the highway patrol just say they hit the guardrail and flipped over in the first place?"

"Hold on, let me finish. That was the sheriff's hypothesis. He brought out one of his buddies, a retired highway engineer for the state, and he inspected the guardrail for hours. He swore no car, or at least your parents' car, ever hit the rail."

"I still don't understand."

"I don't either because..." The deputy shrugged his shoulders. "Well, it is impossible for the car to have ended up there. It just doesn't make any sense."

"You think there was some type of cover-up?"

"No. I think the highway patrol couldn't explain the location of the car, either. They're not idiots. But policemen don't like open or unexplained cases. They had to report something, and since there was no evidence of foul play, no witnesses, or any other explanation, I think they did the best they could, wrote up the report, and closed the case."

Charlie looked down at the spot where his parents' lives had ended. Then he noticed his fingers on his right hand were twitching faster than the needles of a seismograph machine during a major earthquake. He reached into his coat pocket, pulled out three aspirins, and stuck them into his mouth, welcoming the bitter taste they brought as he gnashed them between his teeth.

The deputy put a hand on his shoulder. "Let's go. The chief is waiting."

Charlie followed the deputy back up to the road. They climbed back over the guardrail, where the deputy stopped and reached inside his pants pocket. "One more thing. Take a look at this."

Charlie recognized it immediately. "It's the amulet you found in the mountains by the skinned wolf."

"That's right." He watched the deputy reach into his other pocket with his other hand. He pulled out another identical amulet and held it in front of Charlie's eyes. "I didn't tell you this at the bar, but I found this next to your parents' car the night they died."

Charlie gasped. He wanted to say something, anything, but the words never formed.

The deputy put the amulets back into his pockets. "C'mon." He motioned to the truck. "Let's get out of here."

Charlie had to almost physically force himself to walk back to the truck. He got in, and the deputy pulled back onto the highway. Charlie couldn't think anymore. He slumped down in his seat and stared out the window.

~

Chapter 14

A violent shudder shook Charlie out of his trance. He stretched out his arms while looking over at the deputy.

"Sorry, we hit a pothole."

Charlie rubbed his eyes. "Where are we?"

"Coming into Cherokee."

Charlie stared out the window as they sped past a series of small buildings. They entered the center of town.

The deputy pointed to the right of Charlie. "Those are the government buildings housing the police department, administrator, the chief's office…"

"I thought we were going to see the chief," Charlie said, as they sped past his office.

"The elected chief runs the administrative part of the reservation, but the other chief, the man we are going to see, is the spiritual leader. He holds tremendous influence over all decisions affecting the tribe."

"Why elect a chief then?"

"I'm not saying that the elected chief doesn't have any power or important duties. He does. But wisdom and respect for the knowledge of our elders is an important part of Cherokee society. The chief we are going to see has veto power, so to speak, on all major decisions affecting the tribe."

They continued driving down the two-lane road, eventually passing the largest, most kept-up building in the entire town.

"What's that?" Charlie asked

"A museum."

Only a few cars parked near the front occupied the enormous parking lot. "Doesn't look like they get a lot of visitors, do they?"

"They don't," the deputy said flatly. "Back in 1998, the tribal council, our supposed elders, pressured the elected chief into a major renovation project. It was not the greatest monetary decision in the world."

The deputy lit a cigarette and blew out a stream of smoke that ricocheted off the front windshield back into Charlie's face.

The deputy continued, "They convinced the chief the museum would serve to honor the Cherokee nation and that it would be a successful tourist attraction. They promised the tribal council that after three years, the museum would have been paid for, and then it would turn into a yearly cash flow machine, and the revenues could be used for what we really need out here: schools, healthcare facilities, work training programs."

"Well, what's wrong with that?"

"Nothing, I suppose. The museum gets a decent amount of visitors, and it is really well run, but we still have shitty roads, a rundown understaffed hospital, and a school that can't afford to buy new books. You know, just a lot of poor people. The farther out you get from the town, the worse it is."

Charlie noted the rising agitation in the deputy's voice, and he guessed that he really couldn't blame him. It did seem like a waste of money when there were so many other things that the town needed.

"That's too bad about the museum, but I guess at least future generations won't forget their heritage."

The deputy grunted. "I suppose. It's just kind of sad. No one cares about the Eastern Band of Cherokees or its history."

"You're wrong," Charlie said.

The deputy threw his cigarette out the window. "How's that?"

"You said no one cares about the Cherokees' past."

"I know what I said. No one does."

"You do. The people that live out here do. Don't they?"

"So what's the point?"

"Well, do you care about my Scottish ancestors and the hardships they faced? What about the Asian man down at the gas station where we stopped? I'm sure his family faced many hardships, especially when they first came over. Do you make an effort to study them?"

"I think that is different."

Charlie laughed. "How?"

"It just is."

"No. It's not. Everyone has their cultural history, and everyone thinks it should be important to everyone else in the world. But let me tell you something. You shouldn't go through life expecting anyone to give a rat's ass about you, your ancestors, or your cultural identity. You should only care about what the people in your life think and stop worrying about everyone else."

"Okay, just forget it," the deputy replied testily.

"All right, but you know everyone in the world, every single person, has ancestors that were persecuted and mistreated at one time or another. The only difference is the time frame in which it occurred. I wish people would start living in the present and stop bitching and moaning about things that happened decades and centuries ago."

"I get your point. Drop it." The deputy lit up another cigarette.

They drove another couple of miles until they turned off the paved road onto a bumpy dirt road.

"The chief doesn't live in town?"

"He prefers to live out here, closer to the mountain. Some things you just can't change." The deputy laughed. "The old man could live in town in a nice two-bedroom town house, but he likes his ranch on the edge of the woods, away from everyone."

The deputy pulled up to a one-story ranch house that had seen better days. A clutter of junk surrounded the house: engine parts, chicken cages, wood, and tools were strewn everywhere.

Charlie saw an old man sitting in a rocking chair on the porch. His appearance left no doubt that he was the chief.

The truck stopped, and both men got out. The chief stood up and walked down the porch stairs, allowing Charlie to get a better look. He was about Charlie's height but had a lean, wiry frame. He wore old blue jeans, a dark vest over a flannel shirt, and a faded black cowboy hat. Deep wrinkles were cut into his dark brown face.

He limped slightly, and his shoulders stooped a bit, but Charlie detected a presence of strength that seemed to permeate throughout him. The chief walked over to the deputy, not even seeming to notice Charlie, and gave him a great big bear hug.

The chief laughed and said in a strong voice that didn't fit his frail-looking body, "Soaring Eagle, I am happy you have come to visit me. It has been too long." Then he added in a playful tone, "You should respect your elders more, especially when it's your grandfather."

Charlie looked over at the deputy, who smiled back at him with sheepish grin.

What else did the deputy neglect to tell me? Charlie wondered.

The chief let go of his grandson. "Papa, this is Charlie Parker."

The chief turned toward him with the same warm smile he wore when greeting his grandson. Although his weathered face was tanned dark brown from many years of exposure to the elements, his dark brown eyes were alert and lively.

"Charlie Parker, welcome to my home."

"Thank you, sir, I mean, Chief," he said, as the two men shook hands.

The chief laughed. "You can call me Sir Chief if you like."

Charlie grinned. "Okay."

"He's just joking," the deputy said.

"No, I like the ring to it," the chief corrected his grandson. "Yes. Sir Chief. I like that." The chief laughed again. "Come, let us sit on the porch and enjoy the beautiful day."

Charlie glanced at the dark gray sky and heavy clouds and followed the grandfather and grandson up onto the porch. They each took a seat in rocking chairs, and neither the deputy nor the chief said anything. Charlie watched as both men sat rocking in their chairs, staring off across the barren field. Behind the field was a thick forest leading up the mountainside. The land was bleak, and with the cloudy day, the countryside looked gray and inhospitable.

Finally, the chief turned his attention toward Charlie. "So, my grandson tells me you have an interesting story to tell."

Charlie cleared his throat. "I guess. My family has had property in these mountains for a long time, and, well, I really don't know where to begin, so I guess I better start from the beginning and…"

The chief raised a hand. "Johnny has told me much about you and your family. Our ancestors have also been in these mountains for a long time. Who knows? Perhaps their paths have crossed."

The chief looked across the field again. "These mountains are alive. They are magical, a sacred place." He looked back at Charlie. "But with all magical and good places, evil and bad spirits also conjugate. It is a fact of the universe. Evil gathers like a flock of vultures. It can sense good from far away, and it tracks it, methodically, patiently, but with murderous intent, waiting for its opportunity to pick the flesh from its bones. Evil wants only to take and to destroy without cause or reason."

Charlie wasn't sure what to make of the chief's words. The deputy spoke to his grandfather, "I didn't tell you over the phone. Charlie had a wolf visit him."

"Is this true?" the chief asked.

Charlie nodded. "Your grandson saw the tracks, and he was the one who told me. I knew it was an animal but not that it was a wolf."

"We later found the wolf up in the mountains," the deputy added.

"You saw this wolf?" he asked his grandson.

"We found it. It had been skinned...Rather, it had been mutilated. Charlie thinks he saw two Indians doing this."

The chief's pleasant demeanor suddenly took on a look of concern. "How sure are you that it was two Indians you saw doing this?"

"Pretty sure. I mean they chased me halfway down the mountain with knives. I made it back home, and that is why I called the sheriff."

"Have you had any other unusual sightings, animals around your place?

"No, just the wolf," Charlie said. "No, wait a second." He couldn't believe he had almost forgotten. "When I first arrived in town and drove up to my house, well, it was the darndest thing. Sitting on the railing of my front porch was a giant owl."

"An owl," the chief asked in a concerned tone.

"Yes. And what was so strange about it was it didn't fly away when I pulled up. I even got out of my car and stood there waiting for it to leave. I couldn't have been more than twenty feet away, and it just stared back at me with giant yellow eyes. I mean, it was weird."

The chief looked off into the field again, and after a few moments of silence, stood. "Excuse me. I am going to get my pipe."

Charlie nodded, wondering if he had said something wrong because the chief suddenly appeared very apprehensive.

The chief walked into the house, and Charlie asked the deputy, "Did I say something wrong?"

"No. It's just that owls are considered a bad omen."

Great, Charlie thought. That was all he needed, another bad omen to add to the growing list.

The chief stepped back out onto the porch and returned to his rocking chair with his pipe in hand. He lit a match, puffing a few times to light his pipe. He exhaled a thick stream of grayish smoke that slowly snaked up into the sky.

The distinct smell of pipe tobacco filled Charlie's nostrils, bringing forth a stream of memories. His father had smoked a pipe all his life, and the aroma always reminded Charlie of him.

The chief pointed the end of the pipe toward him. "Birds of the night hold a special place in the Cherokee supernatural world, especially owls. They are dangerous creatures and should be feared."

Charlie was a bit surprised. He always thought of owls as wise, benevolent creatures. "Owls. Really?" he asked, looking back over at the deputy, who nodded his head in agreement.

The chief continued, "The 'Ones That Know' say that owls are the animal bodies that witches choose to inhabit when they need to. They are tricksters and spies. It should be considered a very bad sign that one was at your house when you arrived, especially considering how you described the owl's actions. That is not normal animal behavior. You are under watch."

"'Under watch.' What! I don't know what you mean by that."

"The wolf that was at your house, the one that my grandson found up in the mountains, had been sacrificed."

"Sacrificed, but why?"

"I believe your story about the Indians. I think what you actually saw was either a Nunnehi or some other Indian spirit."

"The immortals you were telling me about?" Charlie asked the deputy.

"For them to allow you to see them is quite extraordinary," the chief said. "I have felt...something in the air recently, and after what you have told me, I believe you are connected somehow, but in what way...that I do not know."

"Should I be concerned?"

"Grandfather," the deputy interrupted. "Tell Charlie about Black Fox. I think his story may help him begin to understand."

The chief nodded. "Perhaps you are right. My great-grandfather was a great warrior called Black Fox. He was chief when the government forced most of the Cherokee tribes of the Southeast to move to reservations in Oklahoma. They called it the Indian Removal Act. We called it the Trail of Tears.

"Black Fox and his small tribe defied the government's order to leave their lands and travel to Oklahoma. He foresaw what would happen if they listened to the government."

The chief shook his head, and Charlie detected a look of sadness. "Those who left on the Trail of Tears endured hardship after hardship. Thousands and thousands of Cherokees perished during the journey to the reservations, and for those who survived, the living conditions on the open barren plains were almost worse than having died along the way. Black Fox led his tribe farther up the mountains into almost complete isolation, where they kept to themselves for decades. Then gold was found, and the last bit of remote land they inhabited was encroached upon by miners, fortune seekers, fools. He was a man of vision, understanding." The chief stopped.

"Grandfather, go ahead. Tell him the rest," the deputy urged.

The chief hesitated then spoke, "The land is all an Indian needs to live, to be happy. But the last bit of Cherokee land high in the mountains was taken away from the tribe, leaving Black Fox with no option. He was in a no-win situation, so he chose the only option that remained. He stole a shipment of gold and hid it in a sacred cave up in the mountains. Gold back then was not desired by Indians like it is among white men. But Black Fox took the gold believing that a future generation of Cherokees would be able to use it to purchase their lands back. The tribe was very small at that point, but he recruited a band of warriors whose sole purpose was to protect the gold. They swore their lives to it."

"Whatever happened to the gold?" Charlie asked.

"Black Fox passed on. His son became chief, and a new group of warriors protected the gold until a white man discovered their secret and tried to steal the gold."

"What did he do?" Charlie asked, although he already knew the answer.

"His greed to possess the gold was so great that he killed his own family, setting it up to look like the Cherokees had done it. Back then a white man's word was always taken over an Indian's. The protectors of the sacred cave and gold were hunted down. A group was trapped in a cave, and the sheriff set off dynamite charges, killing them inside of it. Three more warriors were gunned down, and the chief, his son, and another warrior were hung. The entire group of Indians sworn to protect the cave were killed, so now, the location of the gold is unknown. But some elders say the spirits of those warriors are still up in the mountains, and along with the Nunnehi, they're still protecting the gold."

Charlie's head spun. He could see the image of the Indians hanging in his mind. Could it be that the disfigured Indians he had seen were the Indians who had been dynamited inside the cave? But that was crazy.

"There is something else I need to tell you," Charlie said. "I discovered that Ezekiel McCellan, the man who claimed the Indians killed his family, the man who set up the Cherokees and was responsible for their deaths…he was my grandfather's brother."

The deputy and chief looked at each other with shocked expressions. "Why didn't you tell me that?" asked the deputy.

"Look, I just found out my father was adopted and took his last name. I don't know this for a fact, but his brother Jeremiah, my real grandfather, he might have also been responsible for the murders."

The chief stared off toward the mountains for a few moments. He returned his gaze toward Charlie. "I believe after what you have told me that Nunnehi have been and are protecting the cave. The disfigured Indians you saw are indeed the spirits of the dead warriors."

"It would explain why I never saw any tracks where Charlie saw the Indians," the deputy added.

"It has been foretold that one day, when the spirits determine it is time, a Cherokee of the purest spirit will be led back to the burial spot to reclaim the gold. I think that time is rapidly approaching."

"How exactly do you think Black Fox got the gold?" Charlie asked, wondering if the chief knew about the story of the Bechtler gold shipment.

"Black Fox grew tired of being cheated by the representatives of the white man's government, who reneged on every treaty or agreement they signed. The Cherokees had been cheated so many times that Black Fox came to learn two truths: one, they could not trust the white man, and two, the only tool the Cherokees might have in the future was to take away what the white man cherished the most."

"Which was…?"

"Money," the chief said.

"Gold to be exact," the deputy added. "Black Fox was a man beyond his time. He knew he would never be able to use the gold in his lifetime or even in his son's lifetime. But one day, he believed, the gold would help his people."

"I thought you didn't believe in any of this," Charlie said to the deputy.

"I never said that. I said it was folklore, myth, but some legends are real. Look what is happening around you. I know I was skeptical, and I still am, I guess, but it's hard to ignore what's going on."

"But how can you be so sure the chief took the gold from Bechtler and all of that really happened?" Charlie asked.

The chief smiled and reached inside his vest. He pulled out a gold coin and handed it to Charlie. "This coin has been passed from Black Fox to his son, to my father, and then to me."

Charlie looked at the date—1853. The coin had the same date as the Bechtler gold coin that his father had given him.

Charlie reached in his pocket, pulled out his coin, and handed it to the chief, who looked at it with a wry grin. "Both these coins were minted in 1853."

"Those coins are not supposed to exist."

The chief grinned. "But they do."

"Yes, they do." Charlie handed the chief's coin back to him and asked, "But what does this have to do with me and all these strange things that have been happening?"

The chief stood, walked over to the porch rail, and looked up toward the mountains. "I feel it. Great forces are converging upon these mountains. I believe the time has come. The spirits want the gold to be recovered. The only question is...will good triumph over evil?"

"But what does all this have to do with me and all the crazy things that have been happening?"

The chief exhaled a stream of pipe smoke. "I do not know that answer."

"Grandfather," the deputy prodded.

The chief scowled at his grandson and turned to face Charlie directly. "Like I explained, I do not know the answer to your questions, but I have some guesses. Your family, your ancestors, because of their actions, they are linked to this, meaning you are as well. All the signs are there, but I don't know what side you are on."

"Side—what do you mean?"

"Sometimes in life there is no gray, only black and white. In this case, your case, it is between evil or good. There can be no other choices."

Charlie laughed. "I'm sorry, I certainly don't mean to be rude, but are you saying that I have done something evil or that I am a bad person?"

The chief waved his pipe in a circle. "No. At least, I don't believe so, but the difference between good and evil is not necessarily that easy to distinguish. And sometimes a good person has a seed buried deep within them waiting to..."

Charles cut him off. "Are you suggesting I have some type of evil in me waiting for some event to trigger it?"

"I am suggesting that all people are tested by evil, and sometimes events get out of control and people find themselves in unimaginable positions, and that the right decisions are not always made."

"You still haven't answered my question," Charlie said defensively.

"Have you been having nightmares or strange dreams?"

Charlie hesitated. He thought about denying it, but then thought better of it. "I've had some unusual dreams, but dreams are just dreams."

"Sometimes that is true, but sometimes not. There is a world that exists between dreams and here. Tell me about your dreams."

Charlie figured at this point, he had nothing to lose. "I've had a recurring one where I'm being chased through the woods or up in the mountains."

"What's chasing you?"

"I guess a monster. Typical nightmare that everyone has had at one time or another."

"What's this monster look like?"

"Well, the first couple of times I had the dream, I never really saw it, but as I dream more about it, I catch more and more glimpses of what it looks like."

"What do you see?"

Charlie sighed. "Well, like I said, I can't remember seeing it all the way or too clearly, if that makes any sense. I think it looks kind of like a giant snake, although its trunk is big as a tree. But it doesn't move like a snake, and I remember seeing enormous gnarly horns coming from head."

The chief looked over at the deputy and muttered something under his breath.

"What did you say?" Charlie asked.

"What you've seen is called Uktena."

"Uktena?" Charlie repeated.

"Yes. You have been to the between world, and the reason you haven't seen the Uktena completely is, if you had, you'd be dead. No one sees this beast and lives to tell about it."

"It was just a dream. You can't be serious."

"Let me tell you a story. Long ago, the sun grew angry with the people on earth and sent forth a sickness to destroy all humans. A shaman changed a man into a monster snake called an Uktena and sent it to the sun to destroy her instead. The Uktena failed and returned to earth. Then the people sent a rattlesnake to kill the sun. When the Uktena found out about the rattlesnake, it became jealous and grew angry at the people and made its revenge on anyone who crossed its path. Those Who Know say the Uktena is a great snake with horns on its head as you described. But in its forehead, it has a crest as brilliant as the brightest diamond, and its scales glow like sparks of fire. The crest and scales are so bright that if a person sees them, they are driven crazy, and they run toward the monster snake instead of trying to escape. Then the Uktena devours them. You must never completely look at this thing, Charlie, because if you do, you will perish."

Charlie didn't know how to respond to the chief's words, so he asked his question again. "Do you think I am evil?"

"I think you are in a neutral state. You are being pulled, directed, influenced by both good and evil entities. Somehow, you are a large piece of the puzzle. Perhaps you are the conduit that is allowing this to happen. Maybe both sides need you to determine the final outcome. Like I said, I don't know the answers. I am only telling you my hunches."

The chief banged his pipe against the rail, emptying the burnt tobacco. Charlie caught a glimpse of the stem of the pipe, and a chill ran through him. The mouthpiece was a carved figure. The exact figure of the amulets the deputy had found next to the skinned wolf at the site of Charlie's parents' automobile accident, and the one that was left outside of his door.

The chief tucked the pipe into his pocket. "It was good meeting you, Charlie." He turned toward his grandson, who got up and gave the chief a big hug.

The chief patted the deputy on the shoulder. "Soaring Eagle, it is time I relinquished my coin. It has been passed down in our family, and now it is time for me to pass it on to you."

The chief reached inside his pocket and pulled out a gold coin. He began to hand it across, but the deputy stepped back.

"But grandfather, I can't take this from you. You have many years left."

The chief grinned. "I said the same thing when my father gave it to me. Only I know when the time is right, and it is now."

The chief placed the coin into the deputy's palm. The deputy reluctantly put the coin into his pocket.

"Grandson, you need to visit more."

"I will. I promise."

"But wait..." Charlie protested. "You can't tell me all this, and that's it. Can't you give me some guidance, advice? What should I do?"

The chief turned toward Charlie. "What happens, happens. I am merely a human being. I have no power to stop or start any of these things we have talked about. Many things in life have to be done alone. This is one of those things. What will be done, will be done. That is all I know. I wish you luck in your treacherous journey, and I will be thinking of you."

The chief turned and went back into the cabin.

"C'mon, I'll take you home," the deputy said.

Charlie walked to the truck in silence. He got in and said to the deputy, "Well, I guess we're in this together."

"We are?"

"We need each other."

The deputy lit a cigarette and asked, "In what way do we need each other?"

Charlie smiled. "We're going to find the gold your grandfather spoke of."

"The gold. And how are we going to do that?"

"Don't worry. I have some pretty good ideas. Just give me a little time to check some things out. So, what do you say, Deputy. Are we partners?"

The deputy looked over at him with a wry expression on his face. "I don't need a partner."

"You heard your grandfather. He believes I have a lot to do with this. Who knows? Maybe you are the chosen one," Charlie kidded.

"What?"

"You know, the pure Cherokee warrior chosen by the spirits to reclaim the gold."

"I doubt that."

"You never know. So what do you say? Are you going to help, or am I going to find the gold myself?"

The deputy slowly nodded his head. "We'll see."

Chapter 15

The two men hardly said a word the entire trip back. The deputy chain-smoked, and Charlie's brain felt like it was going to split open. Nightfall had arrived when the deputy pulled up to the cabin.

The deputy stopped the truck and tossed out of the window what must have been close to his fortieth cigarette of the day. He turned toward Charlie but said nothing.

Charlie opened the car door and got out. "Give me a day or so. I need to check a few things out. Then we can start searching."

"Whatever you say," the deputy said with a stone face.

Charlie shut the door and watched as the deputy drove away.

He went inside and dialed home. Thank God, no one answered, so he left a message on the machine and pulled a beer out of the refrigerator.

He started drinking.

The puzzle was taking shape, but instead of the picture coming into focus, it seemed as if the true explanation was even further away. The beer wasn't helping to stop his racing mind, so he found comfort in a bottle of Jack Daniels.

The night passed, and Charlie spent it writing and wishing he could stop drinking. Even with the cloud of alcohol mottling his brain, he felt it was important to keep an accurate recollection of what had occurred, both to help unravel the mystery and to record what he had discovered. The writing seemed to help unburden his mind and actually worked to calm him down.

The pieces of Ezekiel's story were connecting, but there were still holes, and Charlie was afraid if he fell into one of those holes, he might never get back out again. He would have to be careful. Ezekiel had left clues, but there were trapdoors and probably more lies than true statements in his writings. Then, of course, there was the reverend, and Charlie knew their paths were on a collision course.

He set the legal pad down. Charlie stared out of his bedroom window into the night. Blackness was all he could see, and he wondered if the darkness enveloping the safety of his house was what death was like, just an absolute nothingness. He quelled his uneasiness by taking another large drink from the whiskey bottle. He set the bottle on the table with a heavy sigh.

He was drunk.

His muddled thoughts made it even more difficult to write anything coherent. *No one better see these journals,* he thought, feeling his eyelids growing heavy, because he would be committed for sure. Charlie felt his head beginning to nod. His eyelids flickered. He began to drift, when a faint light appeared, deep within the forest.

"What the hell." He stood up, with all senses suddenly on alert. He pressed his face up against the glass, turned off the desk lamp and saw what looked like a bluish light flickering far off in the distance.

Charlie remembered reading in some novel about a legend that on certain nights a blue light was said to be a marker for hidden treasure.

Could it be this simple? he wondered.

He wouldn't even have to decipher the map or the clues or need the deputy's help. He could just follow the blue light to the gold. He took another large swig of the whiskey and made up his mind. He was going to find the blue light even though it meant hiking up the mountain through the dark woods.

He grabbed the legal pad and hastily scrawled:

> *It is well past the witching hour. The blue light high in the mountains is summoning me. The magic of the light will show me the way to the gold.*

Charlie took a last swig of the whiskey and went downstairs.

But what if he found the gold? He hadn't really thought about that part yet. What would he do with it? The chief told him it belonged to the Cherokees.

Screw him, Charlie thought. *They stole it in the first place. Finders keepers, right?* If he found the gold, he could tell everyone, including Roth, to go to hell. In fact, maybe he would buy out the old man's firm just to have the pleasure of firing him.

He dressed in his heaviest winter gear and grabbed two flashlights.

He turned on all the lights in the cabin to help him navigate his way home in case he got lost, which was almost an absolute guarantee. Charlie blinked in rapid succession because the time on the microwave's digital clock caused him to pause. It read *2:17* in the morning, and that number meant something to Charlie because that was the number of the hotel room in the book *The Shining*, and behind that door was a man's worst nightmare.

Charlie waited for the green digital time to change to *2:18*. Then he left and headed off in the direction from where he had seen the blue light.

Luckily, there was very little wind, and the snow had packed down into a hard layer, so hiking was not too difficult. He couldn't see the blue light any longer, but he hadn't expected to at ground level within the forest.

He walked through the trees for some time, gradually moving higher up the mountain. He couldn't believe he was doing this. A wave of euphoria came over him, and he realized he was no longer spurred on by fear but by an overwhelming desire to find the gold.

He'd find the gold. Then he would make things right with everyone, one way or another.

Charlie came through a thick outcrop of trees and up over a ridge. A flat, almost treeless plateau spread out in front of him. He stopped, catching his breath while surveying what lay in front of him.

He turned his gaze up to the full moon. The bright white moon cast down a sea of light, adding not only to his comfort but also to his ability to move quickly and safely up the mountainside.

Despite the full moon, a sea of stars flickered in the sky like a swarm of fireflies against the black blanket of the universe. A pang of complete aloneness swept over him, a feeling so foreign to him that tears fell from his eyes. The reverend was right. Charlie had never experienced what it was like to be all alone.

Until now.

He scanned the horizon to his left. About halfway up to the next peak, he spotted the dull blue light again. He looked back up into the sky, and even though some part of his soul directed him to stop everything and go back, he couldn't help himself and shouted, "I will find you!"

Without hesitation, Charlie set off toward the light. All he could think of was the gold.

Let the reverend or anyone else try to stop me now.

The terrain became rocky, more difficult to navigate, and Charlie felt the energy from the night's excursion beginning to drain from him. Every time he thought he had made some progress toward reaching the light, he would stop for a quick rest, only to discover that the light actually appeared no closer to him than when he first spotted it from his bedroom window.

Was the light just some cruel trick, a mirage set against a barren mountain that was just as cold and inhospitable as any desert?

He trudged on, and a weird thought struck him: He had been walking for at least two hours, and in that entire time, he had heard no sounds except for the constant crunching of snow underneath his boots. No animals, no planes flying overhead, no tree branches swaying in the wind, just complete and absolute silence.

Charlie walked for another half hour. He was growing very tired and fought the urge to lie down to rest because he knew he might never get back up. He didn't want to end up like his grandfather, frozen to death, alone in the mountains.

He cursed. He had lost sight of the blue light, but he kept on until he came to a ridge of rocks about fifty feet high. He stood underneath and looked up. If he was to continue in his search to locate the blue light, he would have to climb.

He shined his flashlight on the vertical rock face for a good fifteen minutes, trying to judge the best route before beginning to climb, knowing that a fall could very well result in serious injury or death.

One step at a time, he told himself as he climbed.

Halfway up the rock face, he looked down, and much to his disbelief, Charlie discovered he wasn't scared. Fear, his constant companion in life, had magically disappeared from his being.

He stood on a tiny ledge thinking about how the irrational emotion of fear had controlled every aspect of his life.

He graduated from college only because he was afraid of what his parents would think if he hadn't. He asked Susan to marry him because he was afraid he might not find anyone else to say yes.

He took no joy in the birth of his children because he was too afraid for their health, and as they grew, he worried constantly that something bad would happen to them. He started his own firm because he feared being fired. And worst of all, he cheated and stole because he was afraid of failing. Afraid of what everyone would think of him.

He was pathetic.

Fear had directed every part of his life, but that was over. All those fears were gone now, and he felt only exhilaration and strength.

Finally, he was the man he always dreamed of being, and it was all because the vise of fear that gripped his soul for so long had suddenly vanished. Charlie took one last look down, turned and continued climbing. Twenty minutes later, he was safely up on the ridge.

Ahead of him, the blue light glowed past a small hill about four hundred yards away. He walked up over the hill, and what he saw caused him to stop dead in his tracks. His heart started to beat irregularly, and an overwhelming urge to run filled every neuron in his brain. Fear, which just moments ago he thought had left him for good, flooded his senses. He was so terrified by what he saw that his legs refused to function. He was completely frozen.

He had found the blue light, and sitting in a circle around the eerie blue light were a half-dozen Indians. Only these Indians were not of this world. Charlie knew immediately these Indians were the Nunnehi and the spirit warriors.

The light reflected off their faces. They seemed to take no heed of him. They were dressed in animal furs and looked similar to the Indians he had seen skinning the wolf. The blue light cast strange and gruesome shadows.

After standing there for what seemed like an eternity, one of the Indians turned and faced him. Then, one by one, they all turned and looked at him in silence. Some had just eye sockets, others had noses that had been mutilated or were not even there any longer. A few had open lacerations with greenish puss oozing out. One of the Indians had half an arm missing, while another had half a leg.

They continued staring at him in silence. Then the silence of the night was broken by a gut-wrenching howl from a line of trees past the Indians.

The sound of limbs snapping and branches being torn was followed by the appearance of the beast from his dreams. He remembered what the chief had said and tried not to look at it directly, but he caught a brief glimpse of the Uktena, and it was of such heinous appearance that it was indescribable. The Uktena moved closer to him, and Charlie thought he had lost his sanity.

Charlie did not even contemplate escape. He knew he was here to serve a purpose, a purpose that perhaps had been chosen for him the day he was born. He was a sacrifice, and now that time had come for him to fulfill his role.

He stood waiting for his fate.

The beast let out another roar, then lumbered toward him…

∾

Charlie opened his eyes and instantly regretted the consciousness that came with it. His body felt like it had been beaten with a sledgehammer. He was curled up in a ball, shivering uncontrollably. As he began to regain his senses, he realized he was lying on his front porch.

Why was he here? And how in the hell did he get out here?

It was still dark out, but it was the kind of darkness that soon brought morning with it. He stood. He had to warm up; he was freezing. He was lucky he hadn't died of hypothermia.

He stumbled inside and wrapped two heavy blankets around his shoulders. His teeth knocked against one another uncontrollably. It took him five minutes to get a pot of coffee brewing because his frozen fingers didn't seem to want to work. He made a fire, and only after three large cups and by practically sitting in the fire wrapped in blankets did he begin to warm up.

As the freezing numbness left his body, only then did his mind begin trying to figure out what had happened the night before. Did he dream about the trip up into the mountains? Could it be possible he had been sleepwalking and had fallen asleep outside?

His head began to ache as the first rays of sunlight filled the sky. He felt exhausted. He needed to call home and check in, but it was still too early. He'd phone in a little while, but first he needed a little sleep.

Charlie collapsed onto the couch and fell into a dreamless sleep.

~

CHAPTER 16

Day Eight

Sunday

The ringing startled Charlie and he jumped up from the couch. It was the phone. He stumbled over to the kitchen, not sure who he wanted to talk to the least: Susan, Simon, Roth, or the anonymous caller who chanted "Nun He" over and over again.

"Hello," he answered.

"What are you doing!" an angry voice demanded.

"Nothing, honey. What's wrong?"

"What's wrong? You haven't called in two days, and every time I call up there, you don't answer. What the hell's going on?"

Susan was not a happy camper, and he would have to tell her something, but his mind wasn't thinking clearly.

"I'm sorry. I'm, well, like I said, I have been really getting into researching the history of the area and my family, and..."

She cut him off. "I ran into Simon at the store yesterday."

Oh shit, thought Charlie. *What'd the bastard tell her?*

"Yeah, what's he up to?"

"Jesus Christ, Charlie. I can't believe you didn't tell me about losing the Roth account. What happened?"

He took a deep breath, knowing he was in big trouble. "I'm sorry, Susan. What do you want me to say? Look, I am devastated by it. Maybe that's why I've been a little, I don't know, short. You know how many hours I put into that account. I'm not really sure what happened. Maybe he just got cold feet and wanted to go with a bigger, more established firm. I just found out about it myself two days ago. I was going to tell you when I got home. I didn't want to tell you over the phone...I didn't want you to worry."

"I can't believe you didn't tell me. I felt like such a fool. You know I don't care about the Roth account. I'm mad because I had to find out about it from Simon."

Charlie doubted that very much. He knew she knew how much money was at stake. "I'm sorry. I really am... and like I said, I didn't want you to worry. You know I was going to tell you."

"But...didn't you have a contract? How can he do this?"

"We had a contract, but... it's complicated. There really is nothing I can do about it. It would take years. Shit, it would probably bankrupt the company in legal fees if I tried to sue him. I mean, he has more money than God. He'd hire a team of the best attorneys to delay and brief me to death."

He stopped talking. Silence filled the line between them.

"Is there something else you aren't telling me?"

"Like what?"

"I don't know. You just seem…I can't explain it except that you are acting strange."

Charlie forced himself to laugh. "No. I swear it. I admit this thing with Roth has me shaken up, but who wouldn't be? I'm disappointed, shocked, and quite frankly, embarrassed about this whole thing. I mean we went out and celebrated. It's just hard to tell everyone that the deal's cancelled. I feel like a complete jerk. I should have waited until everything was official and the check cleared."

"I thought it was official. That's what you told me."

Charlie's hand squeezed the phone. He could have killed the goddamn bitch. Who did she think she was, questioning him like this? Hadn't he given her a good life? Didn't she have everything she wanted? He was the one who provided all that shit for her. What did she do? Nothing except watch crap on TV or gab on the phone all day.

He didn't say a word. Finally, she said, "I'm sorry."

Charlie took a deep breath. "I am, too."

"I just wished you would have told me, that's all. I feel bad. I know how hard you worked on the campaign. When I see Helen Roth, I am going to give her a piece of my mind. This is ridiculous. Roth should at least pay you something for all your time spent working for him, not to mention the jobs you gave up."

Charlie squeezed the phone again. Jesus Christ, that was the absolute last thing he needed. He could just picture Susan berating Roth's wife. That would be a disaster.

He would have to put a stop to that before she caused any more damage. "Honey, please, can I ask you a favor? Don't do anything. Just let it be."

"What! Charlie, the guy completely screwed you. Why are you acting like this? You should be mad as hell."

"Look, like I said, it was a business decision. He had to make the decision that he felt most comfortable with. He has employees and people who depend on him. I know he felt bad about it, but what can I do? He still is a powerful and influential person, and pissing him off by yelling at his wife or trying to get even isn't going to help my business one bit. He said we might do business in the future. Sometimes you win. Sometimes you lose."

"Sometimes you get screwed," Susan added.

"Well, it happens. How are the kids?" he asked, hoping to end the Roth conversation.

"Fine. They want to know when you are coming home."

"Well, I may stay a day or two later."

"Why?"

"Because I want to finish up my research. I think it would be cool to be able to pass it down to the kids. You know, so they know where they came from, who their ancestors were. I'm almost done."

Susan sighed. "All right."

Silence filled the distance between them once again. Then she asked, "Charlie, are you sure you're okay?"

The question and her concern took him aback. Was he okay? Actually, he didn't know the answer. "Other than Roth, I'm great," he finally answered.

"You sure?"

"I'm positive. This Roth thing will blow over, and in a few months, it will be no big deal. I promise."

"Okay. I love you."

"Love you, too. Tell the kids I said hi. Bye."

He hung up and breathed a sigh of relief. She didn't know any of the circumstances about why Roth had shit-canned him. Maybe the old geezer was keeping his word and not telling anyone why he reneged on the deal.

He stared out the window, and a thought occurred to him. The gold would solve all of his problems, but he had to find it first.

Charlie knew the clues to where the gold was hidden lay in Ezekiel's book, and that's why the reverend wanted it back so badly. But he was missing something. He had read the book six times now, and he couldn't figure it out. He knew the clues were there—it was obvious. He just had to acquire the one piece of information or code that put it all together.

Charlie suspected the key to discovering the location of the cave had to do with the Bechtler gold coins. Ezekiel made numerous references to the coins, which had seemed out of place when he had read them. He felt certain that if he could get more information about the coins, he might be able to decipher the clues.

He pulled out the phone number of the local historian that the librarian had given him and called him. Charlie explained that he was doing a little family research, and the man agreed to meet with him immediately. Hopefully, he would be able to give Charlie some useful information.

Charlie turned into the driveway and parked in front of a dilapidated-looking two-story wood house. He walked up to the front door and pressed the doorbell. Not hearing a ring, he knocked on the door. It took three loud knocks before the door finally opened.

A frail man who looked to be close to ninety years old opened the door. "Mr. Bernstein?" Charlie asked.

"Yes."

Charlie stuck out his hand. "Hi, I'm Charlie Parker. I appreciate you letting me come by and ask you a few questions."

"Who?" he asked.

Charlie's spirits deflated. He had just talked to the guy half an hour ago, and the man couldn't even remember their conversation. This was going to be a complete waste of time.

"I got your number from the librarian. I called you earlier about meeting with you to ask you some questions about the Bechtler Mint."

The old man smiled wryly. "I know. I was just fooling around with you."

Charlie laughed, mostly out of relief, and the old man stuck out his hand. "Poppy Bernstein. Glad to make your acquaintance."

They shook hands. "Please come in," the old man said. "Sorry about the mess, but I don't get a lot of visitors."

Charlie walked in and took a good look around. The den was small and dark. There was no TV, and the entire room was stacked with books, magazines, and newspapers.

"Have a seat." The old man grabbed a stack of coin magazines and threw them behind the couch to make room. "Can I get you anything to drink?"

"No thank you. I'm fine."

"Suit yourself. I think I will have a scotch."

Charlie looked at his watch. It was 10:30 in the morning. The old man shuffled over to the kitchen that connected to the den. The entire kitchen was filled with empty Dairy Queen bags, causing Charlie to wonder how Poppy got to be that old eating that stuff and drinking scotch at 10:30 in the morning.

Charlie watched as he grabbed one of six scotch bottles from the kitchen counter and poured a large measure into a dirty glass.

"I know it is early in the morning. But I go to bed at three in the afternoon, so eleven o'clock in the morning is like happy hour to me. Plus, when you get to my age, trying to live a healthy lifestyle doesn't really matter anymore. I used to smoke decades ago, but my wife made me give it up. She said she wanted me to be around in her golden years."

"Is she home?" Charlie asked.

"No. She died twenty-five years ago. Never drank, never smoked. Ate nothing but vegetables. Never even cursed. She was on one of her daily walks. She used to walk six miles a day in rain, sleet, or snow. A bus blew a tire, veered off the road, and ran right her over. Left her flat as a pancake."

"Jeez. Sorry to hear that."

"Yeah. What can you do? I miss her. After she passed, I gave up my healthy living habits to try and speed up my time here on earth. You know, so I could join her. But it doesn't seem to be working. I drink a bottle of scotch a day and eat nothing but cheeseburgers and French fries, but I still wake up every damn morning."

"Why don't you start smoking again?" Charlie suggested.

"Hey, that's not a bad idea. Do you have any?"

Charlie shook his head. "Sorry, my wife made me quit, too."

"Be careful, living a long life is very overrated. Sure you don't want a drink?"

Charlie looked down at his hands. They were shaking. "No, that's all right," he forced himself to say. He looked back at the old man, who had almost finished his entire glass of scotch. "Do you have family in the area?" Charlie asked.

Poppy filled his glass back up with scotch and slowly shuffled back into the den. "No. My two sons have also passed. Damndest thing, outliving your own children. I have some grandkids, and even a few great-grandchildren, but they're spread all over the place—California, Arizona—hell, I don't even know where all of them live. They don't get this way too often. I get Christmas cards with pictures of people I don't recognize."

Poppy sat down in a seventies-style green La-Z-Boy chair and took another drink of his scotch. "But I know you didn't come all this way to hear about my life story, so how can I help you?"

Charlie cleared his throat. "I was doing a little research about the area, and like I said on the phone, the librarian gave me your number. She said you were an expert on the Bechtler Mint."

"Yes. Well, Ms. Taylor flatters me. I am an amateur numismatist."

"Numismatist?" Charlie repeated, because he had never heard of the word.

"The study of coins."

"Oh."

"So what would you like to know?"

"Well, for starters, I guess I'd like to know more about the Bechtlers, the history of the mint, their gold coins."

"They were a fascinating family, the Bechtlers, quite successful. Around 1834, a German immigrant named Christopher Bechtler moved his family from New York and settled in an area just north of Rutherfordton. At the time, the whole region was smack dab in the middle of a gold rush."

"I read about that," Charlie said. "I had no idea that so much gold had been discovered in this area."

"Shoot, in the early 1800s, North Carolina was the leading gold-producing state until the California gold rush. Anyway, those Germans were smart. Bechtler saw an opportunity, and he capitalized on it. Back then, the miners had to transport their raw gold all the way to the Philadelphia Mint so it could be refined and melted into a negotiable currency. In those days, that was no short order. The trip was expensive and extremely dangerous. Bandits and Indians lined the trail all the way to Philadelphia, so Bechtler seized the opportunity and started a mint where he took the miner's raw gold and minted it into negotiable gold coins. He charged a small percentage for his services and became quite wealthy. In fact, the Bechtlers actually produced the first one-dollar gold coin in United States history."

"Wow, I didn't know that."

"Well, eventually the U.S. government started minting one-dollar gold coins. They even opened a mint in Charlotte, but the Bechtlers' gold coins were still the preferred form of currency in the Carolinas for decades."

"What eventually happened to the mint?"

"After Christopher Bechtler passed away, his son, August, ran the mint, and after he died, a nephew also named Christopher operated it for a short period of time, but a combination of events doomed the Bechtler enterprise. The U.S. government opened mints in Charlotte and Georgia, and then gold began drying up in the Carolinas. On top of that, the nation was on the cusp of a civil war, and eventually, the young Christopher Bechtler saw the writing on the wall and closed up shop for good."

"Whatever happened to him?"

"A lot of speculation involves the third Bechtler. It's a bit of a mystery and local folklore. What we know for sure was that he closed the mint and decided to leave Rutherfordton. He sold off most of his possessions, including his property, and left in the spring of 1853. Supposedly, he was traveling to Spartanburg, where he planned on opening a jewelry store, but he never reached his destination, and there has been speculation ever since as to what happened to him. Some believe he was a victim of foul play."

"Do you know if he had a shipment of gold coins with him?"

Mr. Bernstein set his scotch glass down. "I think you know more about the story than you are letting on."

Charlie smiled. "Not really. My family lived in the area during that time, and I have come across old newspaper articles that have spurred my interest." Charlie already knew the answer, but he wanted to double-check his facts, so he asked, "What year was the last Bechtler coins minted?"

"Officially, 1852. But, and this is total hearsay, some people believe Christopher minted one last set of coins for a Charlotte businessman in early 1853."

"Really?" Charlie's interest was definitely piqued now.

"Yup. I knew an old-timer who told me that the Charlotte businessman, I think his name was Posten, was a corrupt banker, and he stole a huge amount of gold from his bank. He convinced Christopher Bechtler to melt the gold bars and remint them into Bechtler gold coins."

"Why?"

"I guess because the coins would be harder to trace or connect to the bank and its stolen money. Times were a lot different back then, especially with communications. You could screw up in one place, move a couple hundred miles to a new town, and it would be like starting all over again. Anyway, the old-timer told me Christopher Bechtler and the businessman left with their shipment of gold, and somewhere outside of Rutherfordton, they were murdered, and the gold was stolen."

"Did he say who might have done this?"

"He believed it was done by a pack of crazy Injuns, and he swore that the gold was still hidden up in the mountains somewhere."

"What do you think?"

"Who knows? I suppose anything is possible."

Charlie shrugged, and Mr. Bernstein added, "I kind of doubt the story though."

"Why?"

"Well, the last gold coin minted by Christopher Bechtler was in 1852, and the year this all happened was supposedly 1853."

"Okay…so?"

"If Bechtler minted those coins, he would have stamped them with the year 1853, and it seems to me that at least one of those coins would have shown up somewhere."

"And none have?"

"Nope. I know for a fact that no Bechtler coins minted in 1853 have ever appeared or been recorded anywhere."

"Let me get this straight. To your knowledge, no coins minted in 1853 exist, right?"

Mr. Bernstein pulled himself out of his La-Z-Boy and went over to his desk. He flung a few books around before holding up a thick book. "This is the most authoritative book published on the subject. It has every coin attributed to the Bechtlers, and 1852 was the last year any coins were minted."

Charlie smiled. He stood and walked over to Mr. Bernstein. He dug inside his pocket and pulled out his Bechtler gold coin.

"Here, take a look at this." He handed the coin to Mr. Bernstein, who looked at the front of the coin. "Ah, nice you own a Bechtler coin."

Charlie smiled. "Turn it over."

The old man turned the coin over and peered down at it. He looked back up at Charlie in disbelief. He looked back down at the coin again before finally saying, "I can't believe it. This coin is dated 1853. Is it real?"

"Yep."

"But...but where did you get it?" he stammered.

"My father gave it to me."

"Where in tarnation did he get it?"

"I'm trying to find that out."

"Son, you have a coin that shouldn't exist. If this is authentic..."

"Oh, it *is* authentic," Charlie repeated.

"If it is, I don't know if I would carry that thing around with you. Do you realize it could be worth a damn fortune? You need to contact the American Numismatic Association or at least a reputable coin dealer like Stacks up in New York City and get them to check this out."

"We'll see. I think there may be a lot more where these came from."

The old man stared at him with a puzzled expression on his face. "You do?"

"Yes." Charlie didn't mind bragging about his secret to the old man. After all, what the hell was he going to do? The old man probably couldn't even walk to his mailbox. "I believe there is a whole stash of these coins hidden up in the mountains."

"You do?" The old man handed the back the coin and looked at Charlie with a cold expression. "There is something you need to know."

"What?"

"I think you may be opening a hornet's nest."

"Why do you say that?"

"Bad things happened in this town back in my early days. Things that are best left where they are buried, if you get my drift. If I'm right, what you are about to try and find will only open those old wounds up again."

Charlie couldn't believe the complete change in Poppy's demeanor in a matter of seconds. He looked at the old man, thinking this entire town spoke in half riddles. "Mr. Bernstein, I don't mean to be rude, but why don't you just tell me in plain English what you mean by that?"

"I know who you are."

"What do you mean?"

"What I mean is, I know of your father, and I know of your family's history."

"What does that have to do with these gold coins?"

"Maybe everything. If I tell you something, will you promise to believe me?"

"All right," Charlie said with a wave of his hand.

"Don't take this too personally, but your family was the cause of everything that went wrong in Wellington, and it took the town nearly a half century to rid itself of the lingering curse."

"What the hell are you talking about?"

"I'm talking about the fact that your grandfather and his brother did something that caused this town to suffer for far longer than it should have."

"What! I don't understand what you are saying."

"Don't act so naïve. It's obvious you know about Ezekiel McCellan and the fact that he got those Indians executed for something they didn't do. You know what I'm talking about—the Cherokees who were hung for supposedly murdering Ezekiel's family."

"That's bullshit. You really believe Ezekiel would murder his own wife and daughters to make it look like the Indians had done it? Why in the hell would he have done that?"

"Because the Indians guarded the cave—the cave with the gold hidden in it. Ezekiel knew he would never get the gold unless he got rid of the Indians, and that was the only plan he could come up with."

"You're crazy. I thought you said that was just a myth, folklore."

"And your grandfather helped Ezekiel."

"I don't believe you."

"You can believe anything you want. It doesn't matter to me one bit."

"Hold on a second. If what you say is true, why didn't Ezekiel get the gold? Like you said, the Indians were disposed of. Why didn't he go to the cave and get the gold?"

"He never got the chance."

"What do you mean, he never got the chance?"

The old man shook his head. "Never mind. I have enjoyed talking with you, but will you please go now?"

"Mr. Bernstein, please tell me why you believe he never got the chance."

"I've already told you too much. Please go."

The old man walked over to the door and opened it. "Goodbye, Mr. Parker."

Charlie walked past him out the front door. He turned and said, "Can I ask you one favor?"

"What?"

"Can I borrow your book on the Bechtlers? I promise I'll return it in a couple of days."

Mr. Bernstein walked over to the desk and grabbed the book. He handed it to Charlie. "Keep it. I have another."

Charlie muttered thanks as the door slammed in his face. He drove home wondering what had kept Ezekiel from retrieving the gold.

Chapter 17

Charlie paced the floor of the cabin. He was pretty sure he had narrowed down the general area where the gold was located, but that knowledge alone wasn't enough. That was like finding the proverbial needle in a haystack. He could spend a lifetime searching, driving himself insane like the reverend.

He sat down at the kitchen table with both Ezekiel's and the numismatic book open, trying to piece together the last part of the puzzle that would tell him where the gold lay hidden.

Charlie poured himself another glass of whiskey and took out the 1853 Bechtler coin, setting it next to the open books. The coin book devoted three chapters exclusively to the mintage of Bechtler coins, with descriptions and pictures of every coin minted from the time the mint began its operations in 1831 until its closing in 1852.

Charlie spent the next two hours reading and rereading every little detail about the coins. The general designs of coins were all very similar. The Bechtlers minted three different-size coins in a one-dollar, two-and-a-half dollar, and five-dollar denomination. The larger the denomination, the higher the gold content, thus the more valuable the coin.

Depending on the years, the coins were generally stamped with the inscriptions *BECHTLER, N CAROLINA, RUTHERFORDTON, CAROLINA GOLD*, or some variations of these inscriptions running along the coin's edge.

The center of the coin was usually stamped with the denomination *ONE* for a one-dollar gold piece, *250* for a two-and-a-half-dollar gold piece, and *5* for a five-dollar coin.

The reverse side normally would have the weight in grams stamped in the center, like *128 G* or *141 G*, and some had the actual carats inscribed underneath.

This appeared to be the general rule about their coins, but Charlie came across many variations, including stars, inverted letters, and varying numbers in grams and carats and dates.

Charlie picked up Ezekiel's book and began thumbing through it. He rubbed his temples. His head was killing him, and the strange inconsistencies in Ezekiel's writings weren't helping any.

The first part of his book contained mostly mundane personal information about his life, including musings about his day-to-day activities. On one page, Ezekiel went so far as to outline, in great detail, a recipe he had made up for possum soup. The second part of the book read more like a horror or suspense novel with all sorts of strange and bizarre goings-on.

The last third of the book was written in the riddle form of an insane man. It was this third part that Charlie believed held the clues to discovering the location of the gold. He had photocopied the last fifty pages, highlighting the sentences he thought were out of place. After reading this part at least a dozen times, he began to notice a distinct pattern emerging in the midst of all the chaos.

In these entries, Ezekiel would write something like "tracking a deer." Then suddenly in mid-sentence, he would interject a sentence or two that made absolutely no sense to the current text. Then Ezekiel would pick back up where he had left off as if he had never strayed.

Charlie flipped back and reread where he had noticed it occurring first:

> I plan on traveling to the general store tomorrow to buy more provisions—**because in 1831, for the cost of one Bechtler dollar, the travel was a little more than twice the number of grams north northeast of the city stamped in gold—** before any more bad weather sets in.

Charlie stared at the highlighted text in the middle of the sentence. An idea flickered in his mind, and he flipped open the Bechtler book.

He slammed his fist on the table. "Holy shit!" he shouted. Could it be this easy?

He looked at the section for 1831 one-dollar coins. Every coin in this series was minted with the inscription *RUTHERFORDTON* and *30 G*, for grams.

He did a quick calculation—twice the number of grams. *That's thirty times two equals sixty. So, go north northeast of the city stamped in gold.* He looked at the 1831 coin. Rutherfordton was stamped in the middle.

Charlie thought for a second, then went to the library and found a detailed terrain map of the area. He spread the map out on the kitchen table. Circling Rutherfordton and Grandfather Mountain, he used a ruler to draw a line between the two locations. He took the ruler and measured the distance and compared it to the map's scale. The distance from Rutherfordton to Grandfather Mountain was approximately sixty miles north northeast.

This had to be it!

Ezekiel had given the directions to the gold in the text, but in order to decipher the information, it was necessary to have and understand the mintage of the Bechtler coins.

So that meant that even if the reverend had Ezekiel's book, it would have done him no good unless he was able to put the Bechtler coins and the text together.

Charlie went through the text, copying down on a piece of paper five more instances where he had highlighted out-of-place passages interjected into the middle of sentences.

When Charlie was done writing them down, he looked them over.

1) In 1831, for one Bechtler dollar, the travel was a little more than twice the number of grams north northeast of the city stamped in gold.

2) In 1832, for 2½ dollars, the Assayer points north toward the profile and surveys a stream x yards from the center due East. Cross the stream to begin the journey.

Charlie looked at the 1832 two-and-a-half coin. The coin was the only one with the word *ASSAYER* on it with the number *250* in the center, so Charlie wrote down:

Start at the Grandfather profile and walk 250 yards and cross over a stream.

He then drew out the course on the map. The next clue read:

3) The backward N with a star at 9:00 will tell you how many miles to travel due east minus one decimal point

The 1837 one-dollar coin had a star at nine o'clock with *28* in the center. So by moving the decimal point over one, the distance to travel from the stream was 2.8 miles due east.

Again, he used the ruler and drew out the directions.

4) Follow the mountainside this far in 2501837's weight in grams and after traveling the distance, hike to the top of the mountain.

The number within the clue took Charlie a little while to figure out, but then it came to him. The 250 of 2501837 actually stood for two and a half, a reference to the two-and-a-half gold piece. The other part of 2501837 was the year 1837. He turned the coin book to that year's mintage, and the book displayed a coin with a weight in grams of 4.45. So, that meant hiking about four-and-a-half miles along the mountain before heading straight up.

> *5) Christopher is no more, but in 1853, his last coin will show you. Follow the edge of the cliff until you come to this marker. Look at the reverse of the 1853 coin and the rocks that look like what is minted on the coin—mark the spot where the cave is. Over the cliff you go, but be careful—you might not want to find what is lurking inside.*

Charlie pulled out the 1853 Bechtler coin, and in the center of the obverse, a small wolf was stamped into the gold, so the cave was by an outcrop of rocks that resembled a wolf.

He had seen this in his dreams. The chief was right. There was another world, in between life and dreams, and he had been there. His mind was churning. He was the chosen one, and they were showing him the way.

Charlie read the deciphered riddle he had translated and wrote down in his notebook:

> *Travel 60 miles north northeast of Rutherfordton. Start at the grandfather profile and travel 250 yards east until you cross over a small stream. After crossing the stream, head 2.8 miles due east. Follow the mountain for about four-and-a-half miles, then climb to the top of the mountain. Follow the cliff's face until you come to the rock formation that resembles a wolf. The cave should be hidden under the face of the cliff.*

Charlie deliberated for an hour about whether to call the deputy or not. His dilemma was that if they did find the gold, how would it be split? Charlie had no interest in sharing it with anyone, but after much thought, he decided to call the deputy, because even after deciphering Ezekiel's code, Charlie was less than confident of his ability to traverse the mountain and find the cave.

He'd figure out what to do with the deputy later.

Charlie picked up the phone and dialed the deputy's number. He answered after a dozen rings.

"Hey, Deputy, it's Charlie. How's it going?"

"Fine."

"Listen, I discovered some pretty interesting clues about where Black Fox hid the gold."

"Really? What kind of clues?"

"In Ezekiel's diary. He left a code to where the gold was hidden. I think I've deciphered it."

"That's interesting."

"Interesting! That's all you can say? I think with a little luck, we could find the cave."

"You know where the cave is?"

"No, not yet," Charlie lied. "But I'm getting there. I am going to do a little more research."

"You do know how big of an area you're talking about?"

"Yes."

"Because if you don't know exactly where it is, you'll never find it. I mean, you have to know the exact location, or you'll just be wasting your time and mine."

"Jesus, Johnny. I thought you'd be a little more excited than this."

"What specifically have you found that makes you think you're so close?"

"I'd rather not talk about it over the phone," Charlie said, stalling for time. "Let me check a few more things. And if they pan out, I was thinking that, when you get a chance, maybe we could take a hike up the mountain to check it out."

"All right. Let me know."

"Good. I'll call you later."

Charlie hung up the phone. Two minutes later, it rang. Charlie stared at it apprehensively because there was no one he wanted to talk to. But it was probably Susan, and he couldn't keep dodging her calls.

He picked it up. "Hello."

"Charlie, hey, it's Simon," a frantic voice said.

Charlie grimaced. Other than Roth or his wife, Simon was the last person he wanted to talk to.

"How's it going?"

"Look, Charlie, I hate to bother you on your vacation and all, but when do you think you're coming back?"

"I don't know. Why?"

"Because we've got some problems, and I'm not sure what to do."

"God damn it," he cursed into the phone. "I haven't taken a vacation in years. I've been gone for one week, and the whole place is falling apart. What do I pay you for?"

"I have been here practically every waking second since you left." Simon shouted back at him for the first time in their boss-employee relationship. "I don't know what's going on, but I'm getting calls from clients, and they seem concerned, very concerned. I don't know what the hell to tell them."

"Concerned? What about?" Charlie asked in a calmer manner.

"About everything. It's like ever since Roth cancelled on us, everyone in town's been...There have been some rumors."

"Rumors about what?"

"Just bullshit."

"What are the rumors about?" Charlie slowly reiterated every word.

"About Roth and you. Questions about the bids and other activities. Look, I didn't want to call you on vacation, but I had to. I felt I wouldn't be doing my job if I hadn't at least kept you abreast of what was going on."

"You're right," Charlie said, trying to keep a more conciliatory tone despite the anger building up inside of him, because now, he'd have to appease Simon, at least for a little while. "I didn't mean to snap at you. Sorry. God damn Roth. No telling what he's been up to. Look, it's Sunday. I am going to be up here for only a day or two longer, and then I'll be back. Hold on till then, and I'll straighten things out."

"All right, good." Simon sounded a little more relaxed. "I'm sorry if I snapped a little. You know I'm just looking out for the company."

Charlie smiled because after he found the gold, the first thing he was going to do was shit-can the little bastard.

"I know you are, and don't think I don't know it. I appreciate everything you've done, and I won't forget it. I'll see you Wednesday."

Charlie hung up the phone knowing his business was imploding, and there was nothing he could do to stop it. He sat in a chair next to the window staring outside, trying to figure out how and why he had let his business, and his life, get to this point.

~

Chapter 18

Around three o'clock in the afternoon, Charlie heard the sound of a car approaching. He got up and quickly put his notes and books into the desk drawer. He walked out onto the porch and saw the reverend standing next to his hearse.

"Reverend," Charlie called out cheerfully. "I've been expecting you. I wish I could have gotten hold of you earlier. I wanted to tell you to come get your book, but, well, you don't have a phone."

"You have my book?"

"Reverend, how 'bout at least a hello. We don't have to be enemies. After all, like you said, we are related. Why don't you come in for a drink?"

"I came for the book, Charlie."

"Don't worry. I promise I'm going to give you the dang thing," Charlie said. "Come on in and have a drink. We'll have a chat, and when you leave, you leave with the book. Okay?"

The reverend nodded and followed Charlie inside.

Charlie went to the coffee table, opened the drawer, and took out Ezekiel's book. "See, I told you. Here it is. It's all yours." He set the book on the kitchen table.

The reverend almost ran over to the table. He grabbed Ezekiel's book, and Charlie watched as he gently caressed it as if it was a newborn baby.

"Name your poison."

"What?" the reverend asked, not taking his eye off the leather book.

"Drink. What would you care for?"

"I'll have whatever you have."

"Perfect. Why don't you take a seat, relax a little."

The reverend went over and sat down on the couch with his back toward Charlie, who went to the kitchen and fixed two strong scotch and sodas.

He set the drink down next to the reverend, who was flipping through the pages of his father's book. He looked like a boy on Christmas day.

Charlie stood behind him and drank his scotch down in four gulps. "Sorry if I was a little standoffish about the whole matter, but you can't blame me too much, can you? I thought you and your story was crazy."

The reverend finally took his eyes off the book, glancing back toward Charlie. "That's all right. I guess it has been quite a shocking week for you."

"To say the least. So I guess you can understand why I acted the way I did."

"Of course," the reverend grunted, as he continued paging through the book with a look of astonishment etched across his ghostly white face.

"I do have one more question, and then I promise I won't ask anymore."

"What is it?"

"The sheriff. He's the son of the sheriff who hung the Indians back in twenty-seven?"

The reverend looked up at Charlie. "Yes, he is."

"Quite a coincidence, wouldn't you say? This little town has sure spun quite a tangled web over the years, hasn't it?"

The reverend nodded but didn't say anything, while continuing to study the book.

Charlie poured himself another strong drink. "Hey, I've got a toast."

The reverend looked up, and for a brief moment, Charlie caught a glimpse of the man behind the surface. He had never seen anything like it before. It was as if he saw through the reverend's physical being down to his essence, and what he saw was pure evil.

Charlie coughed. *Get hold of yourself,* he thought. He lifted his drink. "To our family, Cherokee Indians, and to Bechtler Gold," he toasted.

The reverend eyed him cautiously. He raised his glass toward Charlie and without taking a sip set the glass down on the coffee table. He continued studying the book.

"All-righty," Charlie muttered. "Cheers." He set his drink down.

"There is one last thing I hoped you could answer for me."

The reverend looked agitated. "What?"

"Why did your father not kill you along with your mother and sisters?"

The reverend's head snapped around. The question was supposed to piss him off, but his reaction surprised Charlie. He smiled and then let out a horrendous sounding laugh. "Charlie, you are smarter than I thought. So you think you know the answers, do you? Well, you're right. My father did kill my mother and sisters. They deserved it. But since you're so smart, I'll tell you the rest of the story. Your grandfather helped him do it. What do you think about that?"

Charlie remained silent.

The reverend shook a finger at him. "See, we both have something in common. We are the blood of murderers. Not only that, but we are the blood of the worst kind of killers...men who take their own family for the quest of money. Our relatives killed their own to set up the Indians so they could retrieve the gold. How 'bout that, Charlie, my boy."

"I guess I am about to surprise you, reverend. Because I already knew all that, but maybe you can enlighten me as to why my grandfather killed Ezekiel?"

"I told you, he wanted to get the gold for himself and that was why he dynamited my father inside the cave. But the fool drank himself to death before he could find the cave."

"But how did my father get the book, and why didn't he do anything with it?"

"I suspect your grandfather gave it to him before he died and made him promise to keep it from me. Why he never did anything with it? I'll never know. Maybe he wasn't as greedy as you or me, huh?"

The statement lingered in Charlie's mind for a while before he asked, "So you think there really is a huge cache of Bechtler gold hidden up in the mountain?"

The reverend laughed but didn't say anything and began looking through the book again.

"I'm going to refresh my drink," Charlie said, walking back to the kitchen.

He poured the scotch, minus the soda water, to the top of the glass and gulped the fiery liquid down. The alcohol burned his throat; it felt good. He took a deep breath and reached down underneath the kitchen table.

He slowly walked back over to the couch and stood behind the reverend. Charlie raised the fire poker, and in one quick motion, swung it down as hard as he could straight into the side of the reverend's head.

The sound of the metal striking skull was a noise Charlie would remember for the rest of his life. The force of the blow caused the reverend to fall off the couch onto the floor. Charlie let go of the fire poker, which stuck straight out of the side of the reverend's head at a weird angle.

Charlie walked around to the other side of the couch. One of the reverend's legs was bouncing up and down, while his mouth opened and closed like a fish stuck out of water.

Shit! He couldn't believe the bastard was still alive. What should he do now?

He looked around. He had no desire to pull the poker back out of the reverend's head. Maybe, if he just left him, he would die. The reverend's eyes were open, staring directly at him.

His mouth opened, and the words "Nun He, Nun He, Nun He" spilled out. Over and over the words were repeated in a loud shrill voice.

Charlie stepped back. "Shut up!" he screamed.

"Nun He, Nun He, Nun He, Nun He…" The words came faster and faster.

Charlie put his hands over his ears trying to muffle the horrendous noise. The dead man's chanting grew louder and louder. Charlie felt like his eardrums could burst at any moment.

He couldn't take it anymore! He screamed and kicked the reverend as hard as he could in the side of his head.

Charlie yelled out in pain, falling back against the couch. It felt like he had broken his foot, but at least it had shut the reverend up.

Charlie stared at the reverend sprawled out on his living room floor. *What have I done?* He grabbed the reverend's drink off the table and drank down the scotch in one swallow.

"All right, Charlie, get yourself together. What's done is done. No going back now."

He stood looking over the body. At least blood hadn't sprayed everywhere. Except for some gray lumpy stuff on the floor, the blow from the poker hadn't really caused that much of a mess.

The phone rang, almost causing him to jump out of his skin. It was probably Susan. He considered not answering but then thought better of it. He walked into the kitchen and picked up the phone.

"Hello," he said calmly.

"Hey, darling. How you doing?"

"Fine," he answered, except for the fact that there was a dead man lying in the middle of the floor with a fire poker sticking out of his head.

"What you up to?"

"Oh, a little of this, little of that."

"Hold on, Jeffery wants to say hi."

"Susan, I have to go," he started to say.

He heard his son say in the background, "No, I don't want to talk to him."

The phone fumbled around, and Charlie heard Susan's muffled voice yelling something at Jeffery.

A few moments later he heard Jeffery huff, "Hey Dad. How's it going?"

"Terrific," Charlie said in a cheerful voice. He had to put his hand over the mouthpiece of the phone because he started laughing. "How are you doing?"

"Okay."

"Wonderful. Be a good boy for your mom while I'm away."

"Ah, okay, Dad," Jeffery said as if he couldn't have cared less. "Well, I guess I'll see you whenever you come home. Bye."

"Bye, son. I love you."

"Hey." It was Susan again. "Any luck today?"

"Any luck with what?" Charlie stammered.

"With your family research."

"Nah, screw it, who cares about the past. I'm kind of over all that."

He heard Susan sigh. "All right, so you're coming home?"

"The day after tomorrow. Where's Annie?"

"She's not home yet. She had play rehearsal after school. Why are you not coming home till then?"

"Susan," he said in his 'let's not get into a fight about this' voice.

"Fine," she answered, obviously getting his point.

"Tell Annie I miss her, and I love her."

"I will. What are you doing for dinner tonight?"

Charlie stared down at grayish ooze leaking out of the reverend's head. The sight caused his stomach to churn, and he fought the urge to gag.

"I don't know yet. I may see if Kingsley is cooking down at the Green Man tonight. What are you having?"

"I promised Jeffery tacos."

"Okay. Well, I guess I'll talk to you later. Love you, honey."

"Love you, too. Bye."

Charlie hung up the phone. He limped over to the linen closet and pulled out some sheets. He had to get rid of the body.

~

Chapter 19

Charlie sat on the couch for a full two hours staring down at the reverend because he couldn't figure out how to dispose of the body. Even more of a conundrum was what to do with the black hearse. It wasn't like that damn thing wouldn't attract any attention.

He had to get rid of both of them and quickly.

Finally, after weighing all the pros and cons of various ideas, Charlie got up and went to the toolshed. First things first. He had to take care of the body.

He grabbed the wheelbarrow and rolled it into the house over to the reverend. He hated to even touch the son of a bitch, but he had no choice. After great effort, he managed to pull the body up into the wheelbarrow.

He wheeled it outside onto the porch and slowly started easing it down the stairs. The whole time, he envisioned what he would say to the sheriff or deputy if they suddenly showed up. He imagined it would make for a pretty funny sight to see him wheeling the reverend down the stairs in a wheelbarrow with a fire poker sticking out of his head.

He began laughing because he could see himself saying to the sheriff, "Yes, sir, you won't believe it, but the reverend fell and landed right on the fire poker and the damn thing went straight through his skull. Damndest thing you ever saw and a shame, too. He was such a nice guy."

He was halfway down when gravity took over. He couldn't hold on anymore, and the wheelbarrow with the reverend in it tumbled down the last set of stairs.

The body spilled out onto the ground with a thud, causing Charlie to laugh hysterically. Once again, it took all his effort to get the dead man back in the wheelbarrow. It took a good forty-five minutes of grueling effort to push it through the snow to the edge of his property. His big toe was killing him from where he had kicked the reverend, but he supposed the reverend's pain was a lot worse.

He picked out a spot and began the tedious task of digging a hole with a pickax and shovel. The damn ground was frozen solid, and it was a bitch digging the hole, but he finally got it deep enough after about three hours of backbreaking work. Charlie dumped the body into the hole with the fire poker still stuck in his head. He couldn't bear to pull it out.

He made the sign of the cross. "Dear Lord," he began, "I hope in your infinite wisdom, your higher powers, you will grant the reverend the rest of eternity to contemplate where the gold was hidden and that he can spend that time knowing that Charlie Parker, or I should say Charlie McCellan, was the man who found it. And God, I hate to ask you for anything, but could you please help relieve the pain a bit in my big toe? It's killing me. Thank you. Amen."

He made the sign of the cross, filled the grave back in with dirt then covered it with snow. He limped back inside where he began the long wait to get rid of the hearse.

To kill the time, Charlie updated his memoirs, as he liked to call his legal pads now. He figured it was pretty stupid to write down the fact that he had murdered the reverend, but who was ever going to read his notebooks? Then he thought, *Better safe than sorry.* So Charlie decided he would destroy his writings after he found the gold. After all, he didn't want someone to read them and use his own notebooks to send him to the electric chair.

The time passed excruciatingly slowly until midnight arrived and then passed. Finally, the two o'clock hour chimed on the grandfather clock. Charlie stood from the leather chair, went outside, and reluctantly got into the hearse. He looked in the backseat half expecting the reverend to jump out and grab him. The smell inside the car was awful, almost like some animal was rotting underneath the seat. But other than the smell, the hearse was spotless.

More than spotless, in fact. There were no personal items of any kind. No pens, no eyeglasses, no CDs, no gum wrappers or coffee cups, nothing. He opened the glove compartment. Absolutely nothing, not even a registration card. It was like the hearse had been completely sanitized.

Charlie started it up and drove down to an old abandoned limestone quarry just outside of town. Luckily, he didn't pass a single car on the way. He pulled up to the edge of the pit. He knew the water was deep, probably at least fifty feet, and even though it wasn't a perfect spot to dispose of the car, it was his best option at this point.

Charlie shifted the car into neutral and got out. Using a stick to maneuver the gas pedal, he put it in drive and slowly inched the hearse toward the edge, knowing all he had to do was get the vehicle just over, and gravity would do the rest.

The car's front bumper inched over the cliff, and Charlie jumped to the side. He watched as the car, slowly at first, then with a sudden increase in velocity, began its fall over the cliff's edge.

The hearse went completely over, falling down to the water, where it struck with a loud *whoomp*.

Charlie walked over to the edge and stared down. The hearse was right side up, and it was floating. A terrible thought ran through him. *What if the damn thing doesn't sink?*

After a few gut-wrenching minutes, the front of the car listed and finally began to go under. *Thank God!* Five minutes later, the hearse was partially submerged, with the back end pointing straight out of the water.

He had lain down on his stomach with his head over the edge of the cliff, watching to make sure the car did completely sink.

Damn it! He had left both the lights inside the car and the headlights on. He panicked for a second before realizing that the water would short out the electrical system soon enough.

He stood up and started to leave before deciding to take one last look at the sinking hearse. It was a decision he wished he hadn't made. Charlie's heart seized in his chest. Silhouetted against the back window, with his face pressed up to the glass, was the reverend!

Charlie fell to his knees, watching in horror as the reverend desperately clawed at the back window, trying to escape. He wanted to run, to get away from this madness that he had created, but he couldn't tear himself away from the horrific scene.

He watched in gruesome fascination as the reverend furiously punched the windows with his fists, obviously trying to escape the sinking vehicle. The whole time he watched, neurons fired rapidly in Charlie's brain because he distinctly had the impression he had buried the reverend in his back yard.

Hadn't he? Or had he thrown the body in the hearse? His mind was jumbled up, confused, almost like it wasn't working right.

The hearse continued to sink and was almost completely under water. The reverend had stopped clawing at the window, sealed to his fate. He seemed calm, almost peaceful. Light from the inside reflected off the reverend's face, creating a ghastly image, a sight that Charlie was dead certain he would remember for the rest of his life. Despite the distance, Charlie could see the reverend staring up at him with a broad grin.

Then, with one final pause and a sudden jerk, the car, along with the reverend, disappeared beneath the murky waters. Charlie could still see the car's light beneath the water as the hearse slowly sank to its grave.

He continued watching until finally, the headlights flickered a few times, and then faded out forever.

He stood once again and stared down at the water, shivering, all the time wondering when he was going to escape from the horror movie he was starring in. He closed his eyes. After waiting for a few minutes, he opened them, hoping, praying that he had been having a nightmare and would wake up in his bed back in Charleston.

Unfortunately, he was still at the quarry, so he had no choice but to start the long walk back home. He had measured the distance on the way to the quarry. He had to walk 16.9 miles to get home, and he had to be careful. He couldn't be seen by anyone.

Charlie had dressed in his warmest clothes, but even with thermal underwear and all his cold weather gear, he was freezing. The night was pitch black. He probably hadn't even walked three miles, but he was already exhausted.

A thought occurred to him. He could actually die out here. What would Susan think if she was told by the state police that her husband had been found frozen on the side of the road?

He reasoned he should have been scared that death was a possibility, given that he had always been terrified by the thought, but now, well, maybe that was his best way out.

He trudged on, along the left-hand side of the highway, and as the yards turned into miles, he kept reminding himself to pay attention for any sounds of vehicles approaching. He couldn't afford a state trooper to pull over and start making inquires.

He looked at his watch: 4:30 in the morning. He had been walking for only two hours. He figured with his slow pace, if he averaged three miles an hour, the trip home would take almost six hours, meaning he still had more than three hours to go.

He desperately felt like lying down and going to sleep. He was so tired and cold, and the sun wouldn't even be up for three more hours.

Charlie seriously didn't know if he could make it, and he even began to not care, which he knew was not a good sign. His whole body ached, especially his foot where he had kicked the reverend, and as the seconds turned into minutes, he actually fell into some kind of a trance. His body became numb, unaware of the cold and fatigue.

He looked up at the stars. He hadn't even noticed them before. There were millions and millions of them, and he wondered if there was such a thing as a God, a divine all-knowing, all-powerful spirit. And if there was, did that mean he was going to hell for killing the reverend?

His thoughts about the possible damnation of his soul were interrupted by the steady sound of a vehicle approaching from up ahead. He scurried into the woods to his left and hid behind a tree as headlights appeared from around a bend about a half mile in front of him. The vehicle was traveling slowly, too slowly, causing warning bells to start ringing in his head.

The car came into view. Charlie's nightmare was not over for the night because the car approaching was the reverend's black hearse. The car was traveling no more than ten miles an hour, as if its driver was searching for something, or someone. Charlie couldn't even comprehend who or what was driving the hearse because it should have been at the bottom of the quarry.

If he wasn't already kneeling on the ground, he would have collapsed, because it felt as if his whole body had turned into Jell-O.

The headlights began flicking on and off. Charlie's heart pounded so fast it felt as if it could burst at any second.

The car approached. *Please! Please!* Charlie prayed for it to keep going. He crouched closer to the ground, and the hearse stopped directly in front of him. His mind screamed for him to run, to get away, but his body was no longer capable of responding to his brain's commands.

The hearse sat in the road with its engine idling, water dripping down from the underside. The door slowly opened, and inside the car, in the passenger's seat, sat a mutilated Indian.

The Indian turned its head, staring intently in Charlie's direction.

Next to the Indian, in the driver's seat, was the reverend, who stared straight ahead as if he was oblivious to the whole matter.

The Indian smiled, causing hot bile to crawl up Charlie's throat. Charlie put a hand to his mouth, forcing himself to hold back the vomit creeping up from his stomach.

The Indian began calling out directly to him, "Nun He, Nun He, Nun He," over and over.

The Indian slammed the door shut, and the hearse slowly drove off.

Charlie's mind collapsed upon itself, refusing to think, as if he had moved into function mode only, like some kind of an animal. He left the woods and walked the rest of the way home without having one conscious thought. He only functioned.

He reached the cabin an hour after sunrise. Charlie let himself in and collapsed into bed, where he slept the sleep of the dead—or the soon to be.

Chapter 20

Day Nine

Monday

Charlie awoke completely disoriented, but after the fog of sleep wore off, the remnants of the previous day and night filtered through his mind.

As his actions and the ramifications of those actions began to weigh upon his consciousness, his mind discovered a new ability. He could completely erase any unwanted thoughts by just saying two magic words: "Be gone."

"Be gone. Be gone," Charlie said aloud, already feeling better. He was changing, and he liked the person he was becoming. He was no longer burdened with all the fears and anxieties that tormented him through most of his life.

"Be gone," he repeated one more time and got out of bed feeling refreshed, relaxed. He dressed, ate a big meal, and got ready. Charlie had big plans.

He dialed the deputy, who answered on the third ring. "I know where the gold is hidden," Charlie said, skipping his usual pleasantries.

"Where?" the deputy asked skeptically.

"Come over, and I'll show you."

When the deputy didn't reply, Charlie said, "Hello. Didn't you hear what I said?"

"Yeah, I heard."

"Man, you're a stick in the mud. I would've thought you'd be more excited than that. I promise you won't be disappointed. I deciphered a code from Ezekiel's book. I'm positive I learned the location of the cave. Do you want to come over or not?"

"I'll be over in an hour."

Charlie hung up the phone, and exactly one hour later, the deputy's truck pulled up. Charlie met him on the porch. "We've got some work to do," he called out to the deputy as he was getting out of his car.

He walked over. "We do?"

Charlie motioned. "Come inside." The deputy followed him up the porch stairs.

"Why are you limping?"

Charlie turned back around. "Getting damn old. I pee like six times a night. I smashed my big toe into the bedpost last night. I think I broke the damn thing. It's killing me."

"You should be more careful."

"Thanks for the advice."

Charlie noticed that even in civilian clothes, the deputy wore his gun holster with a nine millimeter in it. He was going to have to do something about that, but that problem could wait for now.

They walked inside, and Charlie glanced over at the area by the couch where he had killed the reverend. He had scoured every inch of the area at least a hundred times, but he was still nervous that some evidence remained.

"Take a look at this." Charlie tried to herd the deputy toward the kitchen. He didn't want him anywhere near the scene of the crime. Charlie unfolded a detailed map of the mountain. Like a chief financial officer delivering a corporate status report to a group of shareholders, he presented all the facts, including the code he had discovered between the Bechtler gold and Ezekiel's clues. He laid out the framework to where he thought the gold was hidden.

After he finished, he looked over at the deputy, who had not said a word. "So what do you think?" Charlie asked.

"Interesting."

"That's it? That's all you have to say?" Charlie stared at the deputy, who continued to study the map. He couldn't read this guy at all. Maybe he was making a huge mistake. Charlie wasn't concerned that the deputy would try to cut him out of the money because he had already planned for that contingency.

The only reason he was even fooling around with the guy was because he didn't trust his own wilderness ability, and he needed the deputy to help him get to the cave. Then Charlie would do what he'd have to do.

The deputy smiled. "Cherokees are known to be men of few words."

"I believe that. So, what do you think?"

"I think you've got something."

Charlie put his hand on the deputy's shoulder. "Okay, let's review what we know. First, a large shipment of Bechtler gold was stolen in 1853. That is a fact. We also have proof without doubt that Black Fox was responsible for the robbery. You agree so far?"

"Yep."

"We also know from Ezekiel's writings and from your grandfather that the gold was hidden by Black Fox in a Cherokee burial cave."

"I suppose," the deputy said.

"You suppose! I know you are playing devil's advocate, but do you believe your grandfather or not?'

"It doesn't matter what I…"

"Yes or no?" Charlie cut him off.

"Yes."

"Ezekiel's writing backs up your grandfather's story. But I've got something else that proves it. Take a look at this newspaper article."

Charlie opened his research folder and handed the deputy the articles about the murder of the McCellan family, the search for the group of Cherokee Indians who were believed to have committed the heinous crime, and their subsequent capture and hanging.

The deputy studied them for a few minutes and handed them back. "You've already told me this. Obviously, the cave where the Indians were blown up is not the right one. I'm sure it has been searched hundreds of times since then."

Charlie smiled. "You're right, Deputy. It was a decoy cave just in case someone got too close. The Cherokees hid out in that cave after finding out that they had been set up for the murders. I guess they figured if they went down, at least the location of the burial cave would remain a secret."

"Except, you believe Ezekiel had discovered the true location of the burial cave?"

"Yes."

"How do you know for certain this other cave doesn't have the gold in it?"

"It would have been found by now. Trust me. I have decoded the clues in Ezekiel's book."

Charlie opened to page thirty-seven of the book. "Listen to this:

"The Indians are more cunning than I thought. They almost succeeded in tricking me into believing that the open cave southwest of Grandfather was the hiding spot. Instead, it's a deception, a trap. The gold is not there.

"But I am also more clever than they can conceive. I hid for weeks in the trees till finally one of the Indians let his guard down, and he led me to another cave. I know, I feel certain, that this is where the gold is hidden.

"But now I must figure a way to get rid of the Indians. After much thought, there is only one way. God forgive me."

"So this is when Ezekiel killed his family and set it up to look like the Cherokees did it?" the deputy asked.

Charlie handed him the other article with the ghastly image of the Cherokees hanging in the gallows. "Yep. He figured the only way he could gain access to the cave was by getting rid of the Indians, and the only way he could do that without attracting attention to the gold was to set them up for murder because he knew the town would hunt them down."

The deputy's mouth hung open as he looked at the photo and read the article detailing the account of the Cherokees' execution for the murder of Ezekiel's family.

The deputy laughed nervously and joked, "I feel like I have landed in the middle of a *Twilight Zone* episode."

"You can say that again."

"Where do you think this cave is?"

"That's where I need your help." Charlie pointed to the map. "Here is the profile of Grandfather." He circled the imprint on the map. "Here is the cave where the Cherokees were killed and captured. He circled where the cave would approximately be on the map.

Charlie pointed to the valley and the river. "There is the cliff leading down to the river, and with the clues and your tracking ability, I don't think it would take us too long to find the cave."

"That cliff face runs for miles."

"I know, but Ezekiel left the approximate distance, plus he wrote about a certain type of rock formation that will show us where the cave is."

"That is, if it's still there. That was eighty years ago."

"We'll find it. Trust me."

The deputy looked up from the map and stared Charlie directly in the eyes. "Why do you need me? You could have found this by yourself."

"Maybe. Maybe not," he answered, knowing there was almost no chance in hell he could have navigated the mountain all by himself. "Anyway, even if I did find the cave by myself, I would still have to get into it, which, by Ezekiel's account, sounds very difficult."

"What if we do find the cave and all of this is true? What do we do then?"

Charlie looked the deputy in the eyes. "What do you think?"

"By all rights, it is the Cherokees' gold."

"By whose rights? They killed a group of men and stole the gold."

"And Ezekiel McCellan and your grandfather murdered not only Ezekiel's wife and daughters, but also my grandfather."

Charlie raised a hand. "Look, we could spend eternity arguing over the sins of our ancestors. I don't want to condemn or defend anyone. I don't care about the money. If I did, I wouldn't have asked you to help. You're right. I could have found it myself, but I asked you to join me. Maybe it is up to us to correct the wrongs of the past."

The deputy stared at him for a few more seconds before replying, "Let's find the cave first and even see if there is any gold. Then we'll figure out what to do with it."

Charlie stuck out his hand. "Agreed."

The deputy shook his outstretched hand. "The weather is supposed to be fairly mild tomorrow. I'll pick you up at sunlight. I'll bring all the gear and provisions we'll need. Dress in your best winter clothes and plan on camping out at least two nights."

"No problem."

For the first time since Charlie had met the deputy, he appeared relaxed and even flashed a smile. "Wouldn't this be something if we found the gold after all these years?"

Charlie grinned. "We'd be famous."

"I don't want to be famous. I'll see you in the morning."

The deputy left, and Charlie started packing for the trip. He was so close, he could feel it. The gold was almost his.

The only roadblock now was how to take care of the deputy.

~

Chapter 21

Day Ten

Tuesday

Charlie sat on top of the front porch railing sipping coffee, watching the first rays of light from the rising sun spread across the base of the mountain. This had always been his favorite time of the day. There was something magical about those fleeting moments just before and after sunrise. The start of a brand new day, a new beginning, and today would be the start of a new life for him.

Charlie heard the sound of a vehicle approaching, and a thought of terror ran through him. What if the black hearse pulled up instead of the deputy's truck?

Thankfully, his panic was short-lived when a moment later he saw the deputy's beat-up truck.

He gathered his gear.

The truck stopped, and the deputy hopped out. "Hey, Charlie," he called out while walking around to the back of the truck.

"Good morning," Charlie called back.

The deputy grabbed Charlie's stuff and threw it in the back.

"So, what's the plan?" Charlie asked, getting into the truck.

"There's a road that ends about two miles from the profile of Grandfather. We'll park there and head up. I figure we'll reach the decoy cave by early afternoon and camp there for the night."

"That's only as far as you think we'll get? I mean, that cave is only about six miles away."

"Charlie, this isn't a leisurely stroll through downtown Charleston. We'll be hiking over hard terrain, and the first rule of survival in the wilderness is to prepare your camp well ahead of sundown. That advice alone has probably saved more lives than any other."

"You're the boss," Charlie replied. *At least for now.*

They reached the dead end, gathered their gear, and set off. The day broke clear and reasonably warm. The first hour was a relatively easy hike, but then the terrain started getting more rugged. The wind began howling, and it seemed that no matter what direction they traveled, the wind blew directly into their face. The deputy was right—a mile in the wilderness with heavy gear hiking over snow-packed terrain was a lot more difficult than a stroll through downtown Charleston.

After two hours of hiking, Charlie's legs burned. His pack, which at first seemed light as a feather, now felt like he was carrying a sack of rocks.

Charlie followed behind the deputy, and they walked mostly in silence. Charlie tried his best to keep up, but he could tell the deputy was getting agitated because he had to stop more and more often to wait up for him.

Mercifully, they took a break around noon to rest and have lunch, but it was a short respite before they set off again. After two more hours of hiking, they crossed over a bluff, and the cave, where the Indians had been trapped so long ago, revealed itself in an outcropping of jagged rocks. Charlie looked at his watch. It was 2:30. He threw his pack onto the ground and collapsed next to it, where he lay for a full ten minutes before forcing himself to get back up, mostly out of guilt, because while he rested, the deputy had been busy setting up the camp without him. Charlie walked over to the cave's entrance and peered into the black hole.

"Why don't you give me a hand setting up the camp?" the deputy shouted.

Charlie ignored him and took a step farther inside the cave. A sudden gust of frigid air blew up from the tunnel, followed by a strange echo originating from deep inside the black hole.

Despite his overwhelming desire not to go into the cave, he took another step in. He could only see about thirty feet ahead because the main entrance narrowed, then curved around a bend.

"C'mon, Charlie," he heard the deputy yell again. "Get the hell out of there and give me a hand."

Another draft of cold air blew up from the depth of the cave, followed by what, he swore, was high-pitched laughter. Charlie quickly walked out of the cave, certain it was just his mind playing tricks on him. It wasn't laughter he had heard, it was just circulating air echoing and reverberating off the cave walls. That's all.

Charlie gave the deputy a hand, and an hour later, the tent was pitched and the fire was going. The camp was set for the night.

Charlie sat on a log next to the fire trying to keep warm. The strenuous hike had left him ravenous. Even after eating three ham sandwiches, he was still hungry, so he opened a power bar and devoured it along with lots of hot coffee that he spiked with bourbon from a hip flask.

He stared up at the mountain. The sun was well into its nightly descent, and long shadows started to grow around their camp, slowly making their way toward the fire.

Charlie felt foolish, but he didn't like the shadows because darkness followed, and he knew it was going to be a long, long night. The sun hadn't even set, and already he longed for night to be over and for daylight to be back in control of the sky. Because night, with its evil companion, darkness, brought strange things. Things Charlie didn't like.

The deputy came out of the brush with another stack of firewood, setting it down next to Charlie. "This should be enough to get us through the night." He sat down next to the fire and poured a cup of coffee into a tin cup. "It's going to be a cold one."

"Yup. Should we take shifts sleeping tonight?"

The deputy laughed. "Shifts. What in the hell for?"

"I don't know. To keep a look out for bears or... whatever."

"Charlie, we'll keep the fire going all night. No animals will bother us. We have a long day ahead of us tomorrow, and we both need as much rest as we can get. Survival rule number two: when not moving, rest, sleep."

Charlie shrugged. "Right." It wasn't really bears he was concerned about, but it was too late to start worrying about those other "things" now.

The two men spent the next two hours drinking coffee, eating, and resting. Oddly, neither of them discussed their final destination and what would happen if Charlie was right and they found the cave with the gold inside.

The deputy threw out the remains of his coffee from his tin cup and stood. "I am going to hit the hay. You should, too. Big day ahead of us tomorrow."

Charlie looked at his watch. It was just after seven o'clock. He got up and took one last look around the campsite. The fire provided a small radius of light, but past that perimeter, darkness was in control, and Charlie fought back a wave of despair.

He followed the deputy into the tent, thinking there was no way he'd ever be able to fall asleep. He crawled inside his sleeping bag, where he instantly fell asleep.

~

Charlie's eyes opened. At first, he didn't know where he was. Then he remembered the hike and setting up the camp. He felt like he had been asleep for only minutes, but when he looked at his watch, it was three o'clock in the morning. He could see flames flickering from the campfire through the tent, followed by an occasional crackle or pop from the smoldering wood. He figured the deputy must have tended the fire at some point since it was still going.

He looked over his shoulder. The deputy was sleeping with his back facing him. The wind gusted, and the tops of the trees began making low swooshing noises. The increased wind caused flames from the fire to pick up, creating long dancing shadows up against the tent.

God, he wished it was morning.

A rustling noise came from behind the tent, causing his breath to catch. Something was definitely out there. He nudged the deputy in the back. "Johnny, wake up," he whispered.

The deputy didn't budge, and Charlie poked him harder in the shoulder. "Johnny," he said louder.

"What is it?" grumbled the deputy.

"I heard some noises from right outside the tent."

The deputy slowly sat up. "From where?"

Charlie pointed toward the back of the tent. The deputy put a finger up to his mouth, and they sat in silence for a couple of minutes until the noise came again, only this time from different spots.

"Deer."

"What?" Charlie said.

"It's just deer. Go back to sleep."

"How do you know?"

The deputy laughed, then rolled back over in his sleeping bag and almost immediately began snoring.

Charlie took a deep breath and lay back down again. He had begun to drift off to sleep when a gut-piercing howl filled the air. Both men simultaneously sat up facing each other.

"I don't think that's a deer," Charlie said in a low voice.

"Shhh." The deputy put a finger to his mouth.

A chorus of howls erupted, causing every single hair on Charlie's body to stand on its end.

"A pack of wolves," the deputy calmly replied.

"Wolves! What in the hell should we do?" Charlie asked, fighting back a wave of panic.

"Nothing. They won't bother us, especially with the fire going."

"What do you mean, do nothing?"

"They're out hunting, probably the deer we heard earlier. We're safe. Don't worry about it. Remember, I've got a gun. If they get too close, I'll fire a warning shot. There'll run off."

"Should I put some more wood on the fire? You know, to keep them at bay?"

"Might as well," the deputy answered before once again rolling over and falling dead asleep in seconds.

Charlie crawled over to the tent's opening. He unzipped the tent and peered out. The flames from the fire had begun to die. The darkness crept even closer inside the camp. The wind had ceased. A dead calm filled the air.

He slipped out, crawled on his hands and knees, and cautiously looked around. He felt as if a thousand eyes were watching him, hiding in the dark forest, waiting to pounce. Charlie hurried over to the stack of wood next to the fire and set four big logs onto the fire. Embers of sparks crackled and drifted up into the pitch black sky.

He stared out into the forest to the right of him and saw a reflection of something that took his brain a few seconds to register what it was he was seeing—a pair of yellow eyes, then another, and another.

He turned around in a circle. Everywhere he looked, he saw yellow demonic eyes reflecting from just within the forest.

"Holy shit," he cursed. Charlie quickly slipped back into the tent, zipping it up. He shook the deputy's shoulder.

"What?" he grumbled.

"I saw—I think they're wolves—dozens of them," he whispered frantically. "They're right outside the camp."

"There's nothing we can do about it. They're probably just curious, that's all. They won't bother us. Go back to sleep. It's late."

"Are you crazy?" he shouted, forgetting about whispering. "Go shoot a few of them."

"The only thing I'm going to shoot is you if you don't shut up and let me go back to sleep."

"Aren't you afraid they might attack us?"

"Charlie, wolves don't attack humans. That's an old wives' tale. They smell us, the deer, and our food from dinner. They're checking it out, that's all. They probably won't even come into the camp."

The deputy pulled his sleeping bag over his head. "Stupid-ass city boy," Charlie heard a muffled voice say.

A minute later, the deputy was snoring.

Charlie pulled the sleeping bag up to his chin, but he still shook, not from cold but from fear. What if they weren't wolves out there but the monsters from his dreams?

And even if they were just wolves, they were outside the camp for a reason. They weren't "just curious," as the deputy suggested. They wanted him, Charlie was sure of it. He could hear them moving closer, inside the camp.

How could the deputy just sleep through this? The fire had died down, but it still gave off enough light to create shadows on the tent. A low growl sounded off to the front of the tent, and Charlie rolled onto his side.

Jesus Christ! It sounded like the thing was only a few feet outside the tent.

A strange shadow started rising on the tent. Charlie pulled his sleeping bag up to his face. The shadow grew larger and larger against the backdrop of the tent. Charlie froze in terror. He knew he should do something—grab the deputy's gun and start blasting—but he was so afraid, he couldn't even move to wake the deputy. He lay there watching the shadows and listening to the noises from the creatures that were now in the camp, circling.

His fate was sealed, and there was nothing he could do about it but wait for death to come.

~

Charlie's eyes opened to light. The darkness of the night was gone, and sunlight streamed in through the tent.

He had survived the night!

A wave of euphoria ran through him. He looked over. The deputy was gone. Charlie figured he had probably gone outside to relieve himself or fix breakfast. He peeked outside the tent. No sign of the deputy. He crawled out and surveyed the campsite. All that was left of the fire were a few dying coals.

"Johnny," he yelled out.

No reply, so he yelled again, "Where you at? Deputy!"

His yell echoed among the trees, and the only response he received was the silence of the forest surrounding him. He walked around the campsite staring down at the ground, thinking it was strange that there were no signs of the wolves that had infiltrated the camp the night before. Not even a single print. How could that be? Charlie began to have a bad feeling.

He walked back over to the tent and looked inside. The deputy's sleeping bag was gone, and none of his other items were inside. He looked down and saw only one set of footprints leaving the tent. He couldn't tell if they were his or the deputy's. But then he realized, no matter what, there should be at least two different sets.

So how could that be?

He scoured the campsite and couldn't come up with a single piece of evidence that the deputy had been there. He had left and taken everything, but why? Had the deputy double-crossed him and set off to find the gold himself?

Charlie sat down on the log next to the dead fire and waited for the deputy to return, even though he had a sinking feeling that Johnny Ridge would not be coming back.

Two hours later, Charlie gathered his gear and headed off. He could find the cave by himself. Maybe it was better this way.

But the disappearance of the deputy deeply bothered him. His mind could not come to terms with the fact that the deputy had simply vanished. Or far more distressing—had the deputy even been there to begin with?

~

Chapter 22

The Final Day

Charlie was oblivious to the blowing snow and freezing temperatures. All he could think about was the gold. It was almost his. He could feel it. He was going to be rich, and everyone who had plotted against him would suffer.

He climbed up a steep slope, where he came to an outcropping on top of a long cliff. He walked over to the edge and stared out across the expanse of the valley. Dozens of scattered streams of sunlight fought their way through small holes in the dark gray clouds.

The sunlight spoke to him. The wind sang a wondrous song. Everything around him—the trees, the snow, the sky—was alive and talking. Why had he never listened before?

He pulled out his notes, checking them for the thousandth time. Now, all he had to do was find the rock formation resembling a wolf. He turned left and followed the edge of the cliff for about a quarter of a mile.

It was slow going with all the gear he was carrying, and with no trees to shield him, the biting wind stung his face. He knew that if he didn't find the cave soon, he would have to stop and set up camp because if he didn't have a shelter and a fire going, there was little doubt that he wouldn't survive the night.

A grueling hour went by, and Charlie was about ready to quit for the day when he stopped dead in his tracks. He closed his eyes for a moment and then reopened. Standing like a majestic sentry guarding the king's castle was the rock wolf, staring directly at him.

He punched a fist toward the sky. "I found you, you son of a bitch!" Now he could claim what was rightfully his.

Screw Roth, the deputy, his wife, and everyone else. He was about to be rich, and he could do whatever he pleased! No more trying to please everyone. He didn't care about buying fancy stuff. The money meant freedom.

A gust of wind kicked up a spray of snow, blinding him for a second. He wiped the cold snow from his eyes and stared at the wolf; it was now facing in the opposite direction, but it couldn't have moved, could it?

He looked up in the sky. A dozen or so eagles circled above, and everything seemed to have suddenly grown darker. He knew it was getting late in the day, but the hue of the sky was strange, almost disconcerting.

Charlie walked around the wolf, giving himself plenty of room, because even though it was only rock, he didn't want to get too close. He walked to the very edge of the cliff, bent down on his hands and knees, and peered under the ledge. He looked up and down the face of the cliff, and twenty feet to his left was an opening just large enough for a man to fit through.

That had to be it!

He ran down to the edge of the cliff just over the hole and began lowering himself over the abyss, knowing any misstep meant certain death. It took all his strength, but he managed to swing his feet under the edge of the cliff, and with a quick push of his hands, he let go of the ledge and dropped his body inside the hole.

Pitch blackness and an eerie silence greeted him.

Charlie sat on his rear, reached inside of his coat, and pulled out a flashlight.

"C'mon." He fumbled with the switch before flipping it on. The light broke the dominance of the blackness, but it made Charlie feel even more uncomfortable. The darkness inside the cave felt like it had a life of its own, as if it had been waiting for him for a long, long time.

But he had come too far and sacrificed too much to let silly fears prevent him from claiming what was destined to be his.

He stared around. The roof of the cave was low. He couldn't even stand all the way up. To his right was another opening that appeared to lead downward. He scooted across the floor over to the hole. He stuck his head into the opening and shined the light down the entrance.

A tunnel appeared. Without giving himself the chance to back down or let his fears consume him, Charlie hoisted himself through the opening and slid downward into the tunnel. Luckily, the tunnel was just tall and wide enough for him to fit, but that didn't stop a wave of claustrophobia from enveloping him. He slowly started to walk. The tunnel snaked around several bends and began to descend more rapidly.

Does it lead toward hell? Charlie wondered.

The air in the cave grew heavier, colder, and his lungs felt like they were being squeezed. He came around another bend, when his light caught something on the wall.

He stopped directly underneath the images and shined his flashlight on them. Painted on the wall was a ring of fire, and inside the fire were hideous-looking images of beasts with Indians circling outside the ring of fire.

Charlie jumped. A noise echoed from somewhere deep in the tunnel. Charlie shined his flashlight in the direction of the noise. There was nothing. A rock had probably fallen, he hoped.

He turned back to the painting and almost peed in his pants. The fire had come to life on the wall. It couldn't be real, his mind told him, but he could feel the warmth from the flames as the fire grew brighter and began to sway. Charlie stepped back from the wall. The beast in the middle of the fire growled, then began walking around inside the fiery perimeter of the fire as if it was trying to break through and escape the flames.

Charlie's flashlight flickered a few times and then died. He stopped breathing and desperately slapped the flashlight against his palm.

Nothing.

"Please, God," he pleaded with growing desperation.

Thankfully, the light came back on, and he shined it up against the wall. The cave painting was, now, just a cave painting.

He continued downward through the tunnel. More and more paintings lined the walls. The deeper the tunnel went the more elaborate and bizarre the paintings became. Much to his dismay, he began to recognize some of them from his dreams. He prayed his flashlight wouldn't go out, cursing himself for not bringing a backup.

Charlie couldn't even rationally comprehend what would happen if he was stuck inside this cave with only the darkness. He would go mad. He looked at his watch because it felt as if he had been in the cave for hours, but his watch said he had only been inside for fifteen minutes.

A noise reverberated from somewhere ahead of him in the tunnel. He froze. It sounded like a scraping noise. Unconsciously, Charlie took a few steps backward. His body screamed for him to run, to leave before it was too late. But his mind already knew that chance had passed. He would either leave the cave with the Bechtler gold, or he would never leave.

That was to be his fate.

He forced himself forward, but his senses were distorted. Charlie couldn't tell if he was going up or coming down, and the concept of time and space suddenly seemed warped, as if he had crossed over to another dimension.

Pitch blackness surrounded him, with the flashlight providing the only comfort from the monsters that lurked all around him in the darkness. Charlie believed that as long as he had his light, he would be safe.

He tried to keep his eyes off the walls because grotesque paintings now filled almost all the wall space, and they were no longer still images. They were moving, changing, and making sounds like images on a television. They were alive.

Charlie came around another bend, and what he saw made him stop dead in his tracks. The place he had visited so many times in his dreams spread out before him. He had reached the burial chamber. Rocks formed a circle in the center of the cavern.

Circling the outside of the rocks were the mummified remains of Indians stacked a dozen deep.

Charlie shined his light into the center of the rock circle. The light reflected like a thousand suns off the gold coins, and a rush of giddiness ran through him. He couldn't believe after all this time; the gold would still be so shiny, so beautiful.

Charlie stifled a laugh. He had found it! The gold was all his!

He cautiously made his way to the first line of mummified Indians. He had no desire to climb over the decayed corpses, but nothing was going to stop him now. He stepped in between two bodies and looked down. A sickening skeleton face smiled back up at him as if it knew some great secret that only it was privy to.

Charlie moved to the next row, forcing himself not to look down. Instead, he focused his eyes and thoughts on the gold in the middle of the rocks.

He reached the circle of rocks but hesitated before stepping over them into the circle. He looked back at the chamber's exit. This was it. Somehow, he understood this was the final test. Either he crossed over the ring of rocks or he didn't. He didn't know what either choice would bring.

He took a deep breath and stepped inside of the circle of rocks.

He knelt down to scoop up a handful of the gold coins and let them slowly fall between his fingers. He started laughing uncontrollably, and his laughter echoed throughout the chamber, which magnified the volume. The louder the echo of his laughter became, the louder he laughed. It was almost as if he couldn't control it.

The gold was all his!

He stopped laughing, and the last gold coin fell from his fingers. Charlie stood looking back at the chamber. A sinister cackle echoed from the tunnel leading into the chamber, and it grew closer, louder. Charlie put his hands up to his ears. The noise was so shrill, it felt as if his eardrums were about to burst. His flashlight began to flicker, and the heinous laughter echoed louder and louder, filling the chamber.

He never knew a noise could cause such excruciating pain.

Charlie's brain felt like it was boiling, and he fell to his knees screaming, only his scream made no noise because it was consumed by the cave.

He slumped over, and just when he thought he was going to explode, the horrible sound stopped, followed by silence.

Charlie lay curled in a fetal position for a few minutes before sitting up. He shined his light around the chamber, and everything appeared as it should. He rolled over and began stuffing coins into a bag.

A guttural howl came from deep within the tunnel, and Charlie instantly knew what had made the noise.

The beast from his dreams had arrived, the Uktena. His life had turned into his nightmares, or was it the other way around?

He stood, desperately searching for any way out. Another howl came from the tunnel. Only this time, it was closer, and Charlie knew there was no escape.

Popping noises from behind him caused him to turn. What he saw drove him to the brink of insanity. The back row of mummified Indians had risen up from their centuries-old slumber, and they stood facing him, staring with empty eye sockets and repulsive skeleton grins. Charlie watched in horror as row after row of corpses began rising. Centuries-old bones and tissue cracked, popped, and split.

He spun around and around. There was no way out. Nowhere for him to hide.

Directly in front, only feet away, an Indian corpse with long shreds of leathery skin dangling off its face stepped inside the circle of stones. To his left, another followed, and another, and another. They moved forward. The entire first ring of corpses stepped into the circle of rocks.

Charlie tried to scream, but nothing came out. Then his flashlight died. He could sense the monsters inching their way closer, and the darkness enveloping him felt like a million hot pokers being stuck into every part of his flesh.

"Nooo!" he managed to scream.

He felt a hand touch his leg, then his back, but not a hand comprised of flesh and blood. It was a hand of bones. A gnarly cold finger touched his cheek, and Charlie desperately swatted at it.

He heard a loud pop and felt the bone from his assailant snap in half. Laughter followed, and then they were upon him.

Instinct caused Charlie to kick and punch even though he knew it was hopeless. He heard a howl fill the chamber, and suddenly the attack stopped. He was on his stomach lying face down in the dirt, and he could sense the things moving away from him.

He scurried backward, and his hand found the missing flashlight. He grabbed it, but hesitated because he wasn't sure if he wanted to turn it on to see what had made the noise. He crawled on his hands and knees till he felt the gold coins. Then he moved back to the circle of the rocks and lay there without trying the flashlight. He knew the Indians were not gone, but for some reason, they had retreated from the circle of rocks.

He heard something moving in the room, and he couldn't take the fear of the unknown any longer. Charlie turned on the flashlight. It came on despite having gone out earlier.

The Indians had parted to form a column to make space for it. Charlie stopped breathing. What he saw finally sent him over the abyss of complete insanity. The beast moved in between the Indians, closer to the circle of rocks and Charlie.

The sight of the monster was so terrifying, so maddening, that Charlie lost all will to live. He only wanted death with complete blackness and without any hope, any fears, or any consciousness. That was all he prayed for, and he wanted it now! The beast moved to the edge of the rocks and opened its mouth, letting loose a gut-wrenching noise that froze the blood in his body.

The beast entered the circle, and Charlie's flashlight flicked once, then went out. He squeezed his body into a tight ball and put his head in his chest, trying to disappear. He sobbed as he waited for death.

He could smell it. Putrefaction, decay, and death all loomed within inches of him.

Charlie felt a swipe at his arm, tearing off half of the muscle and flesh of his forearm. Then his head was jerked almost completely around. Charlie yelled, and felt the left side of his face. Skin from his eye socket to his neck had been completely flayed off. He reached up with his hand, feeling hot blood and a sickening mesh of tissue and bone.

Instinctively, his hand found the flashlight, and he tried to hit the beast with it. The light flickered on, and for the first time, Charlie saw the true face of the beast. He stared directly into the Uktena's brilliant crest, and he learned the true nature of the monster.

Everything became clear, and Charlie McCellan understood.

The face on the monster was his. Charlie knew the monster from inside of him had finally escaped, and now it was going to devour him.

But the complete silence of absolute darkness that Charlie so often prayed for did not come.

Some monsters refuse to die.

~

Chapter 23

Susan slowed the car, glancing over at the population sign welcoming her to Wellington. She wiped a single tear that had sprung from her eye. Sadness, remorse, and an overwhelming sense of loss still filled almost every waking moment of her life.

Almost three months had passed since Charlie's death, and the aftereffects still consumed every moment of her consciousness. The first few days after his death were filled with extreme grief, despair, and questions as to why Charlie had hiked into the mountains by himself.

What the hell had he been doing?

But nothing prepared her for what she learned after her husband had been laid to rest in the cemetery next to his parents. In some ways, what she discovered was even worse than Charlie's actual death.

So many questions remained unanswered that she felt like screaming.

Susan drove down Main Street. She glanced over at the sheriff's office, igniting a rush of painful memories about his phone call notifying her of Charlie's death.

In an apologetic, nervous ramble, the sheriff provided confusing, often sketchy details about Charlie's death, including where they had found his body.

The news had sucked the oxygen right out of her lungs, almost as if she had been punched in the stomach, and for the first few minutes, all she could do was sob uncontrollably.

The sheriff had stayed on the line and had been able to calm her down some. But as she regained a little composure and began asking questions, the sheriff's responses grew more clipped and vague, almost like he was holding something back.

In fact, he never did provide any answers as to why Charlie had hiked so far up into the mountains, alone. He had never done anything like that in his entire life. During that initial conversation, the only specific answer the sheriff provided was that Charlie had been found by one of his deputies frozen to death atop a cliff in a remote part of the mountain. And although, later, the coroner's report was inconclusive about the exact cause of death, it did list exposure and hypothermia as chief factors.

After the devastating phone call, she drove up to the mountains to identify Charlie's body at the morgue and arrange transportation back to Charleston. Then she had gone to see the sheriff, who finally explained that Charlie had been acting very strange, and in the days leading up to his death, his behavior had grown more and more erratic.

Susan had listened in stunned silence as he detailed how Charlie had placed a 9-1-1 call because he believed Indians were trying to kill him. He told her about the night he pulled Charlie over for drunk driving. Utterly exhausted, Susan had remained quiet as the sheriff went into excruciating detail about how Charlie kept calling one of his deputies with some bizarre story about a Cherokee burial cave and that he thought Indian ghosts had been stalking him.

Finally, the sheriff told her that Charlie kept having delusions about a man named Reverend McCellan trying to steal a book from him that supposedly contained the secret to some lost treasure.

But the extent of her shock was magnified tenfold after the sheriff handed over the legal pads Charlie had kept during his ten days in the mountains.

She waited till she got back home to read them. His behavior and ramblings were the first of many disturbing revelations about her husband. The deceptions and lies were almost like a stack of dominoes that began falling faster and faster as she discovered more about him. In a short period of time, Susan had to completely rethink how well she really knew her husband of eighteen years.

How could she not have known?

For the last three months, Susan had relived almost every second, every moment of their lives together, trying to come to any understanding, and it was torturing her.

The bottom line was that Charlie had been living a double life for almost a decade, and she had had absolutely no clue, no inkling.

Then, if that wasn't bad enough, a week after the funeral, Simon stopped by to tell her that Charlie's company was basically broke, and that Charlie had left behind a series of dubious business transactions. Simon also told her the real reason why Charlie had lost the Roth account was because he had cheated, and that wasn't the only one, either. Out of nowhere, creditors and businesses lined up demanding overdue payments on bad accounts, or services promised but not completed. Yet there was no money in the checking accounts to pay anybody. They had been totally wiped clean.

But the news got even worse. Over a period of two weeks, she discovered that Charlie had liquidated their investment accounts, and his life insurance policies had lapsed years ago, leaving no money for the kids or the expenses. He had even forged her signature, giving him power of attorney to take out a second mortgage on the house. Worst of all, the equity in the valuable mountain property had also been mortgaged to the hilt.

Out of desperation, she called the chief psychiatrist who had treated Charlie during his breakdown and told the doctor about the circumstances of his death and what she learned afterward. Even he seemed baffled by the extreme contradictions in Charlie's life.

Susan tried to force the thoughts out of her mind because they were driving her crazy. She drove past the town's park, fighting back tears. Charlie used to take the kids there when they were little. He'd let them swing and play for hours. She felt as if she was drowning in a sea of guilt, anger, and betrayal.

She had been avoiding this trip for weeks but finally decided to come to the mountains, hopefully to put some closure on Charlie's death.

She slowly drove past the town, veering onto a country highway that led to Kingsley's bar. Susan was meeting with Sheriff Thomas, Kingsley, and a doctor friend of the sheriff who he said could probably shed some light on Charlie's "mental" situation.

Susan pulled into the parking lot of the bar. A large red sign with dozens of pellet holes read *Bob's Place.* She looked down at her directions in confusion. The address was right, but this is certainly not what she had expected.

She stared at the sign, just one of the many untruths in a growing web of lies that Charlie had told. For ten years, he had told her that the name of the bar was the Green Man.

Why would he make something up like that? What was the point?

She had met Bob Kingsley at Charlie's funeral, and it came as quite a shock to her that he wasn't an elderly distinguished Englishman as Charlie had described. Instead, Kingsley was a short, fat man with flushed cheeks and a squeaky, almost hillbilly-sounding drawl.

It was mind-boggling because Charlie had asked her to go to the bar with him on dozens of occasions. What would have happened if she had said yes one of those times? How would he have explained the lie?

Susan parked next to the sheriff's car and took a deep breath. No matter what happened, she wasn't going to cry, she promised herself, not in front of these men.

Susan got out, stood straight, and walked into the bar.

The three men stood from the table as she entered. The sheriff walked over to her with a solemn expression. "Mrs. Parker, glad you could make it."

"Thanks, Sheriff."

She nodded to Kingsley, who said, "Mrs. Parker."

The sheriff motioned toward the other man. "This is the doctor I told you about."

A gentleman dressed in tweed pants and a cardigan sweater walked over and grasped her hand.

"Mrs. Parker, I'm Dr. David Covington, and I want to express my condolences about Charlie. I know this must be an extremely difficult time for you and your family. How are your kids holding up?"

"I guess as good as can be expected. I really haven't told them much about the…discrepancies or details of their father's life and death."

"That might be for the best. They're young enough. Let them remember him for who he truly was—a good, loving family man. He suffered from a disease, but the disease wasn't who he was. Again, I am very sorry for your loss."

"Thank you," she answered out of habit.

An uncomfortable silence followed before Kingsley asked, "Would you like a cup of coffee, Mrs. Parker?"

"Yes, that would be great."

Kingsley left to get the coffee, and the sheriff pulled a chair out from the table. "Why don't we all take a seat?"

She sat down at a stained card table and looked around the bar. Kingsley wasn't kidding when he said his place was a hole in the wall. The walls were cinder blocks. A nasty yellow linoleum covered the floor; with peanut shells strewn everywhere, and there were only two small windows.

She almost laughed. Charlie had told her that the place was an exquisite English tavern. *Again,* she thought, *what was the point? Why would he lie about something like this?* It made no sense.

Kingsley set a Styrofoam cup filled with coffee next to her.

The sheriff coughed and said to Susan, "I appreciate you giving me permission to give a copy of Charlie's writings to the doctor. I asked him to take a look at it because I thought he might be able to explain what happened to Charlie's mental condition."

The sheriff looked over at the doctor, who took his cue. He clasped his hands in front of him and looked her straight in the eyes.

"Susan, I know you want answers. I want you to know these are just my educated guesses, but I need to warn you, I may have to be rather clinical, maybe even blunt. Okay?"

"Believe me, Doctor, there is nothing you could tell me now that would shock me after everything I've discovered."

"I understand. I talked to his main therapist in Charleston after you signed the waiver allowing him to discuss Charlie's diagnosis and treatment, and he told me about Charlie's nervous breakdown in his early thirties. Were you aware that he had stopped treatments against his doctor's orders?"

"Not till recently," she said flatly.

"Charlie's psychiatrist told me that, although his condition had improved drastically after he was institutionalized, he didn't want Charlie to stop treatment, and he especially didn't want him to stop medication."

"Which he obviously did," Susan added.

"Charlie's condition was an unusual one in terms of what generally is considered a 'nervous breakdown.' I believe his condition was much more complex than that. I believe the treatment he received helped, but it was not enough. I know his breakdown must have been very difficult, especially with young kids."

Susan sighed heavily. "I thought at the time that it couldn't get any worse." She laughed sarcastically. "Boy, was I wrong. After he was released, he seemed a lot better. I thought he was seeing the doctor. He pretty much quit drinking, and I picked up his medication every month at the drugstore. He really did seem fine, and I thought his episode was just a one-time thing. A fluke."

"Did his behavior change in the weeks or months before he came up to the mountains?"

"No."

"Any episodes of agitation or panic attacks?"

Susan shook her head.

"Was Charlie short-tempered, drinking more than usual, anything?"

Susan sat back in her chair and couldn't help it. She began laughing. The men around the table looked even more uncomfortable after her reaction, and she couldn't really blame them.

"I just can't believe all of this. For three years, he wrote down his doctor's appointment on our weekly calendar in the kitchen, and he never went! How does a person just go insane without his wife knowing it? Y'all must think I am the worst person in the world."

The sheriff reached across the table and put his hand on hers. "No, Susan, we don't think that. Charlie had a disease, and he snapped. It was only a matter of time. I think what the doctor has to say may at least relieve your conscience a little and help explain what happened."

She looked back over at the doctor, who smiled, obviously trying to reassure her, but it didn't help. For some unknown reason, she suddenly didn't like him and began regretting her decision to allow him to get involved.

The doctor clasped his hands together and leaned forward against the table. "Charlie was an exceptionally smart, complicated person who had a serious mental illness. These conditions are organic in basis, and we try not to think in terms of who is at fault or to blame because it is a disease just like if someone has cancer or a rare blood disorder. Doctors, especially psychiatrists, aren't perfect. The human mind is a very complex and unpredictable thing, and I believe it was only a matter of time before Charlie suffered another breakdown. You can't blame yourself. He suffered from a disease."

"That's easy for you to say. If I had known or recognized it, I could have helped. Maybe it could have been treated."

Dr. Covington slowly nodded. "To a degree, his condition probably could have been managed, but let me ask you this: how many of your family members, friends, or co-workers suspected?"

She shrugged. "No one that I know of."

"That's right."

"Susan, I saw him a couple of days before he passed away," Kingsley said. "And I swear to you, he seemed completely fine to me. I had no idea. The doctor is right, you can't blame yourself."

She nodded wearily. "I guess."

The doctor lifted a binder. "The diary he kept while up here is a remarkable clue as to how serious his condition became. And of course, the alcohol consumption was like throwing jet fuel onto a raging fire."

"He never sounded drunk when I talked to him on the phone. Was he drinking a lot here, Bob?"

"No, he only came in twice, and that was only for a couple of beers. That's it."

"Susan, I went to your cabin after he was found," said the sheriff. "There were liquor bottles and beer cans everywhere. He had to be drinking a fifth of whiskey a day, not to mention all the beer. The night I pulled him over, he was so drunk he could barely stand."

It seemed like almost another lifetime ago, but Susan distinctly remembered those last few months before his breakdown when Charlie drank excess amounts of alcohol in order to quell whatever it was inside him that caused so much pain. For years after his hospitalization, she would find empty vodka bottles behind cabinets or stashed in weird places. She should have never let him come up to the mountains by himself.

She looked back over at the doctor, who said, "I think what he did up here was create a real life horror story to block out the reality of his failed business. That, with the onset of an underlying mental condition and the excessive alcohol, made it worse. Bit by bit, it just took hold of him to the point where he really believed the things he was writing about were actually happening to him."

Susan turned to the sheriff and said bluntly, "You mean like the mutilated Indian spirits, the wolves, and all that nonsense about gold being hidden in some cave protected by Indian monsters? I have read his diary at least twenty times. It was written by a person I never knew, someone who…I don't know, someone who clearly was insane."

The doctor put the copy of the diary down and said, "I know it must have been quite disturbing to read your husband's writings, especially describing in such gruesome detail how he 'supposedly' murdered someone in your mountain home."

"Of course, we know that didn't happen," the sheriff said quickly. "It was just another figment of his imagination."

In her wildest dreams, Susan never thought she would ask this question. "Are you sure he didn't kill anyone?"

The sheriff answered without hesitation, "I am one hundred percent positive. Like we discussed on the phone, I had my people search every inch of the house and property. No one was buried anywhere, and we used a blood screener inside. The only traces of blood we found were your husband's. And, of course, the man who he claimed to have murdered, Reverend McCellan, well, like I told you, he's been down at Kearney nursing home for more than a decade. He has advanced stages of Alzheimer's. I personally talked to the nurse over there, and he has been in a vegetative state for close to two years. Susan, I promise you, your husband didn't murder Reverend McCellan, or anyone else, for that matter."

"Charlie believed it, though," Dr. Covington added. "Everything he wrote in the diary, he truly believed was happening. I mean, I don't want to sound glib, but if it wasn't so tragic, his diary would be a fascinating piece of work."

Fascinating! What the hell is this guy talking about? she wondered.

The doctor continued, "I have done some pretty extensive research regarding his writings, and he seemed to be able to take bits of factual information and then distorted it into, I guess, what his mind at the time believed to be reality."

She looked over at Bob. "So, obviously, this reverend didn't make an appearance at your bar like Charlie wrote?"

He shook his head. "Charlie was here along with the usual crowd, and yes, a strange-looking man who was lost did come in. I gave him directions to the Interstate."

"What did that man look like?"

"Like the reverend who Charlie described in his diary. He was easy to remember because he was so odd looking. He was tall, really thin. He wore an all black suit with a bowler hat. I think the guy was an albino."

"The real Reverend McCellan is about five foot six, bald, and before his illness, extremely overweight," the sheriff said. "I knew him personally for years."

She looked back at Bob. "This man, did he give you a book like Charlie wrote?"

"Yes, he did. After I gave him directions, he gave me a Gideon Bible. Said he appreciated me helping a stranger, and that he was a preacher spreading the word of God to all those in need. I'll admit, the guy definitely made me uncomfortable, but he left, and that was the only time I've ever seen him."

"See, Susan," the doctor said in his formal physician's voice, "Charlie's diseased mind had already snapped, and he was mixing real events with newly discovered family history that obviously was quite disturbing to him. He discovered that Reverend McCellan was a relative and still alive, and this preacher became a symbol of evil to him. He started confusing reality with his horror books and his own mind."

"But what parts of his insane writings could possibly be true?" Susan asked testily.

"The McCellan family history," the sheriff answered. "Charlie's father was adopted, and he was raised by his stepfather."

"What about those Indians that were hung for killing Ezekiel McCellan's family? Did that really happen?"

Once again, the sheriff's face took on an uncomfortable expression. "Crimes are committed in every single city in the United States. That was over eighty years ago."

"But it happened?"

"Yes."

"Did Charlie's real grandfather really have something to do with killing Ezekiel's family?"

The sheriff folded his hands on the table and looked down for a second before answering, "Susan, if I knew, I would tell you, I promise. That was a long time ago."

"It must have been a shock to Charlie to discover that his father was adopted and to find out the circumstances behind his real grandfather's death," Dr. Covington said.

Susan sighed. "God, I can't even think about that with all of this going on, and the kids."

"That's understandable, Susan," the doctor said in a comforting tone, "but the family history is true."

Susan looked over at the sheriff. "Did you know about Charlie's family?"

He hesitated for a second before saying, "Yes."

Susan wondered why he paused before answering her question. "So, you knew about his grandfather dying up in the mountains, and that they were responsible for the death of those Indians?"

"Susan, that is all ancient history. It doesn't help anyone to go back and…"

Susan cut him off. "You haven't answered my question. I want to know if that part of his story is true."

"Yes. In 1927, three Indians were hung because they were accused of murdering Ezekiel McClellan's wife and two daughters."

"But did they do it, or did Ezekiel do it to set up the Indians like Charlie wrote?"

The sheriff looked over at the doctor and then back to Susan. "It has never been proven that the Indians were innocent. I wasn't even born then. I can't tell you the answer to that. I don't think anyone can."

She looked back at Dr. Covington, who said, "You know Charlie had an unusual penchant for reading horror novels, and I myself am a fan of that genre. I know this isn't particularly why you are here, but a lot of what he wrote about in his diary, he lifted from horror novels that he had obviously read."

As if it couldn't get any stranger, Susan thought. "Like what books?" she asked, not sure she really wanted to know.

"Well, for one, he told you this place was called the Green Man and that the owner, Kingsley, was an English gentleman, right?"

"Yes."

"Well, *The Green Man* is actually a novel written by Kingsley Amis."

"I mean, this is..." Susan stopped and looked away.

"But that is not all," the doctor continued. "Charlie wrote on numerous occasions about chewing aspirins to help his headaches. Well, the character in *The Shining...*"

"*The Shining*," Susan interrupted. "That was his favorite book. He must have watched the movie at least twenty times."

"We found three large empty bottles of aspirin in the cabin. I guess he had been chewing them like candy," the sheriff added.

"Have you read the book?" the doctor asked.

"No."

"Well, in *The Shining*, the lead character, Jack Torrance, the one played by Jack Nicholson, does the same thing as he begins to lose his grip on sanity. He chews aspirin after aspirin. Hold on."

The doctor opened his photocopy of Charlie's diary. "On page one hundred and fifteen, one of Charlie's last entries, he writes about seeing a blue light that he believes will lead him to the gold in the mountains. That reference to the blue light was an easy one. It was in Bram Stoker's *Dracula*. There was this ancient Bavarian legend that on certain nights of the year, blue lights would appear in the countryside marking spots where treasure was hidden."

"What about those goddamn mutant Indians he kept writing about—the Nunnehi—are they in any horror novel?" Normally, Susan would have been embarrassed by her foul language, but today she didn't care.

"Not that I've read," Dr. Covington answered. "But I'm sure there are many things in his diary that I overlooked."

"I guess he just went insane. What else is there to say?" Susan replied stoically.

"How are you holding up?" Kingsley asked.

"The accountants are telling me I have to sell the mountain house and property. Charlie left us with nothing. I want to get this business over with so I can try and move on. I need to take care of my family."

The doctor put his papers back in his folder. "Of course. They need you. But there is one other thing I'd like to ask you before you leave."

"Yes."

"Charlie wrote that he had a Bechtler gold coin that was minted in 1853. Do you know anything about that?"

Susan thought it was a weird question but answered, "He had a gold coin, if that's the one you're talking about. I don't know any of the details or the date of the coin. He carried the dang thing with him everywhere. Why?"

"I am something of a coin collector myself, and when I read about it, I was just curious because there were no coins minted in that year. Did he leave the coin in Charleston?"

"No. I mean, I haven't come across it. But, like I said, he always had it on him. It's probably somewhere in the cabin."

"No. It's not there," the sheriff said.

Susan looked over at him. Something all of a sudden didn't seem right. "What do you mean, it's not there? How do you know?"

The sheriff looked a bit taken aback by the hard edge to her question. "Well, standard police investigation. After his death, of course, we searched the property looking for evidence. We took an inventory of the contents of your home."

"What for?"

"Standard police procedure. Just in case we had to build a case against someone."

"You never mentioned this before. Can I have a copy of that list?"

"Susan, I called you after his death. My main objective was to give you the information in a way that, well, there is just no easy way. I apologize if I wasn't more specific with you."

"Can I see that report?" she repeated.

"I can send you a copy."

"I'm sorry I brought it up," the doctor said. "I was just curious about the coin. It really is irrelevant to the situation."

"Well, I wonder where the coin went to then," Susan said angrily. "He always had it in one of his pockets. Did you ask the deputy about it?"

"No, but he's a good, honest man. If it was on Charlie at the time of his death, I assure you, the deputy didn't take it. It's probably still in the cabin. It wasn't like I was rifling through every drawer or nook and cranny."

Susan forced herself to calm down. After all, the sheriff was just doing his job. "You're probably right," she said in a conciliatory tone. "When I find it, Doctor, I'll let you know the date."

"No problem. I don't want to sound rude in light of the situation, but the coin is valuable, and if you're interested, I could pay a pretty good price for it."

"When I find it, I won't sell it for any price. I'll give it to Jeffery to remember his father by."

The corners of the doctor's mouth turned down, followed by what appeared to be a forced smile. "Of course, I understand."

She stood, followed by the men.

"Thank you for taking your time to meet with me and help explain what happened."

"Not a problem," the sheriff said.

"Thank you, Dr. Covington," she forced herself to say. "I know your time is valuable, and you didn't have to do this."

"Think nothing of it. You take care of yourself."

She turned to face Kingsley. "Bob, Charlie really spoke highly of you. I want you to know he considered you a good friend."

Bob walked over and gave her a hug. He pulled back and looked her straight in the eyes. "Susan, if you need anything, anything at all, don't hesitate to call." He handed her an envelope.

"What's this?"

"Well, some of the boys…We know it has been tough on you, so we chipped in and…"

Susan opened the envelope and saw the cash.

"It's not much, but we want you to have it."

Four months ago, it would have been inconceivable that she would have taken a handout like this, but now, she had the kids to take care of and nobody to help her. She tucked the envelope in her jacket. "Thanks Bob. I really appreciate it. Tell everyone that I said thank you."

She turned to leave but stopped. She almost forgot. "One more thing," she said to the sheriff.

"Yes."

"The deputy, John Ridge, did he ever go with my husband up into the mountains in search of that cave, the one that supposedly had the gold?"

The sheriff wrung his hands, and Susan saw a sudden look of unease on his face.

"No."

"Are you sure?"

"Deputy Ridge was on duty at the time of your husband's death."

"But he was the one who found Charlie's body?"

"Yes."

"Why did he think that something was wrong? I mean, Charlie had only been missing for twelve hours. How did he know to go up into the mountains to look for him? That seems a bit unusual, doesn't it?"

"The deputy told me that your husband had contacted him a couple of different times…with some crazy story that he had discovered the location of the Indian burial cave with gold in it. He was concerned for your husband, so he drove out to check on him and saw his tracks leading up into the mountains. He followed them, and, well, you know what happened after that."

"Could I have his number? I'd like to give him a call."

"He resigned a month ago. Never left a forwarding number. Sorry."

"Do any of you believe the story about the Bechtler gold hidden in a sacred Cherokee cave?"

Kingsley grinned. "Who knows? Anything is possible."

"Have any of you ever searched for that gold?"

Kingsley's smile disappeared, and the doctor looked over at the sheriff, who looked like he was thinking of an answer.

She studied the sheriff's face before he said, "I have better things to do with my time. No one here is a treasure hunter as far as I know."

The other men laughed at his comment.

"Thank you for time. Bye." Susan left the bar and drove back to Charleston. She decided she would send a moving company to pack up the mountain house. She didn't belong there anymore.

EPILOGUE

Two-year anniversary of Charlie's death

Susan walked outside of her house and took a deep breath. She looked up into the bright blue skies. It was unseasonably warm for February, but Charleston's weather could be like that during the winter.

She couldn't believe two years had already passed since Charlie's death. Two of the toughest years of her life, but she had survived.

She walked down to the mailbox and pulled out the usual assortment of catalogs, junk mail, and bills. She stood in the driveway sorting through it.

A thick manila envelope was underneath. *Strange,* she thought. It was addressed to Mrs. Charlie Parker, and there was no return address on it. She walked back up the driveway and set the other mail down on the trunk of the car.

Susan opened the envelope.

Inside was a newspaper clipping wrapped around something. She carefully unfolded the newspaper, and inside was a large gold coin.

"What the hell," Susan muttered.

The coin looked exactly like the one Charlie used to carry, and it was stamped *CAROLINA GOLD* in the center. She turned it over, and the date inscribed at the bottom was *1853*.

She thought back to the day she had met the men up at the mountains to discuss Charlie's death and remembered that was the year the doctor had inquired about. She had really tried to put the whole episode behind her as best she could, but one thing that bothered her to this day was that she had never found Charlie's coin.

Was this Charlie's coin? Who sent this to her, and why?

She unfolded the newspaper article. It was cut out from *The Mountain Gazette*. A large picture of a new building was in the background with a group of Native Americans standing in front.

Susan read the article:

> The Qualla Town Cherokee Indian tribe has had a lot to celebrate recently. The above photo was taken at the grand opening of the tribe's new hospital. In the last two years, the tribe's fortunes have changed dramatically after the discovery of an ancient burial cave by one of the tribe's members.
>
> Johnny Ridge, a Cherokee who was employed as a deputy for the Wellington Police Department until his resignation two years ago, discovered the cave while hiking through an isolated part of the Western Carolina Mountains.
>
> Mr. Ridge began exploring the forgotten cave, and deep inside, he discovered the remains

of fifty-nine Cherokee Indians who had been buried there from various time periods. A team of scientists are now excavating the cave, and Dr. Anders, the chief anthropologist at the site, believes the cave served as a sacred site where only the most powerful Indian chiefs were allowed to be buried. Results from carbon dating tests show that the oldest remains found in the cave date back to the early 1100s.

But it was what Mr. Ridge also found inside the cave that proved to be the surprise of a lifetime. Along with the mummified remains of the Indian chiefs was a fortune in gold coins.

Haggy Johnson, a numismatist for the American Numismatic Association, told the *Gazette* that "the coins were from the Bechtler Mint that was located outside of Rutherfordton, North Carolina. The private mint produced coins from 1831 until it closed in 1852."

But what was so significant about Mr. Ridge's discovery was that the dates from all the coins inside the cave were from 1853, adding further to the mystery of the cave and its treasure.

Mr. Johnson went on to say, "There is no record of any coins being minted by Christopher Bechtler in 1853, although there has always been speculation by historians and numismatics that Mr. Bechtler did in fact complete one last minting in 1853."

Folklore has it that a stash of gold was stolen from Christopher Bechtler by a tribe of Cherokees as Bechtler made his way to Spartanburg, South

Carolina. It was believed that the Indians hid the gold up in the mountains. And, it now looks like some legends are true.

Most of the lost Bechtler gold coins have been sold at private coin auctions, and the Cherokee tribe located along the Qualla Boundary in North Carolina was the benefactor of the proceeds. Leaders of the tribe have declined to comment on the total proceeds from the sale except to say that "it was significant."

In fact, it has been a not-too-well-kept secret that the Cherokee tribe has made substantial real estate purchases outside of the Qualla Boundary. The Qualla Boundary is a large tract of land designated by the United States government as a national park, and it is located on the Oconaluftee River.

The tribe's spokesman commented that "the Eastern Band will continue to add to their land holdings outside of the Qualla Boundary for some time, and it is their intention to repurchase all the lands that they believed the Cherokees rightfully owned."

Repeated efforts to reach Johnny Ridge for comment were unsuccessful.

Susan looked back inside the package. There was a white envelope at the bottom. She pulled it out and turned it over, studying it. The envelope was sealed, and there was no writing on either side. Susan wasn't sure if she wanted to open it or not.

After a brief hesitation, she carefully opened the envelope and pulled out some type of a legal document. It was a notarized deed to the property in the mountains. The property that she had been forced to sell after Charlie's death.

Susan gasped as she read the deed. Her hands shook as she read it again in disbelief. The deed was registered in her and the kids' names. She turned the deed over and stared at the signature turning the land back over to her and the kids. The signature read: *Johnny Ridge, Chief of the Eastern Band of Cherokees.*

Susan looked up toward the sky. "Maybe Charlie wasn't as crazy as they thought after all."

She closed her eyes and prayed that he had finally found his peace.

The End

Authors Note

The Bechtler Gold Coins

I hope you enjoyed *Ten Days To Madness.*

The Bechtler gold coins featured in my story were produced at a mint in Rutherfordton, North Carolina from 1831-1852. Rutherfordton is located in the foothills of the Blue Ridge Mountains and the mint was operated by a German émigrés named the Bechtlers.

The Bechtler mint was the first mint in the United States to produce a $1 gold coin and their coins were among the most successful and long lasting of all territorial coins. The mint successfully ran for two decades until gold deposits dried up in the Carolinas and the United States opened a government mint in Charlotte. Today, the Bechtler coins are highly sought after among collectors and they sell for thousands and even tens of thousands of dollars.

In W.C. Jameson's book, *Buried Treasures of the Appalachians,* Jameson recounts a legend that in the early 1850's Christopher Bechtler Jr. disappeared under mysterious circumstances while transporting a shipment of Bechtler Gold to Spartanburg, South Carolina. No trace of Bechtler or the gold coins has ever been found.

The Bechtler Gold Coins play a unique role in *Ten Days to Madness* and my story may provide an answer to what might have happened to the last Bechtler Gold.

To learn more about Jamie Clifford and his books visit his website: www.jrclifford.com